GIRL IN REVERSE

ALSO BY BARBARA STUBER
Crossing the Tracks

GIRL IN REVERSE

BARBARA STUBER

Margaret K. McElderry Books
NEW YORK   LONDON   TORONTO   SYDNEY   NEW DELHI

MARGARET K. McELDERRY BOOKS
An imprint of Simon & Schuster Children's Publishing Division
1230 Avenue of the Americas, New York, New York 10020
MARGARET K. MCELDERRY BOOKS is a trademark of Simon & Schuster, Inc.
For information about special discounts for bulk purchases, please contact Simon & Schuster
Special Sales at 1-866-506-1949 or business@simonandschuster.com.
The Simon & Schuster Speakers Bureau can bring authors to your live event. For more information
or to book an event, contact the Simon & Schuster Speakers Bureau at 1-866-248-3049
or visit our website at www.simonspeakers.com.
Book design by Russell Gordon
The text for this book is set in Minion Pro.
Manufactured in the United States of America
2 4 6 8 10 9 7 5 3 1
Library of Congress Cataloging-in-Publication Data
Stuber, Barbara.
Girl in reverse / Barbara Stuber.—First edition.
p. cm.
Summary: "Lillian Firestone is Chinese, but the kids in her 1951 Kansas City high school can't
separate her from the North Koreans that America is at war with. Sick of the racism she faces at
school and frustrated that her adoptive white family just sees it as 'teasing,'
Lily begins to search for her birth mother"—Provided by publisher.
ISBN 978-1-4424-9734-4 (hardcover)
ISBN 978-1-4424-9736-8 (eBook)
1. Chinese Americans—Juvenile fiction. [1. Chinese Americans—Fiction. 2. Racism—Fiction.
3. Adoption—Fiction. 4. Birthmothers—Fiction.] I. Title.
PZ7.S937555Gi 2014
[Fic]—dc23
2013024720

For Jack

GIRL IN REVERSE

The Lie
by Lily Firestone

When I was four I swallowed a lie.
It sunk inside me, grew a shell, stayed hidden.
But the lie became restless.
It broke into bits and surfaced so I could not ignore it anymore.
The lie dissolved into truth and
showed up in the mirror.

Prologue

SISTERS OF MERCY CHILDREN'S HOME
KANSAS CITY—1938

"Say it, Lily."

I bow my head, close my eyes, press my hands together. "Choose me."

Nancy bends down and whispers, "Again . . . like a magic prayer."

"Choose me. Please."

"That's right." Nancy smiles, tucks my hair behind my ears, smooths my dress.

My good shoes clatter on the steps. I hear Sister Evangeline talking to the lady who wants a girl.

Step. Step.

The lady walks out of the shadow. She has shiny black hair and a bright pink sweater.

"M—Mamá!" I stumble, grab the railing.

"No!" Nancy says. She reaches for me, but I'm free. I run to Mamá, grip her legs.

She wobbles, twirls around, and looks down. Her lips are red. Her eyes are blue and crinkled. She says, *"AH!"* She is *not* Mamá.

Her hair swings. She bends down and lifts me into her arms. I hug her neck. She does not smell like sweet wood. She is flowers.

. . . This time I won't let go.

Chapter 1

JANUARY 1951

I hold my face as if it has been dipped in plastic, slide down in my seat, and stare at the doodle—a tornado-shaped ink spiral gouged in the desktop.

Five rows ahead Neil Bradford faces our class in his ROTC uniform. He holds out a cartoon taped to red construction paper that he has brought for current events. His eyes glitter. "See? It's an army tank stuffed with Chinese commies about to crush all these little kids in the crosswalk. Each of the kids wears a name tag of a country in the United Nations." His lip curls. His gaze skims our class. "Don't be fooled, folks. They're out to get us!"

The Chinese soldiers in the tank are fiends with crossed eyes and nasty bucktoothed grins. They aim their bloody bayonets and machine guns at the poor, helpless United Nations.

He slices me with a glance, pats his chest. "My brother is in Korea right now fighting the Red Chinese." Neil's voice gets pushy. "The *Evil Empire* is attacking our boys this very minute. Their next target? The U.S. of A."

Neil pivots and salutes the flag. Kids whoop and applaud. He starts the cartoon around the room.

I tuck my hair behind my ears, remembering last Friday's current events cartoon. It showed a Chinaman's mask over the muzzle of a crazed, razor-toothed bear—the global symbol of Communism.

I glance at Neil's cartoon when it is handed to me. But when I try to pass it to the guy beside me, he yanks his hand back, holds it suspended in midair. He bucks his teeth at me, crosses his eyes, and fake coughs, "Commie." Neil covers his mouth, as if suppressing his own commie cough.

Another comrade of Neil's sneezes, "Chink!" Somebody snickers. The air sizzles, all eyes on me. *Commie. Chink.* My hands fly to my cheeks. My insides buzz. The cartoon falls on the floor with the machine guns aimed right up at me. I glower at Miss Arth seated at her desk—*God!* DO *something*.

But she doesn't.

No. Miss Arth is preoccupied with her ear. She grimaces, pulls off a tight earring, and massages her fleshy earlobe. The fat gold glob wobbles on her desktop.

Two rows up Patty Kittle turns to me with an expression full of pity. *Sorry, Lily.* I look from one to the other of my classmates. Even the nice kids stare right past me out the window.

"But . . . ," I squeak. "But."

The Communism-is-contagious guy beside me swivels in his seat, jiggles his hands palms up, silently mimicking— *but . . . but . . . whad?*

Neil stuffs his hands in his pockets, smug as can be. Miss Arth removes her other earring. She runs her finger down her grade book, announces the next student's turn, and boom! The attack is over.

I sit back, slapped. Trapped.

My hands and face tingle.

The next thing I know, right in the middle of fifth hour, I am standing on Neil's cartoon, grabbing my books. The janitor, on a stepladder at the back of the room, catches my eye. He salutes me with a lightbulb raised in his fist. Neil hops back as if giving the enemy a wide berth as I square my shoulders and step around him, out the door, and into the empty hall.

I yank my coat from my locker. The school secretary tracks me walking past the front office window. I bump the building door open, run down the front steps, through the crosswalk, and up the street.

Lily Firestone, unhooked from the world.

You did it—you did it—for once—you did the right thing. The rhythm of the words propels me for blocks, through

Southmoreland Park and across the lawn of the art museum. I sit on a stone wall, clutching my books. It's spitting snow and windy. Cold seeps through my coat, but I feel a little fire in me—a right and true flame. I unload my books, pull my knees up, remembering a different rhythm, a jump rope chant from grade school: *Jap-mon-key-girl-Jap-mon-key-girl.* Kids chanted it during recess after Pearl Harbor was bombed. I didn't know if I was a Jap or not. I didn't know *what* I was. I thought it was supposed to be funny. I hopped and scratched like an ape until something shifted inside and I realized *I* was the joke.

Easy as pie, without trying, I've changed from being a monkey to a commie.

Wars come in all sizes: whole world, playground, classroom, even inside your own skin. My mittens are fists. I wipe my eyes, furious that I didn't protect myself way back then. I should have stood up, fought back. But I didn't. I didn't know how. And now I'm still just me, still trying to ignore it.

. . . *until today.*

I rock side to side, hot tears on my face, recalling still another rhythm—the cadence of my first mother's steps and how her hair swayed when she carried me around the puddles and scary dogs and steamy gutters filled with the trash of Chinatown. *If we ever get lost from each other, Lily, look for my bright pink sweater. You can always find me.*

She was Mamá, my birth mother, who sailed here from China and delivered me in California before the Iron Curtain and the Bamboo Curtain divided the world. After three years she put us on a train to Kansas City, pried my arms from around her neck, lowered me to the floor of the Mercy Children's Home, and walked out. Mamá disappeared and became Gone Mom.

But today she has walked back inside me. Right where I don't want her. "I'm here, where you left me, Mamá, a truant Chinese speck in the middle of America."

I blot my eyes on my coat sleeve. Squirrels chase around the oak trees, scramble through piles of dead leaves. I look up. Shiver.

I am not alone.

Across the wide sidewalk in front of me sits a huge naked man. He's on a tall, blocky pedestal, with one fist clenched under his chin and a squirrel on his knee. I walk over and squint at the engraving on the smooth stone base below him:

THE THINKER

RODIN

His face looks worried. I circle him, study the curves of his backside, his biceps and massive bare back. He's weathered gray-green metal with rain streaks down his sides and between his thighs and fingers. His whole body is clenched.

He looks like he has muscles in his brain.

Behind him is the Nelson-Atkins Museum of Art, with its rows of columns and steps. I watch a shadow slide slowly across *The Thinker*'s jaw and down his chest. It's getting late. I rub his frigid toes. "So, I've gotta go now. But where to? Home or someplace else?"

No reply.

Snow gathers on his eyebrows and the crests of his ears. I guess *The Thinker* is like me today—lots of problems and no answers.

Chapter 2

I slump against the bus seat feeling split between the quiet, shrinking Lily Firestone before two o'clock this afternoon and the truant me.

By the time I get home, kids will already be home entertaining their families with the big news: *Lillian Firestone, you know, the adopted Chinese girl at school, ran away.*

Or they're saying—*Lily Firestone is a Communist spy.*

Or—*Lillian Firestone is missing in action.*

Or—*Did you know that the Jap girl is really a chink?*

The vice principal, Mr. Thorp, will have called my mother to report me truant, and our whole house will have collapsed.

But, amazingly, Mother is cooking, not crying, when I walk in. Nothing weird, no ripple in the air. I slip into the living room and check the phone—it's working.

No ring from Mr. Thorp all through dinner.

"We had a speaker at our patrol meeting today," Ralphie says at the table, sneaking a napkin full of too-chewy min-ute steak into the pocket of his Boy Scout pants. "Jerry Newcomer's uncle talked about being in the air force. He's heading out to Korea." I picture Neil Bradford's brother straddling a machine gun in a frozen Korean foxhole. "Dif-ferent guys in our patrol are bringing people to inspire us for our Citizenship in the Nation badge, like someone from their family tree who has done something brave and impor-tant."

My mother perks up. She turns to Dad, mouth open, but he waves her off.

"Vivian, I am not going to bore those Scouts with tales of twenty years in the real estate business. They need inspi-ration, not the *glory* of my bad-back deferment." He takes a long sip of his bourbon and water.

My brother shifts in his seat. "Well, do we have any-body else, any relatives I could bring?" He waves his arm toward Mother and then toward me. "Uh, well, I guess Lily wouldn't have . . . uh, anybody . . ."

The radiator gurgles as if it's about to throw up. *Shut up, Ralph.*

Our mother brushes an invisible crumb off her lip and stands, her voice staccato. "*Our* family tree is charted in the front of the Firestone Bible." Her apron looks as if she ironed it after she put it on. She marches to the kitchen with a bowl of Waldorf salad that does not need refilling.

She always refers to our family tree as if it is the source of all life on earth, the only reference we will ever need. Ralph and Dad share an eyelash of a glance. They look just alike, round heads, thick middles, except Ralph's not bald.

My brother shifts on his seat, tilts his head at me— *sorry*—and pokes a fork at the marshmallow bits floating in his dish of peaches. Mother goes upstairs without another word on the messy topic of family roots. If a little Ajax powder can't fix it, she's *gone*.

Our father pats Ralph and me on the shoulders. "I guess you two better handle the dishes tonight." He heads to the living room, evening paper in hand.

Dinner is done.

I lean across the table. "You need a bar of soap for dessert!"

Ralph makes a saliva bubble, smiles. "I know. Sorry. I'll do 'em."

I truly feel sorry for Ralphie, though. There's nobody from our family I'd call brave or courageous, except maybe him for bringing this up in the first place.

Cars snake around the traffic circle in front of our house. Headlights wash the dining room ceiling. Dad's radio news filters in from the living room. *One-kiloton nuclear test bomb dropped on Nevada flats . . . the grisly aftermath of Seoul, Korea's capture by the Communists . . . Mao on the move . . .*

Ralph reaches around me and grabs the meat platter, spilling a few drops of cold minute-steak juice on the carpet. He grinds them in with his sneaker.

After the dishes Ralph clomps upstairs and bursts through my bedroom door with the Firestone Bible under his arm. His face is flushed, his sleeves wet to the elbows. "Disappear, Ralphie." He pulls the chewed steak from his pocket, tosses it in my wastebasket.

"Ick."

He shakes his head at the trash can. "Man, I need to teach Mom how to cook. I know how to make jelly horn. You just wrap raw dough around a stick, cook it over the campfire, and smear it with jelly. And I can steam wild greens in a fire hole and—"

"Wow, that mouth of yours did it again. You lit the ol' Firestone family fuse with your tongue and ended up with the dishes."

He shuts my door, narrows his eyes at me. "So? God! What'd you do?"

"What do you mean?"

"At school! What happened? The vice principal called. Mr. Thorp. Mom was out so I, uh, took the message."

"*You* took the message?"

"I took the information," he says in a confidential tone.

I shake my head. "Wrong. Mr. Thorp wouldn't give *you* information."

Ralph raises his voice an octave. "He would if he thought I was Mom. I can still do that voice thing when I need to."

"You pretended you were Mom?"

"Yep."

"Oh my God. You are amazing. What did he say? Did he apologize for how Miss Arth didn't—?"

"He said you left school without permission and that you need to report to his office Monday morning. That's all." Ralph looks about to bust. "I mean . . . *you*. I can't believe it. What happened?"

Snow twirls in gusts in the streetlight out my window. I sit cross-legged on my bed and tell him everything, including the janitor's lightbulb salute and *The Thinker*. For the first time in history Ralph doesn't interrupt. "Usually it's just one or two kids, but this was the whole class *and* the teacher. I am so sick of it. I just stood up and walked out."

"That took guts," he says. "Did everybody clap?"

"*No*. They probably thought I was running away."

His eyes are saucers. "I swear. I'm bringing *you* to Scouts. You're a hero. It'll be so neat when you walk into school Monday morning."

"Sorry, but walking into Mr. Thorp's office will not be so neat."

Ralph thinks a minute, puts the Bible down. "Uh . . . what're you gonna do if it happens again, you know, somebody else coughs something bad?"

"It's not *new*. You wouldn't remember it, but in grade school kids teased me all the time thinking I was Japanese. I didn't even get what was going on." I chew my thumbnail. "But it's switched. Everybody's prejudiced against Chinese people because they are Communists now and they're trying to take over Korea. I've become the enemy because I'm Chinese even though I've never been there and I know exactly zero about it."

Ralph's quiet a moment, thinking. "So what *did* you do—run away, or stand up for yourself?"

I rub my face, my stomach in a knot. "I don't *know*. Both, I guess."

Ralph's eyes are bright. "Well, you can't stop now. You gotta keep going. You can't put the toothpaste back in the tube."

"Wow. Is that a quote from the Bible?"

"No, it's from the Dental Hygiene merit badge." He sighs, rubs his eyes with the heels of his hands. "Well, at least Mr. Thorp's call is over."

"Yeah. Thanks. But that's not exactly Boy Scout code, is it? Faking who you are."

"No, it's part of the help-your-older-sister code of honor."

We open to the genealogy page of the Bible, with four generations of Firestones perched on little branches. In Mother's neat script "Lillian Catherine Firestone—b. December 20, 1934" is written under "Donald and Vivian." Perched next to me is their miracle, natural-born son "Ralph Laurence Firestone—b. July 13, 1939."

Ralph points to two crossed-out, smudgy names. "Who are those guys?"

"Relatives on death row."

He nods. "Nice." We sit quietly for a minute studying the chart of our heritage, or at least Ralph's heritage, but we know almost none of them. It's as if our mother has used the Bible, the literal bulk and solemnness of it, to stand in for the actual people, even on Dad's side.

Ralph rattles the junk in his pocket, pulls out a rock. He flips it off his thumb, catches it back and forth, and then tosses it in my lap. It looks to be a piece of greenish shell.

"Ew. Did this come out of your nose?"

"Yep."

"What is it?" I ask.

Ralph gives me an odd look. "I thought maybe *you'd* know."

I lob the shell over him into the wastebasket by my vanity.

"*Hey!* Careful. It's part of my Scout collection," he says, scoping my room.

I hop off the bed, plaster my hands over his eyes. "You may not touch, move, or *re*move one single, solitary speck of dust from my room for your collection."

"Okay. Okay."

Dad's cigarette smoke snakes up the stairs. Ralph hoists his lumpy self off the floor. He retrieves his rock, then takes a split-second detour by my closet on his way out.

"*Halt!* I saw that."

He turns, hands behind his back, all innocent acting.

"Give it!"

He pulls my sneaker from behind his back. "Oops . . . wrong shoe. Meant to take the other one. I'm, uh, practicing my tracking and stalking skills for Scouts. No muskrats handy, so I picked *you*. Should be interesting, especially after today." He studies the sole of my shoe. "I need your *paw* print."

"Stalking? Really?"

"Careful observation is important." Ralph squats in stalker position on the carpet with his pants wedged up around his butt. He creeps—stomach to rug—across my floor. "Use toes and elbows only," he grunts. "Rest your weight on the insides of your legs."

I squish him to the floor with my foot. "In stalking," he grunts into the carpet, "always remember that your shadow is not overlooked by your quarry." He cranes his neck to look up at me. "Constantly watch your quarry. Be prepared. Freeze if necessary. Never approach from downwind.

Don't breathe until your quarry resumes feeding or other natural activities."

I pull Ralph to standing, load the Bible on his arm. "Here. You take it. It's missing a few chapters."

He walks out backward. "Don't you mean verses?"

"No, chapters." I shut my door in my brother's goofy face.

... *the true creation story of me.*

Chapter 3

I could grow a beard waiting for Mr. Thorp to get off the phone in his office. All weekend I obsessed over what rumors had been spread about me. I have rehearsed and re-rehearsed my side of the story until I can say it without crying. But so far, walking into school has been a carbon copy of every Monday, except for the pretzel twist in my stomach.

Mr. Thorp, of the clipped-caterpillar mustache and poochy eye bags, finally puts his caller on hold and looks up blankly. He mentions not one word about social studies. He does not ask a single question. Over the weekend my humiliating incident seems to have fallen into the empty wastebasket between his ears. He says nothing about Neil or commie coughing or the deaf-and-blind Miss Arth. "Since this is your first offense, if you successfully complete your detention, your truancy will be expunged from your permanent record."

Mr. Thorp reaches over, punches the blinking button on his phone, and that's it.

I walk out with my punishment—eighth hours on Wednesday and Friday for the next four weeks. Art room cleanup.

Sorry, Ralphie, all I got is a pink slip—no floats, no ticker tape parade for me.

Outside the front office I stop. I stare at the buffed brown floor, thinking *I hate this place*. But who cares? Nobody. My *heroic* departure was nothing that the swipe of a pink slip couldn't wipe away.

Outside, the ROTC honor guard is in formation around the flagpole. Neil Bradford holds a precision salute as the flag is raised. He's starched and serious. Neil will not receive a detention. Miss Arth will not receive a detention either. People don't get eighth hours for adjusting their earrings, even if right before their very eyes an innocent person is getting crushed by a tank.

In the lunch line Patty Kittle and my other former best friend Anita ask me how I'm feeling now. They both wear pearls, an essential part of the sorority girls'—better known as *cupcakes*—school uniform.

"What?"

Patty says, "You went to the nurse's office during class, right?"

"No. I wasn't sick. I walked *out*." I hold up my detention slip.

"Oh!" She nods, wide eyed, with her hand cupped over her mouth.

Anita's eyes shift all over the place. "Well, I'm so glad it was just because of . . . *that*, I mean, I'm so happy for you that you weren't sick or having . . ." She holds her stomach, cringes, and mouths *cramps*.

Is feeling prejudice more pleasant than cramps?

These are the only conversations I have the whole day except the ones in my head.

Oh, Patty and Anita, maybe the nurse could medicate you two for your phony sincerity syndromes. You know, the ones you use to hide the fact that you dropped me, the smiles that scream sorority girls and rice girls don't mix.

If I had done a handstand on my desk everyone would still have avoided looking at me in social studies. Miss Arth yawn-talks her way through a lecture on the future of the oil industry in America, followed by a Cold War film so dull it shreds itself in the projector.

Mr. Thorp reads the afternoon announcements—*the Student Council Ideals and Ethics Committee meets today. . . . Glee Club will practice its repertoire of religious, popular, and novelty songs for the Brotherhood Week assembly. . . .*

The final bell. The dreaded Monday here and gone.

*   *   *

On Wednesday afternoon the art room smells of turpentine and wet clay. It's big and messy. A freezing draft from outside comes through a ground-level door that isn't latched tight. Prisms hang in the long windows overlooking the icy track and football field. They cast patches of rainbow across the floor. I shiver, fold my arms. I remember sitting in here last year full of my parents' assurance that Patty and Anita and I would be fine starting at Wilson High School together. We'd stay loyal and watch out for each other after transferring from Our Lady of Sorrows. We would not become ladies of sorrow ourselves.

No one would have predicted that the polite, straight-A former Girl Scout Lillian Firestone would become a juvenile delinquent.

I sign the detention form on the art teacher's desk and read a list of "Cleanup Procedures" posted on the wall: 1. wipe tables, 2. soak rags and brushes in turpentine, 3. rinse eyedroppers, 4. sort pastels, 5. wash mirrors, 6. alphabetize glazes.

How would anybody ever know if I just signed in and left?

On the wall is a diagram showing how to shade a flat two-dimensional circle to create a sphere. Another poster, titled "Principles of Portraiture," outlines the proportions of the human face. Student self-portraits are tacked to cork strips around the room. They're terrible! Every one looks like an electrocuted zombie.

The side door thunks open, followed by a swoosh of freezing air. I wheel around. In sweeps a tall guy with messy brown hair, glasses, and a long coat. *Elliot James!*

"Self-portraits are a pain," he says, tossing me a glance. He flops his portfolio on the table. "Don't laugh until you've tried one."

What? "I wasn't laughing."

"But you wanted to," he says.

No I didn't.

He sits on a stool at a drawing table with photos taped to it. His boots are paint splattered. His knit scarf falls on the floor. "Girls don't get detentions. What'd you do?"

I ignore the question, grab a rag, and wipe an arrangement of bottles and shells sitting on a pedestal in front of the window.

"Don't touch that! It's a still-life model. You'll change the shadows. And don't clean the tables, either. Nobody'll notice. It's just stupid crap to make you sorry for what you did."

"Do you have one too?" I ask.

"One what?"

"Detention," I say.

"No!" *Stupid. Stupid. Elliot James is the king of the art room. Of course he doesn't have an eighth hour.*

"Yearbook stuff." He points to his drawing paper. "Caricatures."

I must look blank because he says, "You know, *carica-*

tures, drawings where you exaggerate people's features and personalities." He waves his pen. "It's sort of like Chinese calligraphy. Just a few perfect strokes and no more. But with a pen instead of a brush."

Continued blankness.

"Chinese calligraphy, you know, handwriting. I'm learning how. Practicing the techniques." He tilts his head, speaks slowly. "*China*. Right? That big ancient place across the ocean?" He makes a wavy pattern with his hand, then hunches over the table, rubbing his boots together as he draws. He has a rolled towel propped under his forearm to keep from smearing the ink, and an expression as intense as *The Thinker*'s.

I wring the life out of some sponges, thinking that at least he said China like it's a *place*, not a slap in the face. I prop the sponges behind the spigot. I looked dumb about calligraphy because I am. I know exactly zero about China—we haven't studied it yet—except that it's now *Red* China and that pandas live there and so did Gone Mom and my birth father. But I didn't. Babies living in Chinatown, San Francisco, don't learn Chinese handwriting. And little Chinese orphan girls who move to Missouri and get adopted and go to Catholic school don't learn it either.

I check the clock. Thirty minutes to go. Now what? Clean up or don't clean up? I straighten the stools around the blocky wooden tables and empty a coffee can into the rust-stained sink. A greasy swirl slides down the drain. "That was turpentine. You don't dump turpentine down a *sink*," Master Elliot says.

Too late now.

"And you can't rinse oil paints with water," he says.

What else can I mess up?

He blows on his ink drawing of our head football coach blasting a whistle. It took him all of four minutes, maybe less. Elliot turns. "So . . . what *did* you do for the detention?"

"I walked out of social studies in the middle of class."

"Because . . . ?"

". . . of a cartoon, a political cartoon this guy brought for current events. . . . Kinda dumb, but anyway . . ."

"Cartoons aren't dumb. What was it?"

"Uh, well, these creepy Chinese soldiers in an army tank are killing United Nations kids in a crosswalk, and this guy coughed 'commie' at me because I'm, you know, Chinese, so he wouldn't touch the picture after I *contaminated* it, and it got worse and I finally walked out."

Elliot looks up at me, curls his lip. "*That* was stupid." His face shifts. He glances at the clock, says, "Damn," stands, slides his drawings into a folder, and in another whoosh of freezing air bolts out the door.

It bangs hard against the frame. The self-portraits flutter. I pace between the tables, telling my audience of zombies, "So he thinks *I* was stupid for walking out. Well, that's perfect. An eighth hour plus insults!"

I whip Elliot's scarf off the floor, stuff it in the trash can, grab my books, and walk out on my own detention.

Sleet taps the bus windows. We wheel past the Country Club Plaza—the World's First and Finest Shopping Center, my father's *baby*. Every day my real estate developer father tramps between the restaurants, construction cranes, fountains, and cement mixers in his hard hat, yakking into his walkie-talkie. By the time I get home I have decided to tell my parents that I am volunteering in the art room after school. They won't like it. It's not Future Homemakers of America Club or Pep Squad. They are allergic to anything arty.

When I walk into the front hall they are talking in the kitchen—voices hushed. Dad comes out still wearing his overcoat and carrying a highball glass full of ice. He motions me into the living room.

Surging panic. I perch on the edge of the couch.

He removes his hat and smooths the hair on the sides of his head. The flesh of his neck bunches when he loosens his tie and undoes his top button. He steps to the bar and pours a generous jigger of bourbon over the ice and then water.

Mother enters with a tortured expression and a letter that she hands to him. I recognize the Wilson High School letterhead. My father holds it at reading distance. His gaze bounces across the page. He reads aloud the section reporting my truancy and detention.

"Is this a mistake?" Mother asks.

Dad lights a cigarette, takes a deep drag and a deeper gulp of bourbon. He clears his throat, looks longingly at the evening paper on his footstool.

"*No*," I say. Next comes a prolonged pause where the question "Why?" should be. Their bewildered silence nudges me on. "Do you want to know *why*?"

My father nods.

"Because the guy sitting next to me in social studies called me a commie and other kids sneezed 'chink.' And Miss Arth just sat there and did *nothing* to stop them. She acted like I didn't exist!"

"You walked out of school because of a sneeze?" Mother turns to my father, palms up. "A *sneeze*?"

"*I* did not sneeze, Mother."

"I *know* that." She shakes her head. "Yours was an extreme reaction, Lillian."

My mother's words are tacks in me. I turn to Dad, search his face. "What your mother is saying is that the class's conduct did not warrant you getting yourself in trouble, Lily."

How would you know that?

Dad rubs his eyes. I'm glad he's not wearing earrings he can fiddle with. I poke my parents with a slow and overly elementary explanation. "They did this because I'm Chinese and we are currently fighting the Red Chinese Communists in Korea."

Mother fixes me with a look, shakes her head. "You are not the same girl you used to be, Lillian."

Thank you for noticing.

My father turns to my mother with a slight smile. "Well, the world isn't the same place it used to be either, Vivian. Our Lily hasn't changed." *I haven't?* "The world has—the Germans and the Japs, the Cold War, Korea, the Communist takeover in Red China . . ."

Mother holds up a hand. Her eyes shift between my father and me. "Why should all that concern Lily?"

I look right at her. My eyes fill up. "I am not talking about the war *over there* in Korea. This happens to *me* at my school every day. Who else's concern *would* it be? Miss Arth and the vice principal were horrible. Everyone was."

I wipe my face, expecting her to get back to asking about the consequences of my detention, but instead she says, "Who knows about this, Lillian?"

I count on my fingers. "Miss Arth, Mr. Thorp, the janitor who was changing a lightbulb in the room at the time, all the people in my class, the art teacher . . ." I do not mention Ralph deflecting Mr. Thorp's phone call. "I've tried to tell you lots of times before that I got teased and insulted. Even at Our Lady of Sorrows. How was I supposed to understand it?" I turn to Dad. "You always said it was just goofy kids' stuff. Don't let it bother me."

My mother's mouth turns down. "We were trying to help you get along, protect you."

"From what? Myself? All that did was make it my problem." I stare at my lap. "My face is Chinese and it's not going away!" I do not look at her. Can't. We fall into our ocean of silence where hurts old and new crash against each other.

Why in the world did you adopt me?

I take a long breath and another, and explain about my punishment cleaning the art room. My mother looks as if she has swallowed turpentine. She glares at Dad and heads to the front hall. She stops a moment, turns back, and holds her hand palm facing out, as though bestowing a blessing. "Never forget. You are an American, Lillian. You are a *Firestone.*"

I watch her climb the stairs, imagining the sentence she doesn't say—*So act like one.* I listen to her creak across the floorboards in the upstairs landing. My father leans in, filling the emptiness she left, and says in a confidential tone, "Your mother is scared for you, Lily. The world situation has everybody terrified. She wants you to adjust, fit in. She has tried to put her own hardships behind her and she wants you to do the same."

I nod, but I don't mean it.

Dad opens the newspaper. My parents' bedroom door

clicks shut. I sink back into the sofa, squeeze my fists thinking that this is exactly how she always operates. She hears something and she *owns* it. *She* determines if it counts, if it matters in the world. And I have let her determine if *I* count, if I matter exactly the way I am.

I cannot stand her.

This is why we should never try to talk. This is exactly why.

Chapter 4

"Hey," Ralph says, tapping on my bedroom door after the house has calmed down. He tilts his head toward our parents' shut door. "What gives?"

I shake my head. "They got a letter from school. God. I'm so sick of everything. I can't talk about it anymore."

"Okay." He waves his hand. "Then just come look at this. It's different."

"No."

"Please!" He pulls me into his bedroom and opens the door by his closet that accesses the attic steps. He turns on the light. Displayed on the step right under his candy collection, which is mostly empty Bit-O-Honey and Necco wrappers, is his Boy Scout collection. He painted the attic stairs bright blue, something our mother allowed during the period right before now when she believed he could do no wrong. Before Ralph turned eleven he could have painted his carpet blue or built a campfire in the bathtub without a peep from her. He is still a master at working around her. Much better than I am. He plays smart, then dumb, he tiptoes, has tantrums—whatever works. Dad knows it too. "Crazy like a fox," our father calls his protégé.

Displayed on the stair is a scraggly strip of fur, an old stick of polished wood, the chunk of swirly rock he threw at me the other night, and the cap to a bourbon bottle.

We kneel on the floor. "It's not finished, yet," Ralph says. "I'm looking for more stuff."

"Ralph, *normal* Boy Scouts collect coins or stamps, or how about matchbooks?"

"Well, this was easier than Hog and Pork Production or Bugling or writing a report on the dangers of laxatives or bandaging my own finger."

I point at the fur. "Where's the rest of the squirrel?"

Ralph slashes a flat hand across his neck.

I shiver. "Ick." I sit back on my heels and rub the stick. It's about a foot long, wider than a ruler, with one flat side and another that's curved, like a wooden cylinder cut in half lengthwise. "What *is* this?"

Ralph shrugs. "Don't know. I thought you might."

"Why not collect things that go together, have a theme?"

"Oh, I *am*." He raises three fingers. "Scout's honor." He

puts the stick back, organizes his measly junk, and glances up into the dusky rafters. "I've found lots of strange stuff up there."

Saturday night.

My parents are out. So is Ralph. If I joined the Boy Scouts I'd at least have an indoor campout tonight instead of sitting here with a stale popcorn ball stalking myself in last year's yearbook. I guess it's better than reading our Bible, although lots of people at school think the yearbook *is* the Bible. The freshman pictures look like God dealt a bad deck of miniature face cards: *I giveth you pimples. To you I bestow a hooked nose. You shall look like a turtle. But ye, oh blessed one, can have a smooth, sculpted white face and blond hair.* Actually, every single face is white, cover to cover, except mine. Mine's grayish. My mouth is a dull dash mark, my eyes black pinpricks, and my hair flat. No wonder I never look at myself.

The yearbook makes school seem shiny and organized, all of us packed between the padded silver covers. Everybody is lined up, achieving great things—winner after winner. Yearbooks don't include the taunts and discrimination and cliques. There is not a group picture of the Students Prejudiced Against Chinese People, because the members are secret, or they used to be, until Korea. Now prejudice is free to eat in the lunchroom, ride the bus, join fraternities, sneeze, cough, speak up. Prejudice is *big* at Wilson High School.

Also *unpictured* are the sorority girls, because sororities and fraternities aren't school sponsored. They're social clubs outside high school. Patty and Anita are dying to become cupcakes despite our old oath of allegiance.

And there's no picture of the gang of greasy guys who grab their chests on the bus and whisper, "Hau ru, Tea Cups?" as if I wouldn't comprehend what "cups" of mine they're talking about.

A bus is a battleground if you look like the enemy.

What would Mother say if I asked her for advice? *Go quietly to the bathtub, Lillian, and soak in bleach water.*

Dad's advice? *Make a joke of it.*

Ralph's? *Be a hero.*

My advice to myself? *Carry Kleenex.*

When I walked out of social studies, it looked like running away, but it wasn't—it was the first Chinese thing I have ever done. But what now? Fight back every time somebody says something? Walk out? Drop out? Gone Mom must have felt tested living here with illegitimate me. Or maybe she was really a spy or a tramp or she was sick or broke. Who knows why she left me in Missouri and sailed away?

I flip more pages.

Elliot's caricatures are everywhere. He drew the Future

Homemakers of America Club as hobos. The ROTC rifle team holds boomerangs. The Typing Club president is all thumbs—slightly funny, but not very. I see his drawing of himself in the Brush and Pencil Club—thick glasses on a lanky stick figure with paintbrushes for fingers.

I see my tiny face peeking out of the Red Cross Club group picture. Ugh. I shut the yearbook, look away, close my eyes. I won't be in this year's photo because I quit going. I'm too *Red* for the Red Cross now.

On Wednesday Elliot James says, "Thank you so much for throwing my clothes away." He flips the fringe of his scarf. "I dug it out of the trash."

Thanks for calling me stupid. I tilt my head, shrug, neither admit nor deny it.

Mrs. Van Zant, the art teacher and yearbook sponsor, walks through the door carrying a thick folder. She steps around me, makes a beeline for Elliot, because they are getting an early start on the yearbook. They consult about page layouts and his drawing of the front of the school building. "My vote is a double spread for the title page. *The Sentinel 1951.* You will make Wilson High look regal." She moves her hands together in prayer point and bows to Elliot.

They talk about the theme this year, "Patriotism," and the Student Council's vote last fall to eliminate homecoming because of the Korean War. *Boo hoo hoo.* Not everybody liked it, but I guess patriotism was more popular than popularity.

I look at Mrs. Van Zant bent over Elliot. I imagine a cartoon with him holding an umbrella as she drools all over his talent. "I hope you're planning something wonderful for our Fine Arts Showcase in March," she says, shaking a finger at him.

From their conversation I learn that he takes advanced life drawing and sculpture classes at the Kansas City Art Institute. I learn that Mrs. Van Zant believes Elliot should be *teaching* the classes.

She glances at my whisk broom. *Yes, Mrs. Van Zant, I am the truant with no artistic talent. I am the custodian's apprentice.* "I remember you," she exclaims. "Lillian Firestone, isn't it? Why haven't I seen you in here this semester? You showed promise your freshman year."

I did? I smile to be polite, but she's wrong. "I—I'm left-handed," I stutter as Mrs. Van Zant heads out the door.

Elliot stares at me like I'm crazy. "So what? So am I! They tried to make me switch but I couldn't." He sharpens his pencil with a pocketknife, drums his fingers. He gestures *come over here.* He's about to prove his left-handed drawing brilliance.

I meander over with my dustpan.

"Tilt your head up," he says. "Turn this way." I don't. I stare at the pile of pencil shavings he is creating on the floor. "I'll clean it up," he says. "Just turn here a sec."

He holds a pencil vertically, horizontally, and diagonally in front of my face. He squints, covers one eye, and measures the space between my eyes by sliding his inky thumb along the length of his pencil. His glasses look like he has finger painted them with dust and spit.

"Drawing *your* face," he says, pointing the pencil right at me, "I'd exaggerate the triangle shadow along your nose, and the cleft in your chin, and your cheekbones." He taps his own cheeks, looks off, puzzled, as if my face is an unsolvable geometry problem. "You know, the combination."

Elliot stretches to get a side view. My cheeks burn. I turn from his dissection of my face. "When did you come from China?" he asks.

"I didn't." I stare at spots of paint the color of dried blood on the floor. "I was born in San Francisco. In Chinatown."

"Interesting," he says. I know he's figured out that I'm adopted. No secret there. Elliot dives back into his yearbook drawings, his pencil turning paper into people.

I remember almost nothing of Chinatown. My new mother explained my history to me when I asked about her big stomach. She had gotten pregnant with Ralph soon after my adoption. *I didn't have you in my tummy, Lillian. A lady who came here from China did. We know nothing about her. That's all over now.*

My new mother couldn't carry me because she worried that the baby inside her would stop growing like all the others had. So she lay on the divan, and whenever she sat up, the lap I wanted to climb onto disappeared. Even before he was born Ralph overtook it.

In sixth grade, when Patty and Anita and I discovered the facts of life, I tried for the first time to imagine the man "involved" with Gone Mom. We didn't dare mention it out loud, but we all thought my birth mother wasn't married to him and had committed a mortal sin and would go to hell if she didn't get forgiveness. I actually pictured her coughing and moaning in hell, all smoky and overcrowded. How could I know if she had ever properly asked for forgiveness? Done penance. Chinese people were heathens, not Christians. She might not have even known she was supposed to confess.

Any other record of her existence is sealed forever. She has been sealed off inside me, too. But since I walked out of class, Gone Mom has been creeping in—turning my tear faucets, twisting my stomach, and unwrapping memories, like the one that awoke me last night. We were together in a dark room reaching for a giant, glowing pearl hanging from the ceiling by a chain.

And now Elliot James has started poking at Gone Mom with his pencil.

The door bangs open. I jump. Elliot is off without

a word. I watch him tramp across the empty practice field to his car parked on the street. I mop my face with a handful of damp paper towels that smell like dirt. I straighten the stools and wipe a cluster of round mirrors on gooseneck stands. They're self-portrait supplies. Broken flashes of my face bounce up at me—my teeth, the view up my nose, a Cyclops.

I squeeze my eyes shut, hold my cheeks. *Go away, Lily.*

Chapter 5

I'm cold and jittery positioned in the streetcar shelter at the Country Club Plaza with my hat pulled down and my muffler up, praying my father doesn't walk by. Traffic slides between the shelter and the Chinese restaurant across the street. The House of Chow is a *leasing experiment*, as my father calls it. He described his dilemma about offering the Chows retail space. "Orientals are . . . *shrewd*," he said over his glasses. "So far they're okay, but . . ."

Mother had dabbed the corners of her mouth and given him a smug *we'll see* kind of nod.

A banner stretches across the wooden overhang of the restaurant entrance announcing: CHINESE NEW YEAR CELEBRATION FEBRUARY 5. It is written in English. Another hanging banner, written in Chinese characters, could say anything at all.

I am here because Elliot made me feel like a stooge about China. Hopefully one of the Chows will walk out and at least I will have seen a Chinese person lately.

And sure enough, in a minute two people do. Mr. and Mrs. Chow, the owners. Mrs. Chow is loaded down with a ladder and a long string of red and gold lanterns. They probably need help, but if I walked over this very minute they would stop and gawk, wondering, *Who are you?* And I would reply that I am a Chinese character without a plot.

I've held a teeny fantasy that Gone Mom might be Mrs. Chow, which is nuts because Mrs. Chow is obviously a planner with foresight and guts. Good for her. She and Mr. Chow would not have a baby girl, feed her, clothe her, love her, and then abandon her. They would have helped their daughter. They would have taught her Chinese cooking and fancy napkin folding and calligraphy and how to be true in the world. They would have had a proud bamboo family tree and dragon decorations for her birthday party. They would have clapped when she stood up for herself for the first time and walked out on prejudice.

Mrs. Chow's loud voice carries across the street. She gestures wildly to her husband. *"Siu sam!"*

He flaps his hands at her. "Okay, okay." He's got a yellow stocking cap, baggy pants, and foggy glasses. With raised arms, she points with her chin where he's supposed to position the ladder. Between the tops of her rubber boots and the hem of her bulky green coat are sections of bare leg. Her calves are thick and sturdy as she struggles up the rungs with the string of lanterns cascading on the ground behind her. *"Mou dit douh!"* he yells.

The clink of wind chimes floats across the street. They sound free and flighty. But the Chows don't. They're all business. Mr. Chow strains to hook his end of the lantern string. He says, "You the boss," and she says, *"Siu sam, siu sam."*

Mr. Chow plugs in the bulbs. The entrance gleams, with rows of glowing lanterns nodding in the breeze. Passersby stop to look. Clap. Mr. Chow grins, extends his hand, bows. *"Xie xie.* Good see you. Long time no see!"

The Chows are not huddled behind the Bamboo Curtain. They are not avoiding themselves. They're loud and colorful, making a living off their Chineseness.

I feel like clapping too, when a gong sounds in my head: *Siu sam, siu sam*—be careful, be careful. *Mou dit douh*—don't fall down. *Xie xie*—thank you. It's Chinese and I understand it! I whisper, *"Siu sam, siu sam"* and *"Leih li douh"*—"Come here"—and "Mamá," with the accent on the second syllable. I hear her voice and mine mixed, amazed by this singsong Chinese music box still wound in me.

I squint across the street. Somebody is helping hold the door for Mr. Chow while he carries the ladder inside. He's chubby with a Boy Scout hat.

Ralph!

He waves at me. *Oh, God! Please, please don't tell them I'm over here.* Ralph bows. Mr. Chow answers heartily, *"Joi gin."* Good-bye. Good-bye.

My brother trudges toward the streetcar shelter. There is only one Ralph Firestone in the whole world, but somehow he's everywhere! He hands me a fortune cookie. "From the Chows' place."

I put it in my pocket. Crumbs go flying when he cracks his. The paper fortune strip falls in a puddle. I do not help him get it. "What are you doing here?" I snap. "Has there ever been a day in your life when you were not bugging me?"

Ralph shrugs.

"If I needed a pet I'd get a hamster. If I needed a shadow I'd rent one. *What* are you doing here?"

"Shopping."

"What?"

"At the Chow House they've got a neat gift shop. And I'm also stalking you. Polishing my tracking skills. Remember?"

"Real stalkers never wave at their quarry."

He gives me a sidelong glance. "What are *you* doing here?"

"Observing Chinese people." I do not add that I already checked the encyclopedia and our world history textbook, which have only distant pictures of people constructing bridges or working in factories with faces no bigger than the head of a pin. The pictures of the Chinese soldiers in the newspaper and newsreels are too scary to face.

We walk to Cooper's Drugs a few blocks away. I need a notebook. Ralph needs a mirror—more stalking equipment. We're safe here. If Dad shows up now, we can talk our way around being at the counter drinking hot chocolate together on Saturday afternoon.

I shove a napkin at my brother and shudder. "There's marshmallow globs in your braces and crusty chocolate ick on the corners of your mouth." He gives me a wide grin. His hair is plastered to his forehead and his ears stick out, pink as petunias.

The door swings open and in steps a slew of older sorority girls and Patty and Anita. I shrink on the stool, turn to Ralph. "Oh, God. *Cupcakes.*" I cock my head. "Let's go."

"Hey, there's Anita," Ralph says, "and Patty and Maureen. What do you mean—*cupcakes?*"

"*Sorority girls.* Let's *go.*"

So Ralph does. He goes right over and says in Mr. Chow style, "Hi, Anita. Long time no see."

I have no choice but to follow. They give me quick, flashy waves and smiles and squiggle into their corner booth—the Cupcake Corral. Maureen, my former locker partner, smiles, turns to my brother, and says, "Wow, Ralphie, you're taller!"

Anita stands, facing me across our deep pit of crippled awkwardness. "Are you gonna get a chocolate Coke?" I say. *Why do I care what she orders anymore? I don't.* Her eyes flicker. She moves her head—maybe.

"Your current event about the Red Cross was great." I hear the whole drugstore—even the cosmetics consultants and pharmacists—gasp at the most pathetic nonsense sentence I have ever uttered. Anita and I both know I quit the Red Cross Club because I didn't fit in. My face tingles. Even Ralph looks surprised.

Anita looks down. "Yeah. Sorry you stopped coming to club," she says, and slides back into her seat. She and Patty and Maureen wiggle their fingers. "See ya."

I bump out the door—a cliqueless alien. Ralph goes back to the counter and pays.

I head to the streetcar, silent. I'm done. Permanently. I can't trust my mouth and I can't trust my whole self not to get up and walk out of class or throw Elliot's clothes in the trash or stalk the Chows.

Ralph nudges me. "What's a sorority?"

"Uh . . . like Boy Scouts . . . but it's for high school girls, except it isn't Girl Scouts either. You can't join if you want to. You have to be *asked*. Anita and Patty are grooming themselves so they'll get in next year. No merit badges either, Ralphie. Just tryouts."

"Tryouts?"

"Number one: You have to be white. Number two: You must act cupcakey sweet on the outside. Three: Wear pearls. Four: Swear off your pre-sorority friends, and if you are Jewish or poor or something, hide it. No pandas

44

or yellow monkey girls allowed. Oh, and you have to be cliquey and . . ."

Ralph looks up. "What's 'cliquey'?"

"Keeping with your own type. Labeling people, talking behind their backs, and being two-faced and . . ."

"Oh, neat! You mean like *you* talking behind their backs, calling them *cupcakes*?" Ralph gives me a sorry look. "I'm stickin' with Scouts. At least there's a handbook."

On the bus he asks about the Chows. "Okay . . . so, why were you spying on them? Do you think they're your real parents or something?"

"No!" I squeeze my hands. "That's impossible."

"Grandparents?"

"No."

"Aunt and uncle?"

"God! Forget it. I just wanted to see some Chinese people. That's all."

Ralph's not convinced. "You thought Mrs. Chow might be your first mom, didn't you?"

"*NO!*"

Ralph's tone turns soft, curious. "Have you ever seen her?"

"Uh, *duh*. I only *lived* with her for three years."

"I mean, like in pictures."

I do not say that currently it feels like any Chinese lady

in the universe could be my birth mother. I do tell Ralph that I call her Gone Mom, because it sounds kind of Chinese and it fits her perfectly.

"Do you have any of her old stuff?" he asks.

"Nope." I sigh, retrieve my fortune cookie from my pocket, and crack it open. It reads:

Bodhisattvas surround you.

I turn the strip over. No translation. I hand it to Ralph.

"What's *bo-dee-sat-vaas*?" he asks, holding the fortune up to the bus window.

"Who knows?" I close my eyes.

"We gotta go eat at the Chow House sometime. They've got an aquarium full of red fish and a shop that sells finger tortures and these neat dragon kites."

"I won't ever go in there. Plus it's not *Chow House*, which sounds like a cowboy diner. It's the House *of* Chow." My voice sounds a little haughty.

"Right. Chinese cowboys only." Ralph tosses part of my cookie and catches it in his mouth while I sit back wondering why in the world I care what the Chows' restaurant is called.

When we get home Mother is playing solitaire at the kitchen table with the radio on: *Yes, folks, we bring the world to you.* . . . I hear Ralph sneak to the attic. I sit on my bedroom floor, hold my new notebook between my palms, and let it fall open to a random page. I write, and then whisper the name: "Gone Mom." I tape my "Bodhisattvas surround you" fortune on another page. I stretch my legs and shut my eyes. More scraps of my Gone Mom memory-dream appear.

I'm little. She's standing and I'm sitting on her arm. The room is dim with lacy shadows on the floor. We look up at a ceiling filled with lighted dragons. They bite each other's tails with pointy fangs. Gone Mom holds her palm flat against my backbone so I won't fall. She counts and says, "*Gau luhng.*" *Nine dragons.* Footsteps echo around us. A glowing ball, the dragon pearl, hangs from the center of the ceiling. I stretch my hand to grab it.

My eyes pop open. I look up at my own raised hand. *Where in the world were we?*

My vanity mirror reflects snowflakes shoved by the wind. I walk over, sit down, and search my face for bits of Gone Mom. My door bangs opens. No knock. I grab a Kleenex and turn. Ralph stands in the opening hiding something behind his back. "Hey! I—"

"Disappear, Ralph! Have you ever heard of the term 'privacy'?"

He looks from me to the mirror and back. "Staring at your face isn't gonna *change* it, Lily."

"Well, don't *you* ever try it," I snap. "Yours is getting all bumpy."

Ralph blinks, shrugs. "I was gonna say your face was *fine*, but forget it." He flips off my ceiling light and slams the door.

I'm sorry. I'm awful. I touch my cheeks in the dark. They're wet. I wipe my face, imagining Gone Mom's fingers are mine, wondering if the only place in the whole raging world she exists is in me. I slide my new notebook between my bed and the wall. With her name written in it, it's already too full . . . and too empty.

Chapter 6

I have cleaned out my bobby pin box, tossed the rusted clippies, finished my geometry homework, and started reading *Jane Eyre* for extra credit. I have emptied the wastebaskets, dusted the downstairs, and now I am in the basement plowing through the ironing basket without being asked. The reason?

Guilt.

I am sprinkling and pressing my father's cotton boxer shorts because guilt will make a person do many fantastic and insincere things. Guilt will motivate a person to iron underpants and complicated pleated skirts.

Why do I feel guilty? Because I stood up for my Chineseness. I stalked the House of Chow. I gave my birth mother a name and wrote it in my notebook and if my parents knew, they would die.

Unlike me, Ralph is not bullied by guilt. He can fake

his voice to sound like Mother, hide his cruddy Scout collection, grind gravy into the rug, and feel fine. He can do anything. He's free because he's their natural-born son. He fixed our mother's life by being born. He is the guilt-free answer to everything.

I should hate him, but I don't. He is real smart and loyal and funny and always thinking.

Pinned to our basement clothesline is an army of Mother's girdles. Two white, one flesh-toned, and a black one with a lace front panel. Ralph refers to her putting on a girdle as the "Fat vs. Elastic" battle. The girdle always loses.

Our basement is the opposite of the art room. It smells like Spic and Span and it stays exactly the same—tidy stacks of canned beans and tuna fish, snow chains on hooks by the furnace, the crate of empty pop bottles rinsed and wiped. Ash bin spotless. Neat as a pin.

With a few additions it would make a perfect fallout shelter. Or if the Pope dropped by our basement one day, he'd hire Mother to be God's housekeeper. She could organize His medicine cabinet, arrange His manicure kit, and starch His halo. She would wipe God's fingerprints off His bottle of Squirt.

Ironing, my contribution to the clean and orderly world of our house, is better than going to confession if I want to be rid of guilt. It's the perfect penance.

I gather Dad's handkerchiefs, Ralph's rolled socks, which I did not iron, and head upstairs. Out of nowhere I picture Elliot James's paint-spattered pants, the scarf hanging around his neck, and the gray sweater stretched across his shoulders. He looks like he lives in an art studio. He sure doesn't try to look like everybody else. He seems unaffected by what people think, except maybe his girl-friend if he has one. Surely he does. I drop Ralph's socks. They bounce behind me all the way down the steps.

No trace of Elliot today. Mrs. Van Zant's art quote for the week on the chalkboard reads:

If you want to understand something, try drawing it!

She has just walked out after hanging posters of famous artists along one wall. Each has a biography and an example artwork: Winslow Homer, Claude Monet, Salvador Dalí, Vincent van Gogh, Pablo Picasso. I scan the artists. The only fact I know about any of them is that Vincent Van Gogh cut off his own ear. His own *ear*! How could he?

One poster describes Michelangelo, who painted the ceiling of the Sistine Chapel in Rome, Italy. God wears a blue nightgown that needs ironing while riding across heaven with a squad of angels. He reaches to touch fingers with "Man," who is naked. They are both white. Man's and God's fingertips almost touch, but not quite.

Did they ever touch? What did Michelangelo believe was supposed to happen then?

A stained-glass window at Our Lady of Sorrows showed God on His heavenly throne with fiery eyes and His sword of righteousness. He isn't reaching out to touch anybody. He's in a bad mood. His helper angels look miserable. God's hard to work for.

Salvador Dalí's surreal poster is a nightmare landscape— melted pocket watches crawling with black ants. *The Persistence of Memory*. Memories of what?

Pablo Picasso's *Girl before a Mirror* painting looks like two exploded clowns staring at each other. The background is clashing red and black diamonds and green polka dots. It's crazy, more hideous than all the self-portraits combined.

I grab some rags, turn and bump the pedestal with the still-life arrangement. The water bottle wobbles. I grab it and knock the pipe and shells on the floor. I put it back all wrong. "Why do people *care* about this junk?" I bark at the ruined arrangement. "Can't a normal person just *see* something and go about their day without drawing it?"

"I knock it every darn time I clean in here," a voice answers. It's the janitor, Mr. Howard, who seems perfectly fine to have witnessed me yelling at a pile of pure junk. "I just sorta"—he walks over, patting his big hands on the air—"put it back." Mr. Howard scrutinizes it and adjusts the bottle. "It needs to be closer to the edge, and the cloth needs to be slightly more crinkled over the pipe. There, that's a nice reflection on the candlestick. Don't you agree?" He steps back, tilts his head this way and that. He kisses his fingertips. "Perfect. Nobody will notice. They never do! Art rooms aren't supposed to be *clean*, they're supposed to be cluttered with inspiration and new ideas." He pauses a moment. "How are *you*, Miss Firestone?"

I know he's referring to the horrible social studies fiasco he witnessed from his ladder. "Okay," I mumble, the way I might say it's *okay* that my house burned down or that I have contracted polio.

Mr. Howard nods. He checks the kiln, rewraps a block of wet clay, then turns with a hand against his chest. "As you may already know, Miss Firestone, I can *work* here, but my kids can't go to school here. Negroes can't live in this neighborhood."

I blink at him, tongue-tied. He stands there ten feet tall. I can't tell if he thinks it's a good or bad thing not to be able to live around here. For an awkward moment we both turn to Picasso's mirror painting. On the left side is a girl whose face is a mix—half-yellow, half-white. The white part is a profile with a triangle-shaped nose, a black oval eye, and black slash for a mouth. The yellow part looks forward with pink cheeks and red lips. "I think Picasso's saying that people can treat an artwork like a mirror and find themselves in it," Mr. Howard says.

Really?

He empties the waste can, turns with his cart, and says, "This is my favorite spot in the whole building, best place in the world for a detention." He smiles. "Good afternoon, Miss Firestone."

I walk closer, squint at Picasso's crazy painting. The girl's reflection in the mirror on the right side is mysterious and disturbing. Her profile is dark purples and blues with a thick orange tear hooked on her eye and a pregnant-looking stomach that's hollow—no baby inside. *Gone Mom.* I cover my face with my hands. *Go away.*

I grab my coat and walk out the side door onto the practice field. I swallow the chilly, busy air, my coat flapping against my legs. An airplane whines. I follow the sound up to a speck of glitter crossing the pale sky. I imagine the passengers as tiny, distant dolls. If one of them really needed God, she could break the rules—just open the airplane window, reach out, and brush fingertips with Him.

Chapter 7

Toward the end of dinner these words pop from Ralph's mouth and crash on the table. "Say, everybody, I have something!"

Uh-oh . . . here come the Chows.

Ralph gives me a look. My eyeballs return bullets. "It's more a question, really." He turns to Dad.

Dad holds up his hand—*halt!* "Ralph, if this is another rendition of your when-are-we-going-to-get-a-television-set campaign . . ."

"No, Dad. It's a legal question." Ralphie takes a deep breath. "When kids get adopted . . ." He pauses. "Adopted" shatters our chandelier, pierces the ceiling. Mother dabs her mouth, leaving two mauve smears on her napkin.

". . . when they are four or five years old or something . . . does the orphan get to bring all his stuff with him to the new people—pictures and clothes from the orphanage, or, you know, what happens to all his stuff?"

Mother leans in, grips the table edge, and glances at my father. "It is gotten rid of." Dad tips his head, blinks, presumably considering the correct legal answer.

Our mother shivers, turns to her husband. "It's best. Why should a child be encouraged to live in reverse?" Her face looks a mix of *amen* and *dammit*.

My mind exits the dining room and enters the little girls' dorm at the Sisters of Mercy Children's Home. I see the scratchy green wool blanket on my metal bed—seventh down on the right side—and my pink plastic hairbrush labeled "Lillian" and my locker stacked with pajamas and undershirts. I smell the incense smoke floating in the chapel. My *reverse*.

"But, technically, shouldn't the things still belong to the kid?" Ralph insists.

Dad does not look at me. He chuckles a phony *ho-ho-ho, now there's a doozy* kind of laugh and says, "If you don't follow in my footsteps in the construction business, son, you've got the makings of a fine attorney."

No one has asked Ralph why he's asking such a question. No one has asked what *I* think. Mother stands like a juggler who has lost her pins. She turns and studies her face in the mirror above the buffet, then glares at her precious crystal cabinet. She walks out, lifts a new *McCall's* off the mail pile in the front hall, and heads upstairs to that tidy upholstered place inside herself with no adopted Chinese daughter, no smarty eleven-year-old Boy Scout, no old orphan belongings, no commies or chinks or Korean War—just bridge club, manicures, darning, and solitaire.

Don't live in reverse! That's my mother, always summing things up, exiting a difficult conversation before it starts. In our house hard topics are either swirled away in a glass of bourbon or wrapped in sandpaper and swallowed.

"Why are you stealing my misery?" I ask Ralph upstairs. "Why are you so interested in *adoption* all of a sudden? You're all rooted here and fertilized and growing your nice branch on the family tree."

"I was asking a general question."

I nod. "Sure you were."

The phone rings. Ralph leaps downstairs to answer it. "Lily!" he yells, loud enough to awaken our neighbor's dead parakeet buried in the side yard.

I walk down slowly, reviewing who it could be. Patty Kittle? No. Anita, who acts married since she and Neil Bradford's best friend are going steady? No. Mr. Thorp reporting that I walked out early on my detention?

"Hello?" I croak.

Deep voice. I grip the phone. Elliot James! *Oh, God!* "Mr. Howard found your books and purse and stuff in the art room." *What's in my purse? Oh, God. Did you look in my purse?* "The side door doesn't lock every time, so somebody could just come in there. . . . Anyway, I left them on your front porch."

"Yes, w . . . w . . . well . . . Okay. Bye."

I squeeze the receiver of our magical telephone. Ralph is standing one and a half inches away, coating me with Wrigley's spearmint breath. *Git!* I bump him with my knee. "Go away—*now*—or die." I walk to the front hall and creak open the heavy door. My textbooks are in a neat pile with my purse on top. I look up and down the block. No Elliot.

I flutter upstairs, past Dad with his newspaper spread on the kitchen table. I unclasp my purse and paw through it—just dull stuff: an elastic headband, comb, my detention slip, Tangee, pen, money. Thank God.

I sit on my vanity stool, lean in, and stare at the mirror. Same face, *new* me. I have been telephoned by the mysterious, know-it-all, future artistic genius of the century Elliot James. "So there!"

Like clockwork Ralph is at my door demanding, "Who was that?"

"Michelangelo." I know Ralph has no earthly idea who Michelangelo is, but he'd never admit it. "He brought my books over."

"Yeah," he says, "thought I recognized him. Hey, check this out." He drags me to his room and opens the door to the attic. The bottom stair holds his Scout gear—binoculars, a camping heater, ditty bag, magnifying glass, his *Handbook for Boys*.

The next step houses his newly revamped Scout collection. "I've got a theme now, like you suggested." But it doesn't look like it. There's the odd polished stick and the fossil shell. The rotten squirrel tail has been replaced with a bundle of bamboo poles and string. "Wind chimes," Ralphie says, lifting them in front of me. He sits back on his heels. "For my pigeons."

"Why, yes, of course. How excellent." I shake my head. "*What* pigeons?"

He points. "Up there. I'm doing the Pigeon Raising merit badge. You know, *squab*."

"No."

"For racing and flight contests and carrying secret messages. There's coop sanitation and seeds and grit and record keeping . . ."

"Ew. Where'd you buy them?"

"Didn't. The pigeons were already up there. Now all I have to do is raise 'em." He jiggles the wind chimes. "These'll keep them in a good mood."

"No, stupid. Where'd you buy the wind chimes?"

"Chow House gift shop." Ralph backs away from the steps on his knees and turns to me. "We've gotta eat there sometime."

"I told you, I'm never going in there."

"Their shop is neat. They also sell *wrist rests* like this. New ones. Chinese artists use them to prop their forearms up while they paint. Gives a better angle for the brush. But this one of mine is *old*. An antique." Ralph gives me long look. "Have you ever seen one before?"

I hear a car cruising slowly down our street—*Elliot?* I hop up, peek out of Ralph's window, but I can't see a thing. I turn back. "Huh?"

"Like I just *said*, they sell these at the Chow House."

Ralph waves the stick in front of my face. "Ding-dong, anybody home?" He puts it in my hand.

I look down "What'd you say this was?"

"God! Never mind." Ralph puts it back on the step. Sighs.

My brain is fuzz. What a day!

It started in Kansas City and ended in Weird Town.

Chapter 8

Neil Bradford's brother, Tom, is missing in action in North Korea.

After attendance is taken Friday morning the principal announces an all-school gathering outside by the flagpole. Neil and his sister, Susan, who is a freshman, stand by the principal. Susan is crying. She looks scared to death. Neil has his arm around her. Everybody is shivering. After a moment of silent reflection, the ROTC honor guard raises the flag. It is regal and reassuring lifting in the wind, snapping strong against the Red Scare. Neil salutes. The flag helps everybody focus.

Anita glances over. She actually looks scared of me. I stare at my feet, feeling responsible for Neil's missing brother. The principal pledges that the school will keep a vigil for Tom Bradford and his family. I feel terrible for a thousand reasons, especially for the possibility of Elliot and these other guys joining the army someday and trudging across Korea dodging bombs and bullets.

We say the Pledge of Allegiance and dismiss, but the Bamboo Curtain blocks my way. Kids literally sidestep around me. I see ching-chong head tilts. I hear "commie" coughs. A thousand students and staff head back into school, but not me.

My heart pumps glue. I hate my impossible self and the impossible warring world. I sink onto a low brick wall by the bike racks. Go back into school or go away? I could take a quick walk across the street and become missing in action too. What's the right thing to do in this wrong world?

Mr. and Mrs. Chow must rise above slights and slurs every day, just go on about their business. What did Gone Mom do? I guess she gave a big part of her *problem* to the Sisters of Mercy and went on about her business. I pledge to the flag: "I will never do that to anybody!"

Mr. Howard comes down the school steps. He walks past the flagpole into the crosswalk in front of the building to retrieve the portable STOP FOR PEDESTRIANS sign. The base of the pole is stuck in a tire filled with cement. He spots me on the wall, pauses. Cars gather on both sides of the crosswalk but Mr. Howard is in no hurry. He glances at the flag and then back at me. He seems to read my mind. He tips his hand toward the stop sign—*are you going to be a pedestrian or not?* For a frozen moment our eyes lock. The second-hour bell sounds. I stay put. In the wind the metal hooks on the flag rope clank against the pole. Mr. Howard straightens his back, salutes me, and walks toward the building, rolling the sign along.

A gust of wind whips the flag around the pole until all but a little red corner disappears. I get up and disappear too, back inside the building.

Social studies is torture. I feel like everyone expects me to confess which of my chink relatives captured Tom Bradford.

Lights off. Thank God. Venetian blinds closed. Miss Arth starts a newsreel about the war. She sits at her desk and slides a nail file from her drawer. I have concluded that showing movies is a way to avoid teaching us something. The first film features a man who is finding homes in America for "war waifs"—unbaptized babies with mixed Asian and American blood that nobody wants. A beaming crowd of dignitaries applauds as the orphans are unloaded from military planes. The man and his wife wave, surrounded by six waifs they have adopted themselves. The kids look too petrified to blink, despite the flashbulbs.

I think back to the second grade at Our Lady of Sorrows. Patty and Anita and I played a game called "pagan babies" in which we acted out the dynamics of our real Pagan Babies classroom project. I was always the pagan baby who got saved, which I now understand was because I was foreign and lesser. In our real classroom Pagan Babies activity we were all encouraged and coerced to bring pennies, nickels, and dimes for the coffee can on the teacher's desk. When we had five dollars we sent it to a Catholic mission in a heathen country to baptize one baby and save its soul. We got to vote on the name. Once somebody put my name in the ballot box. Sister read it out loud before realizing the *joke*. Everybody laughed at me. I laughed too, but I never played pagan babies again and I never stopped worrying that I might become one someday.

Maybe I have.

Another newsreel shows blasted bridges and blood-stained snow and marines cooling their guns with river ice after an attack by "the Reds who are trying to split the free nations of the world apart." Another has Chinese Lieutenant General Wu speaking at the United Nations, blaming UN troops for the criminal acts that precipitated the Korean War. Only the Russian delegate shakes hands with the general after his speech, evidence of commies sticking together.

To close, the announcer asserts, "We must not capture the enemy; we must *destroy* the enemy. Red China's atrocities will be judged by the parliament of the world."

Friday after school I'm lying on my bed when Ralph barges in as usual. "Scram. This waif has a horrible headache."

"Waif?"

"Orphan."

"Hold on." He exits to the bathroom and comes back with two aspirin and a glass of water. Ralph chews his thumbnail, rocks back on his heels, looking down at me. "Tell me as soon as it's gone, 'cause I've gotta show you something."

"What?" I say, rising onto my elbow. Ralph's hair is stuck up funny in the front. "I am not doing a guessing game. I had a humiliating, horrible day."

"With Mom?" Ralph asks, as if everything impossible in my life has to do with her.

"At school." I rub my eyes and explain about Tom Bradford being missing in Korea and the devil Lieutenant General Wu newsreel and the traveling waifs and how I feel responsible for the invention of Communism.

He nods. "Bad day." Then holds up a finger. "But not as bad as Tom Bradford's day."

"Right." I picture Susan Bradford looking so dumbfounded and Tom in a grisly prison camp with U.S. soldiers stumbling and starving and dying. Ralph sits beside me on the bed. I lean on him, my heart stopped. He's quiet for a change. I think he's crying a little bit too.

I start sobbing. "Don't ever go in the army, Ralph. Or the navy or the marine corps. Promise. I know it looks all brave and everything, but please, promise me you won't go."

"I thought you *had* to enlist with the selective service or something if you're a guy."

"Then get a bad-back deferment like Dad, or a hernia, or flat feet, or . . . get married."

"Getting married wouldn't keep an eleven-year-old out of the army."

"You're right. But being crazy would."

"Okay. I won't get married." Ralph stands. "Is your head better? There's something I need to show you. Don't move."

He runs to his room and returns with his hand behind his back. He shuts my door, breathing hard.

"Now, close your eyes and put out your hand."

I start to, then pull back and make a fist. "Is it gonna be wet?"

"No."

"Alive?"

"Nah."

"Dead?"

Ralph sets something in my hand.

It's the same wooden wrist rest from his collection.

"Oh, this is certainly exciting," I say. "You've shown it to me a million times already."

"But see the carving on the bottom?" Ralph points to the flat side.

It has engraving so faint I have to close my eyes to feel

it. I rub my thumb over the gouges and swirls. "Yeah. So? Do wrists really need to rest?"

"Allow me to demonstrate." Ralph puts the stick on my vanity, grabs paper. He holds a pencil, props his forearm up on the wrist rest, and writes his name. "This holds your arm steady if you're doing calligraphy, you know, Chinese writing, or painting with ink."

"What's the joke?" I ask.

"No joke." Ralph looks right at me. Pink creeps up his neck. "This one's used. A rare *Chinese antique*. Like you'd find in a museum."

"No way. Where'd you get it?"

"Found it."

"In the Chows' trash?"

"Nooo."

I take a breath, then another. A bell chimes in my mind. I turn to him. "Where *did* you get it, Ralph?"

He looks like he is trying to swallow a straight pin. "In our attic."

"You found this in the . . . ?"

"Yep! You have to swear not to tell, Lily. If you don't swear—Boy Scout's honor, I will join the army tomorrow."

Before I know it, Ralph has me holding up three fingers and repeating that on this day of January 26, 1951, I will never divulge that he found a Chinese wrist rest in the Firestone attic.

I rub my forehead. "My headache's worse."

"Yeah, well, it's gonna get *real* worse in a sec. . . ." His look has a story behind it.

"Why?"

"Well, I also found that swirly carved rock in our attic." Ralph's eyes narrow.

I sit back on my heels. My insides hum. "When?"

"When I was building my pigeon coop. I found a box hidden under a tarp." Ralph's face is sweaty.

"What box?" I ask.

He points, swallows. "It's up there. Chinese stuff. It's yours."

My hands fly up. I leap off the bed and face him. "Why didn't you tell me about it? *God!* You should have told me the second you found it!"

He shakes his hands at me. "I *am* telling you. I tried a thousand times—before Michelangelo called. And before that, I showed you that shell thing and pretended I was making a Scout collection, which I'm really *not*, but you didn't catch on. I thought you might recognize the wrist stick from your past and figure it out yourself so I wouldn't get in trouble and . . ."

"You *never* get in trouble. What else is in there?"

"Paintbrushes."

I blink at the curved pattern Mother's vacuum has made in the carpet. I run my foot back and forth until it's gone.

Ralph stares at me. He looks miserable. I rub my cheeks.

"And tools and rocks and sticks," Ralph adds, "and Oriental dust and . . ."

"So that's why you asked about the adoption belongings."

"Yeah. I thought they'd confess," Ralph whispers. "But of course they didn't because they hid it. And if Mom finds out that *I* found it, I'll be dead before I ever get to go in the army."

The house is silent except for Ralphie's pigeons. I've never been in the attic because the stairs are creepy and it's full of squirrel poop. I can't imagine my mother ever setting foot up there. "Is it big?" I ask.

Ralph spreads his hands. "No. Just a beat-up wooden case with a latch."

"Maybe it belonged to the people who lived here before us?"

Ralph shrugs. "Nope."

"Why not? There's no proof it belongs to me."

"Uh, just your *name* on it, plus a vampire door knocker and . . . Don't you wanna see it?"

My name? Liquid fear slides through me—a hand grenade from my past in the attic. "I . . . I don't know. I can't think. Not yet."

Chapter 9

I cannot go to sleep. Gone Mom is awake too, pacing the attic, waiting for me. "Ralph, wake up," I whisper at midnight.

"I already am." He struggles to sit up in his bed, digs his flashlight from under the covers. "I *knew* you'd wanna go up there."

I nudge him. "Go get it. Please."

He hands me the flashlight. "You go. It's yours."

"You're the better stalker. Come on! I might step in something."

Ralph stands facing me in the dark. He tests his flashlight just long enough to highlight his red striped pajamas buttoned up to his chin. He climbs the splintery steps in bare feet and disappears into the dark hole at the top. I hear grunting and faint rattling. I track him crawling across the ceiling. Something drops. He hisses, "Shit!"

"Shh!" I whisper up the stairs. I cross my arms. My stomach is a circus.

Ralph's flashlight beam reappears at the top of the stairs. It flashes—on/on/off, on/off. "Morse code," he whispers.

"Meaning what?"

"I don't know! I'm just learning it." He climbs down the steps backward. "Okay, I got it." He sets the case on the floor, blanching it with his flashlight beam.

It's wooden, more toolbox than treasure chest. The outside is scarred with dull metal hinges.

"Go on," Ralph says.

It's heavy. Whatever is inside rattles when I flip the latch. On top is a sheet of crumpled stationery with the letterhead:

SISTERS OF MERCY CHILDREN'S HOME

8400 Waldo Avenue

Kansas City, Missouri

Under it is written: "Lillian Loo."

Ralph and I stare at each other. I curl over my knees. Ralph pats me on the back. His hand sticks to my nightgown. His pigeons coo through the ceiling *loo . . . loo . . .* My old name— I'd nearly forgotten. In a moment my birth mother's name surfaces—*Lien Loo*. "Lien Loo," I whisper.

"Who?"

"Lien Loo."

"Who?"

"My birth mother. I called her Mamá until she became Gone Mom." My insides shivering, I reach into the box and lift out a dirty cloth tape measure, a compass, a square of screen, a hammer, wooden stakes, the broken shell, and a carved red box that won't come open. The hairs in two bamboo-handled paintbrushes are brittle. They leave dust trails across my palm.

I hold the shell, shine Ralph's flashlight on it. It's a stone actually, greenish tan. "What kind of rock *is* this?" I whisper.

Ralph shrugs. "I don't know. Probably jade."

"It's carved."

Ralph looks up at me. "Yeah. I noticed that. A swirl."

I pick up the metal chunk Ralph had referred to as a vampire door knocker. Lots of the gold is worn off. It's got a flat monster face with protruding fangs. I hold it to the light. "Not friendly." I turn to my brother. "I mean, is this what mothers normally leave for their little girls? Broken junk and rusted fangs? Where are the soft booties and monogrammed baby cup?"

The round red box fits in my palm. It's bigger than a compact, with a carved deer on the top.

"Let me see what's in it," Ralph says, digging for his pocketknife.

"Don't break it!"

Ralph's all business, heavy breathing and grunting,

wedging his knife blade twice around the seam. He tries again and again to twist the lid loose. His hands are sweaty. So is the rest of him.

"Let me try," I say.

He hands it over.

With another turn, the lid lifts off. The scent of Gone Mom springs into the room. I gasp. In a split second I'm crying. Ralph looks over like I'm nuts, then he smells it too. Incense dust. Proof of Lien Loo. The exact smell of her neck.

I take a deep breath and replace the top. My eyes turn her dust into tears.

Ralph's face lights up. "So . . . either she was a spy and these were her tools of the trade or they are *clues*, a trail she left for you to find her."

I'm a bundle of battling nerves. "Or maybe she left it so she wouldn't have to haul it on her trip to wherever." Ralph and I look at my stuff a while longer. I repack everything but the wrist rest. In the flashlight beam I notice something, a faint carved radish on the curved side, aligned with a bulge in the wood grain. "It's a radish," I whisper. "I swear. Look, Ralph. A *radish*!"

He shrugs. "Yep! I know. I saw it already. Kinda weird. Kinda loony. Well . . . sweet dreams anyway," he says, heading back to the attic with my box.

* * *

My mind pings and chatters all night. What kind of person—*mother*—would save these crazy things for her daughter? Nothing goes together except the stationery and my
old name. But the box didn't float to the attic by itself.
Maybe my parents *knew* she was loony and weird and were
protecting me from knowing it too. *Or* maybe they hid it
because they knew it was a case of clues. Why didn't they
just throw it out?

I wake up early Saturday with Gone Mom on my mind—
her straight black eyelashes, her long hair gathered in a gold
barrette, her smile. I pull up the covers. Which of the Sisters of Mercy nuns would have met her the day she left
me at the orphanage? Either Sister Immaculata, who was
ancient and decrepit even back then, or Sister Evangeline,
who was tall and kind and watched over me.

I picture the staircase there, with its wide strip of worn
brown carpet, and remember stepping on the wooden part
by the wall so I could hold on, except once when I was
crying and Sister Evangeline pulled a huge white hankie, a
"dove," out of her sleeve, lifted me, and wiped my nose—
stopping all the dinner traffic just for me. The hankie was
soft and smelled like bleach.

That staircase spilled into a big entry room that echoed,
with rows of hooks for our coats and hats and scarves—
pine green, red, navy. Walking by, I swept them like fringe.

I grip the wrist rest and I sit back on my heels, my face

wet. The Sisters of Mercy Children's Home feels so real, as if we are all still eating peanut butter and begging the nuns to hug us. Still desperate to be *chosen*.

Right after breakfast I am on the bus headed for the Mercy Home even though I know it's become a retirement place for old nuns now. There's just one in-between stop, so I will only have to fight chickening out once. All I will do is sit in the shelter across the street, the way I did at the House of Chow.

I step off the bus, check the return schedule.

The orphanage is a block of red brick, smaller than I remember, with a bulky front porch, lace curtains, a rusty fire escape, and a heavy front door with sidelights. I sink back on the bench, having awakened this place that's been hibernating inside me.

The front door swings open. *Oh, God. Oh, God.* Sister Evangeline! Her long black coat is wrapped over her habit. She carries a sack. After brushing snow off the little roof, she shakes seed into a hanging bird feeder. She checks the mailbox fastened to a fat brick pillar, checks the sky, and heads inside, leaving a solitary trail of footprints in the snow-dusted walk.

I imagine Gone Mom walking down that front walk thirteen years ago, the wind blowing her hair and the leaves in the gutter. Or was it calm that day? Or maybe summer? Was she wearing gloves and a scarf? Was she crying?

I look down knowing that this is the same spot, next to the same rusty manhole, where she stood waiting for the bus the day she disappeared. After you give your baby away, I guess it would come down to this—just you, all by yourself, on a square of cement.

Were you sick or in trouble? Was it just a choice you made? How long did you wait for the bus? Long enough to change your mind? Long enough to run back and pick me up and never let go? You could have . . . in the time it took the bus to come.

My heart shrinks small as an empty locket.

The traffic heaves past me. I rest my face in my hands and have the wild notion that Gone Mom and I are still hooked by animal instinct and if I just keep sitting here she'll show up. Since I've come back, she will too.

There are no orphans here now, just Sister Evangeline, whose "family" has rippled away from the rock she was for us. But it is still her home. The limbs of my family tree should include her and my orphan sisters and the nuns. Weren't we a family? Didn't this count? Should a waif's *reverse* vanish when she gets chosen? That's what Mother tried to do—make my birth occur at age four.

I check down the street. Now that I need the bus to come, it doesn't. I'm waiting the way Gone Mom did that day, unless she didn't take the bus. Maybe she hopped an airplane all the way back to China. Who will ever know?

Chapter 10

I watch *The Thinker* taking a chilly sunbath on his pedestal. He seems to have forgotten something important, so I don't bother him. It's got to be so frustrating to worry and worry without being able to get up and do anything about it. But not me—I am going in the museum to view the shelf with the display of Chinese art.

I feel small and nervous heading up the steps. Everything, including the fancy glass-and-bronze doors, seems monumental and immovable and famous. I yank the thick handle. My saddle shoes squeak across the entry floor.

Rows of shiny black columns line both sides of the main hall. Voices ricochet like darts piercing the three-story ceiling. The air smells old and warm, like the radiators at the orphanage. I check my coat. The man at the information desk says there is no fee for students. He unfolds a map for me and points. "Our modern artworks and Asian collection are on the second floor. And here's information about our special exhibitions."

Tapestries as big as movie screens hang around the main hall. They depict scenes from Jesus's life. At least I recognize Him and Mary, but this is nothing like church—a place the Firestones rarely go. Dad called church a "winter sport" before he put his foot down and refused to go altogether. That's about the only time I've seen him take a stand. Mother won't go alone—"It wouldn't look right." In her world looks are everything.

Donald Firestone also doesn't like art, as if it is a universal fact that men and museums don't mix.

Mermen leap from a splattering indoor fountain. A massive marble lion stares out from the ancient gallery. It is surrounded by sculptures labeled "Athena," "Hadrian," "Hercules." There are huge Egyptian statues—stone bodies without heads and expressionless heads without bodies. I wonder, what if museum owners adopted Mother's philosophy and decided, hey, let's just throw this old stuff away? Why live in reverse?

Before I head upstairs I dart into the bathroom. No art in here, only ladies tinkling and an old-timey fainting couch with a rolled back. If Ralph's stalking me today, I'm safe in here. A woman comes in pushing an old lady in a wheelchair. They both look tired.

I stop cold halfway out the door. He's headed across the main hall carrying a folded easel and an artist's suitcase and wearing a flannel shirt and the scarf I threw in the trash.

Elliot James.

His shoes do not squeak. He walks into the Sculpture Hall like he owns the place.

I sink back into the bathroom, sit on the couch, my hands turned to ice. I haven't talked to him since he brought my books over. I haven't thanked him, so he definitely knows I am thankless and mannerless and just plain—*less.*

Go do it right now.

I walk out, sneak over, and stand in the shadow below a tapestry of Jesus carrying the Cross, titled *The Way to Calvary.* I peek around the corner, the perfect spot to watch Elliot, my quarry. He unloads his supplies onto the floor, assesses the lighting, and positions his easel by a twice-life-sized sculpture of two naked people sitting on a giant, scratchy-looking pig's head. They embrace, inches away from a kiss.

Elliot clips dark gray paper to his easel, opens his charcoal box, and stares forever at the lovers, who stare forever at each other. With his gaze fixed on the woman, he moves his charcoal stick through midair as if he's touching her with it and begins to shadow the very spot where her breast brushes her boyfriend's chest. My face burns. I look away, then look right back. Shadows and curves grow on Elliot's paper.

Sharp dashes of black.

Highlights in white.

Life drawing.

The wheelchair woman and her daughter stop to watch. It's fine to stare at bare body parts in here. You're supposed to.

Elliot squints, shades her jawline, bends to deepen the shadows of her armpit. He twists like the boyfriend, gripping the stone floor with his feet. His shoulders drop and rise. He smudges the contours of her cheek with the side of his thumb, closes one eye, adjusts his position, lost to the world. I lean against the wall thinking—here I am obsessing over an old stick of Chinese wood while Elliot James is twisting himself into love scenes.

Without one bit of warning, he stretches and swivels around so fast he's looking right at me. I jump, a termite caught in the light of day.

Oh, God. Oh, God. I wave—*hi.*

He nods.

I walk to his easel. "Th—thanks for bringing my books over."

"Yeah."

Say something else! I sweep my hand. "I just came by to see the Pablo Picasso painting, you know, *Girl before a Mirror.*"

"Fat chance. She lives in New York City in the Museum of Modern Art."

"Oh, well. Yes, uh . . . I mean, I like that poster in the art room. . . ." Excruciating pause. Colossal embarrassment.

I walk around the sculpture trying to appear captivated by the artist's signature, which is etched into the woman's hip. The marble is milk-colored, silky, and glowing, as though it's heated from inside. The title is: *Atalanta and Meleager with the Calydonian Boar.* The label explains that Atalanta is the woman, the huntress who has shot the boar. The upcoming kiss must be her reward.

"They're characters in a Greek myth," Elliot says.

I nod, like I already knew that.

He shrugs. "I'm going to enter this in the Fine Arts Showcase at school."

Wow. That's brave. "How do you want them to look?" I ask, instantly recognizing my second stupid, unanswerable remark. He wipes his hands on his pants and walks around the whiskery boar and its naked riders. He looks up and down their curving spines, around their pulsing necks. His gaze slides across their lips, over their navels, and down their legs. The man, Meleager, has a handful of Atalanta's cascading marble hair. She grips his long curls, pulling him in. Their shadow on the gleaming stone floor is huge and beautiful—curving and complicated.

Elliot stops, glances over at me, and points to his easel. "Do you want to know how I want them to look?" There's a raise of his eyebrows and a slight smile. *"Sweaty."*

Unh!! I blink . . . blink, blink. Morse code for: Bring assistance. I am going to permanently *die.*

Elliot goes back to work. It takes guts to expose your naked lovers to the students and faculty of Wilson High School, especially the rusted hearts of Miss Arth and Mr. Thorp.

Other visitors watch Elliot draw. A tall, willowy girl, probably from the Art Institute, walks up. Her hair is in a messy blond ponytail. Her hands are covered with charcoal and she has a smudge on one gorgeous cheek. She wears a man's shirt with a belt around it and boots. She looks at his drawing, then at him, and shakes her head. "Dammit, Elliot," she says in a low, mocking voice, "how do you get your foreshortening so *perfect?*" She fake stamps her foot. *"How?"*

Next to her, I feel like a human lump with a Chinese facial problem that no eraser or coating of charcoal smudges can resolve.

Elliot does not introduce us. The blond girl leans down. Her golden hair falls over his shoulder. He describes how to foreshorten the lovers' giant, dimpled knees so they appear to jut forward. She throws her arms up. "I know, I know . . . but *still* . . ." She blows him a kiss and walks toward her easel, exasperated—or pretending to be. Her blown kiss is cleverly mixed—part real, part kiss-*off.* But either way Elliot has got to feel kissed by that exotic, arty, curvy girl who would fit perfectly on any one of these pedestals.

In a few minutes I stand on the museum steps staring across the Sculpture Park lawn. The shadows of the bare elms look so real, so black and stark that if they were tilted upright, they could be trees themselves. Only after I've walked past *The Thinker* do I remember that I came to see the Chinese antiques.

Chapter 11

"There's more in that box," Ralph remarks, chewing the side of his thumbnail Tuesday morning before school. Dad is warming up the car. Mother is on the phone in the living room. "Under the bottom."

I give Ralph a *you are so full of it* look.

"Photographs are under the false bottom of the box," he says flatly.

"Of . . . ?"

Ralph leans toward me and whispers fast, "Crime scenes and camels."

"Crime scenes?"

Ralph grimaces, nods.

"Whaddayamean?"

"Body parts," he says.

Body parts. *Body parts?* "Dead-people body parts?"

"They usually are." Ralph raises his eyebrows. "Sorry, Lily." He holds out his arm, chops his other hand across it above his wrist. "The arm is cut off here. There's a handcuff and dead fingers hanging down. Another's a face with a bullet hole in the forehead."

I picture the newsreels of Chinese torture camps in Korea, the bloody snow and wooden watchtowers. So Gone Mom was a spy, a pregnant spy—the perfect disguise.

After school I weave through cars parked in our driveway, dreading the next five minutes. It's Mother's bridge club day and our living room contains two foursomes of ladies, "Girdles," as Ralph and I call them.

Our front hall is smoky and smells of perfume. I hang up my coat and—*ugh*—run into Anita's mother coming out of the half bath. She says she's the dummy this round. I half expect her to act afraid of me, the way her daughter does, but she's friendly, in a distant way.

I fix a pleasant anticipatory expression on my face, unclench my fists, and follow her into the living room. Everyone looks up—blink, blink, smile. Most of them have kids at my school. *Hello. Hello. Yes. Fine. Thank you. Good to see you, too. Thank you.*

Each lady has a little silver bowl of bridge-mix chocolates, an ashtray, and a tally. After the last hand they will switch from coffee to sherry.

Someone asks me about Neil Bradford and his sister and how they are managing. "We can't concentrate on our play today thinking about poor Tom," my mother says. They shake their heads. The Red Horde has invaded our living room and sabotaged their bridge party.

I describe the flag ceremony and our club projects to support the war effort. I do not add that, for me, school is a war zone. The Girdles nod at my mother in an approving way—*Lily is a good girl, Vivian, such a brave thing to adopt her. And how beautifully you've raised her—such manners and poise.*

I start upstairs, then swivel and bump through the kitchen door, shoved by my phony, perfect-daughter self. I survey the mess. Washing dishes is a *guilt fixer*. It is also a detour from the secret stash of gory pictures burning a hole through the rafters. I stack everything in the dish rack. I put the leftover orange cake in tinfoil. I wipe the crumbs into the garbage, rinse and rerinse the dishrag, check my watch.

I have the remainder of their card time plus the sherry-and-cigarette hour. Mother is preoccupied, Ralph and Dad both gone. Time to prowl the attic.

I lock Ralph's door, get his flashlight, and open the attic door. I clear the steps containing his Scout gear and climb toward the disgusting pigeon coop.

There's no floor—just raw boards on their edges running parallel, with gray insulation between. My eyes adjust.

I see *stepping-stones* of scrap plywood straddling the boards. Two trails—one to the window and another to a tarp by the chimney stack. My heart races. How in the world did Ralph find my box?

The single window is broken. The wind chimes rattle softly in the cold breeze. I bite my lip, stifle a sneeze, train the flashlight on the tarp, and crawl, propelled by raw nerves.

I imagine my brand-new father straddling the rafters, hiding my box under the tarp, and declaring: Lillian Loo's past is finished. Lillian Firestone's future can begin.

I sneak down the attic stairs and dart in the bathroom as the Girdles tromp upstairs to get their coats off my parents' bed—*Those were my worst cards, ever! I should have bid no trump. Ha ha-ha. I must have that orange cake recipe.* I lock the door, sit on the floor, and prepare to meet the dismembered body parts of my past.

I spread a bath towel and lay everything out—door knocker with fangs, greenish jade piece, compass, wrist rest, incense box. I pry the bottom with a nail file and, sure enough, there's a flat red package underneath. Ralph has left the twine in a knot that requires tweezers to undo. I arrange the pictures in a line facedown—the gory game of solitaire Gone Mom has dealt me.

Each has the same Chinese word and the year 1934 written on the back.

I hold my breath and flip the first picture over. It's blurry, but I can see it's a hand. A pale, drooping hand, chopped above the wrist, with long, stiff fingers and a handcuff exactly the way Ralph described. The index finger sticks up as if the person was pointing to his killer at the time of his death. The background is plain white.

I sit back, shiver, and turn the next picture. It is a headless person's bare back with a hole dug out between the shoulder blades. For a sickening moment I imagine it's Tom Bradford with his arms hanging limply. There is something in the hole—bones or stringy guts or sticks. I don't know. I don't want to know. In the background is a fence with other body parts propped against it.

The third is what look like two bloated, severed toes. I flick it away, my shoulders hunched to my ears, and swallow hard.

One of the remaining pictures is going to be the head. I dread the head. I need Ralph for it. I gather everything back in the box, turn off the bathroom light, slip into my room, and hide it in the closet.

Later, after Dad is snoring, and Mother's cold cream has gone to work for the night, I sneak into Ralph's room, shake him. "Wake up!"

He stirs, grabs for his flashlight. "Have you become nocturnal?"

"Shh! Bring your magnifying glass." I tug his pajama shirt. "Stalker feet. Please. In my room."

We sit together on the floor. Ralph rubs his eyes. He's all pudgy and alive with bad breath and stinky feet. I tell him how I crawled through the attic. His eyes get wide. I can tell he's impressed.

"But I can't look at the head by myself." I put the unviewed photos facedown.

"By the way, the word on the back of these is 'Shanxi,'" Ralph says.

"*What?* How do you know that? Did you show these to somebody? The Chows?"

"No. I just copied down the word on a little piece of innocent paper and I showed it to them. I didn't do anything bad. It's okay. Really! Shanxi is a province in the north of China. That's all." He turns to the pictures. "Okay, you pick."

I turn one over. We lean down. It's the head all right, gray and dusted with snow. The blank eyes are partly open. There's a blurry bullet hole in the forehead.

I drop the picture and start crying. "It's Gone Mom. It has to be her."

Ralph shines his flashlight, positions his magnifier. After a long moment he taps my leg. "How could your first mother put a picture of herself in a box for you if she's already dead?"

I say nothing. I can't talk above the clink and clatter of my heart.

"And . . . this can't be her unless she lived on after dying of a bullet wound that didn't bleed and then somehow put her picture in your box and then traveled across the ocean and had you after she was already dead."

"You're the one who said they were body parts."

"Right. But I didn't say of *what*!"

"You are not making sense," I say.

"No, *you* aren't. Plus 1934 is *before* the Korean War." Ralph scrutinizes the picture.

I turn the other pictures over. One is a shaggy camel with saddlebags and reins hanging down. Another is a crowd of gypsies in a dusty pit. It's impossible to distinguish their faces. *"Why did she give me these? I mean it. Why?"* Ralph squints into the magnifying glass. Says nothing. "Regular babies have albums with pictures of them inhaling birthday cake and standing all proud in their poopy diapers with popcorn stuck up their noses. But I've got pictures of dirt and camels and frozen hideousness. Not exactly cuddly and sentimental. No wonder they hid it from me. It's sickening."

Ralph arranges the body parts one above the other— head, hollow back, hand, toes. "Maybe these make a Chinese totem pole."

I put my head down. Bewildered. "Is this some sick joke? A game?"

Ralph says, "Well. Who can you ask? Who would know?"

Chapter 12

I wake up Wednesday with the Sisters of Mercy Children's Home so real in my mind that I feel like I've slept there. The school nurse thinks I am staying home with cramps. Mother thinks I am at school, but actually I am about to do something impossible.

I get off the bus, cross the street, and walk up the sidewalk to the front door. Rock salt crunches under my shoes. The yard is a mat of icy grass and oak twigs. The cement floor is swept, with a little bowl of kitty water not yet frozen by the door.

I will ring the doorbell and count to ten. If no one answers, I will leave. I push the bell and count fast. *Okay!* But as I turn, the door opens. "Ha! Lillian! Oh my goodness." She starts to reach out and then pulls back, her hand on her heart.

Out of my mouth rattles, "Hello, Sister Evangeline." We stand together a long moment, then she motions me inside.

Votive candles still burn in the alcove by the visitor's room—a smoky, welcoming spirit. There's the big old desk with the gooseneck lamp we couldn't touch. I look up the silent staircase to the landing, turn to her, and say, "I remember that the hem of your habit was always wet."

Evangeline looks amazed. "Yes, from the dew when we hung the wash." I picture the backyard clotheslines, the corridors of waving sheets. "And from mopping the floors and watering our garden."

I study the row of coat hooks. Only two occupied. Sister and I lock eyes. Hers are greenish and tired looking. A wave of longing seems to move between us. "I've kept up with you, Lily. I know you have a brother and that you do well in school. I . . ." She stops. Maybe she can tell she'll knock me flat with another word.

"Yes . . . Ralph is m—my little brother."

She nods. A black kitten pads toward us, weaves around my ankles and the folds of Evangeline's habit. "This is Joy. Black cats are better than white ones around nuns," she says. "Her mother, Mystery, lived here when you did. Cats make good pets for a home where so many come and go. They don't miss a thing and their purr is the perfect lullaby, at least for some."

I pick up Joy and scratch her ears and, of all the insane

things, wonder if Mother will find cat hair on my coat and figure out where I've been. "Who lives here now?" I ask.

"Just Sister Immaculata and me and Joy."

Joy jumps out of my arms and curls up on the bottom stair. Sister Evangeline sits at the desk and I sit beside Joy. The entry hall fills with old sounds—clattering shoes, recited prayers, the dinnertime bell, laughter.

"I remember Nancy the best," I say. "She was an orphan too, a fifth grader. I was her 'charge.'" I picture Nancy's smiling mouth full of teeth too big for her face.

"Yes, she took good care of you."

I glance into the visitors' room, with the same doilies and dish of stale butterscotch candy.

"Is your school out?" Evangeline asks.

"No. I called in sick but . . ."

Sister Evangeline's eyebrows shoot up. "We nuns are familiar with managing secrets."

"I was wondering how long I lived here."

"About a year, Lily."

"Is that long for an orphan?"

"No. Some children aren't ever placed." She looks off.

I stare ahead and say the lines I have rehearsed. "I found a box of my belongings from my birth mother, Lien Loo, in the attic at home and I wondered if there might be anything else?"

Sister Evangeline sniffs, blinks, reblinks, and stands up.

She seems trapped by her wimple, unable to scratch her head or comb her fingers through her hair or even tug her collar. She folds her hands—grips them, actually. I remember her strong hands—the look of them, not the touch.

"Or if there's something I should know. The pictures in the box she left for me are awful. . . ." I cover my face. Tears slide between my fingers and onto my coat.

I hear Sister Evangeline sigh, but she doesn't say a word.

"She was definitely Chinese, wasn't she, my birth mother?" I say.

"Yes, and a very determined young woman, as I recall."

"Sh—she wasn't married, right?"

"That is correct, Lillian."

"So she was alone when she brought me here?"

Sister stands, leans on her fists on the desk. "Yes. And she was very much alone when she left."

Evangeline's nun-ness verifies Gone Mom's realness somehow. The strong, upswept *pillar* of Sister Evangeline would not lie. She locks her attention on her desk calendar, clears her throat. "I will check regarding your additional belongings. Come back a week from today, *after* school. Policy dictates that all belongings go with the child, but occasionally . . ." Something ripples behind her words. She grimaces and nods slightly as if concluding a conversation with herself and says, "A complicated past is best understood a bit at a time."

Chapter 13

On Saturday morning I walk across the track and practice field with no plan, pulled by the lights in the art room. Hopefully Mr. Howard is here. He sees me out the window and waves, pushes the door open. "Did you forget something else?" he asks.

"Uh . . . yeah." I freeze. Elliot James is here too! He glances up from his drawing table. They've got a bakery box of doughnuts. The steam from their coffee thermoses fills the air.

"Miss Firestone, in case you hadn't noticed, Elliot does not sleep. He is a drawing machine." Mr. Howard sweeps his hand, grinning. "The world doesn't grow trees fast enough to keep him supplied in paper." Mr. Howard brushes crumbs into his dustpan. "He's gonna be real famous—actually he already is."

"Okay, enough of the commercial," Elliot says.

"I guess *I'm* a sweeping machine," says Mr. Howard, "and of course my bucket and broom are gonna be real famous someday too." They look over at me, as if I should grab a doughnut and join the game, tell what kind of machine I am, how I'll be famous someday. But I stand there like a toadstool with nothing but orphan cat hair stuck to my coat. Mr. Howard checks the wall clock. *Don't leave, Mr. Howard. Please don't leave.*

"Well, gotta go to *work.* Pull that door, will ya?" He taps Elliot's shoulder and is gone.

Elliot's voice seems to have walked out with Mr. Howard. He does not ask why I'm here on a Saturday. I have no idea either, except the world tilted funny and rolled me in the door.

"I—I couldn't find my protractor last night," I stutter. "I thought I might have left it in here." *Last night—spending Friday night hunting down my protractor?*

Elliot says, "So . . . getting back to Picasso . . . he wants *us* to make our own sense of his paintings. He starts it and we finish it." He points to the *Girl before a Mirror.* "What do you see?"

"She's got two faces in one. The profile's white, and the full face is yellow. One face split into two." My mouth has not tripped and somersaulted. It has just performed a miracle—uttered the truth, plain and simple.

"Yeah, but if you let your eyes go blurry they combine into one."

I soften my focus and the miracle happens—the girl's two faces blend, then separate into the yellow side and white side, and then meld together again.

Elliot flips to a blank page on his tablet. "Face me a minute," he orders, all business. "Now turn to the side. Now back."

He works fast, looking from me to his paper, then back at me. "Now the side again." He chews his lip. His pencil scrapes the newsprint with confident-sounding strokes. Elliot turns his sketch to me. "See? Drawing works if you need to understand something. Two perspectives, two sides mixed."

I squint at the shading on the sides of my nose and chin, and the upward curve in my cheeks. My lips are open, as if I'm about to speak. My eyes look focused on something intriguing that's just outside the picture.

It looks like me, but better. Much better.

Elliot lifts the corner of the paper like he might tear it off, then stops. *Are you going to give it to me?* "Still needs work," he remarks, I guess to himself. He takes a deep breath and shuts his tablet on my face.

Wednesday after school Evangeline opens the orphanage door before I ring the bell. Sister Immaculata dozes in a rocker in the living room, the baptismal stole she's mending draped over her lap. It has replaced the babies she used to rock in that very chair. She taught me how to do it—cradle the head and keep the swaddle tight. I used it on Ralphie when he was freshly home from the hospital, barely two weeks old. I taught the technique to Mother. She'd never held an infant before, but I had, lots of times.

Sister Evangeline hurries me to the kitchen and shuts the door. Unless it's hidden in the bread box, I do not see a belonging from my pagan past anywhere. I start to remove my coat, but she says to keep it on. She checks the clock, motions me to a kitchen stool. "The transfer sisters will be here any minute." She's tense and businesslike today. Maybe she's sorry I came.

"Transfer sisters?"

"New residents. Retired teachers. One is allergic to cats," she remarks, putting a saucer of milk on the floor for Joy. Sister's ring flashes in the fluorescent light—a wide silver band with an incised crucifix. Nuns are brides of Christ, a *marriage* of commitment.

I have no idea why we are waiting for the transfer sisters, but that is exactly what we are doing. As much as I want my mystery belonging, if there is one, I grab the chance to ask something I'm dying to know. "How does it work when a couple wants to adopt a child?" This is a safe version of the question I really want answered, which is why Donald and Vivian Firestone picked *me*, out of all the orphans to choose from. There were thirty occupied beds in the little girls' dorm, plus the cribs.

"If a child was adoptable, then I . . . well, each match was unique." She appears to be reliving something. "On rare occasions the child picked the parents."

"Did you learn the stories, why mothers brought their children to be adopted in the first place?"

"It wasn't always the mother. Regardless, I didn't ask, but it was frequently offered. The young women needed so desperately to explain themselves. They were so often ashamed, overwhelmed, and distraught. They just couldn't go on."

I inch toward Gone Mom. Evangeline must feel it too. "Did you think the girls who had babies, you know, and left them here were *bad*?"

"Are you wondering if I thought they'd sinned and required forgiveness?"

"Well, yes, that they were, you know . . . that my birth mother might go to . . . hell." The air tightens around us. "That she was deprived of her relationship to God."

Sister Evangeline straightens her back. "The God *I* believe in doesn't punish people, Lillian."

Really? An impossible thought lights my mind, then blurts out of my mouth. "Y . . . you mean you pick your own . . . *God*? Not the *real* one?"

Sister Evangeline's words gain conviction as she talks.

"I pick forgiveness and compassion and grace and second chances. Women who bear children they can't raise should not be condemned. And women who can't bear children shouldn't feel they have failed God."

"So you don't believe in . . . *hell?*"

"I've known many young women who think hell is where they live on earth." Sister Evangeline folds her hands on the countertop, her face like *The Thinker*'s. *Amen.*

I recall Ralph's Catholic sister philosophy: Don't push nuns. They won't budge. They're half mule. Ralph should know. The teachers at Our Lady of Sorrows dig in their hooves whenever they see him coming.

We hear the front door and voices. Evangeline grabs her coat on a hook by the back door and practically yanks me outside.

I follow her across the frozen side yard to a shed—a place that used to terrify me because wasps floated around their nests in the rafters. Without a word we slip in the door. She pulls the chain on the light—a single hanging bulb dimmed by dust.

Sister Evangeline stands under it in her habit. The dusky shed takes shape as my eyes adjust. Dead vines rustle around the black oilcloth window covers. A lawn mower and rakes and hoes fill one corner. There are stacks of apple-gathering baskets and shelves full of coffee cans and tools. It smells of dust and dry grass.

Did Gone Mom leave me a wheelbarrow or a bucket of nails?

"I believe everything of importance," Evangeline says, "a move, or an opening of the heart, or a birth, requires a *gestational* period, a critical time for development. To everything there is a season."

But I am not waiting nine more months. It's already been thirteen years.

Sister Evangeline takes a cardboard container the size of a recipe box off the shelf. She stares at it as if she's forgotten I'm here. I reach out, then withdraw my hand. She's obviously not ready to let go.

"It's from your birth mother. Extremely fragile," she says, her voice husky.

Oh, God. I want to ask if she left any instructions or a message, but the look on Sister Evangeline's face stops me cold. *She* looks fragile, about to crack. We stand together, shivering. "I'll be very careful," I say, my heart drumming as I take the box. It's light as air.

"Open it at home. Not here and not on the bus. Use a pillow."

I glance up at her and nod. She holds my gaze a long moment, and then looks into the rafters, blinking away tears. A strange loneliness seems to have settled over her, over both of us. "I'll come back and visit," I say.

"I'm quite concerned for Joy," she says, looking off. Her cheeks are pale. She stands so tall and regal, armored in her habit, the bulb spreading light over her. She raises two fingers in a blessing. "John chapter eight, verse thirty-two . . . know the *whole* truth, and the truth shall make you free." Then Sister Evangeline steps around and pushes the door open for me. I walk outside bewildered, but she doesn't.

Chapter 14

I skirt Ralph shoveling in the backyard and creep upstairs as if I'm transporting a bubble under my coat. No one else is home.

I place the box on my pillow, shut my eyes, and take a breath. In a moment I will touch the secret of Gone Mom. It will explain the pictures and the wrist rest and the camels. And me. This will be a message directly from *her* to *me*.

I pull the string knowing that she tied it, wishing I didn't have to undo something she did. The cardboard is dark, stained. I work the lid off.

Inside is cloth—powder-blue silk with a swirling design of dragons. They are not fire-breathing dragons, but cute, with pug noses and big eyes. They are playing tag in heaven. I work my fingers down the inside of the box and pull out the blob of fabric. I try to believe it smells like Gone Mom's incense, but it's just old and musty. There's something hard inside. As I unroll the cloth a miniature Cinderella slipper tumbles into the palm of my hand. It's thin as an eggshell and no longer than my pinkie finger. I hold it up to my lamp. I can see light through the delicate ceramic. I could crush it just looking at it too hard. But no foot, even a new-born's, would fit it. It's not a baby bootie or even a doll shoe, because the toe is molded up at a funny right angle, creating a fan-shaped bumper. The slipper is packed with shredded silk that I'm afraid to remove for fear the whole thing will crumble in my hand.

I understand why Sister Evangeline didn't give this to me before, and why she didn't turn it over to my new par-ents' *safekeeping*. But that's all I understand.

Mother had Ralph's baby shoes dipped in bronze. They're shaped like his goofy toddler feet. They show his personality. My bootie has the personality of a hollow, paper-thin, breakable question mark.

Maybe there's a note inside. Sitting at my vanity with tweezers, I pick out stuffing the consistency of dandelion fluff. It floats all over the place, including into my mouth. I'll never get it all stuffed back inside. Sandy grit trickles out when I tip the shoe. That's it. No note or tiny picture or Chinese writing.

I sneeze, face myself in the mirror, and start crying. The personal present Gone Mom left for me is a maddening,

useless, Martian slipper—odd as can be. Odder than everything in my other box combined.

Okay, Sister Evangeline, what is the truth that will make me free?
I open my Bible and turn to John 8:32. It's Jesus talking:
"Then you will know the truth, and the truth shall make
you free." I sit back. *The truth, the truth* . . . That's not how
Sister Evangeline said it. She made a dramatic point of saying *whole* truth. But the true Bible verse doesn't distinguish
whole truths from half truths.

Ralph is making a racket outside. I walk to the window.
His tent is pitched. He is crushing tin cans from our trash
and tossing them in a hole he dug in the frozen garden dirt.
I open the window. "Hey! What're you doing?"

"Cleaning my campsite," Ralph yells.

"But you're not camping!"

"I *know* that. I'm just doing the cleanup part for my merit
badge." Ralph has stacked twigs for kindling and is burying
the cans. He points to his pitched tent. "I'm achieving the
badge in parts, not all at once." He smooths the dirt he has
shoveled over the trash and then starts unpitching his tent.
"I'll need a witness to check off on all this." He points to
his *Handbook for Boys* lying on the dead grass. "I'll be up in
a sec."

I shiver and shut the window.

Minutes later he barges in my door in his socks with the
manual in hand. His eyes get wide, focused on the world's

weirdest little bootie on my vanity. "What gives?" he asks, walking over.

I dash to block his way. "Don't touch it! Do not blink on it."

"*Blink* on it?"

"I will tell you what it is if you promise to stay a safe distance away—like outside on the driveway. We can use Morse code."

He sits on my bed. I explain about Sister Evangeline and how she has kept the bootie all this time just waiting for me to come over and get it.

"Did she know about the other stuff in the box?"

"She knew there *was* a box, but I'm not sure if she knew what was in it."

"Why's the toe mashed up?" Ralph says.

"How should I know?"

"Where's the other one?"

I shrug. "I guess it belonged to a one-legged, midget Chinese Martian who my first mother also gave birth to."

Ralph nods, stroking an invisible beard. "It looks real old."

"Yep. Probably buried for a thousand years, until she found it and thought it'd be the perfect memento for her temporary daughter."

"What'd the nun say?"

"Nothing. She wouldn't let me open it there." I explain

about our sneak into the shed. "I'm gonna ask her tomorrow."

I sit at my vanity and rub the tiny shoe against my cheek,
touch it on my tongue, blow into it, sniff it. I stare at it
cradled in my hands—so precious, so fragile, so empty.

I try to sketch it in my notebook before it crumbles to
dust or simply floats out the window, but I can't get the
shape or the shading right. The hairline cracks in the glaze
are roads leading nowhere. Every sketch looks worse. I
drop the pencil. Wad the paper.

I need help.

I need Elliot!

After school I step off the bus and squint into the orphanage side yard wondering if Evangeline might be waiting
there for me. I am a nervous wreck. No one on earth but me
is obsessing over a miniature shoe as dingy as an old cracked
tooth. I ring the bell. Joy weaves around my legs. I pick her
up. Her water bowl is frozen.

Sister Immaculata swings the door open. She looks up at
me, her eyes watery and luminous.

"Hello. I've come to see Sister Evangeline."

Joy jumps from my arms. Sister Immaculata says, "The
laundry man is going to take him; in fact I thought he
already had. Our new sister is allergic."

"It's freezing out there. Plus Joy is a girl, a *girl* cat." I am practically yelling in her face. "Sister Evangeline?" I say again.

Sister Immaculata shakes her head.

Dread floods me. I search her face. "Is she . . . here?"

Sister whispers, "Gone."

"When will she be back?"

"Yesterday."

"She'll be back *yesterday*?"

I scour the coat hooks. Sister Evangeline's black coat and boots are gone.

"She's not coming back, dear."

"Why? Did she leave me a note or an address or . . . ?" Sister Immaculata is so feeble it seems my words are shoving her.

"Sisters aren't allowed to explain. Only Mother Superior knows."

Sister Evangeline *knew* I'd come back. Ralph's wrong! Nuns *do* budge. They disappear.

Sister Immaculata shuffles into the living room, folds herself into her old chair. She's infuriating. Everything is infuriating.

I am heart-slapped. Run-over. Maybe there's a note in Evangeline's room or in the shed. *Something.*

I shoot upstairs behind Joy, a sharpened arrow with no target. Nothing in her room except a wilted African violet.

I check the little girls' dorm—thirty beds and nine

radiators. I remember my weekly orphan chore of wiping the buckled green linoleum under each heater with a wet rag. Everybody, no matter how young, had a job.

Tilted against the wall is the same huge push broom Nancy and I used to play witch. She wrapped the bristles with a towel and I stood on the broom, straddling the handle. Nancy *sailed* me across the wooden floors while I perfected my cackle. I wonder if she remembers me, if she became a nun or maybe a witch?

Joy and I sit on my squeaky old bed, seventh on the right side. Our big sisters kissed us good night because the dorm mothers wouldn't, no matter how much we begged. The big girls swore it was a Bible rule that nuns can't hug or kiss anybody, ever.

"Where *is* Evangeline?" I ask Joy. "You know every story in this place. Why can't you *talk*?"

I walk down the hall and turn on the chapel light. I am eye to eye with a statue of Mary with Baby Jesus on her arm. We learned endlessly about her devotion and how losing Him was unbearable. She swooned and grieved forever.

But not all mothers are named Mary, and not all mothers are alike.

I check the shed. Find nothing. Minutes later I wait for the bus in the same spot a different traveler waited yesterday. Did she just undo her headpiece and hop on the bus? Evangeline unhooked from the world. If Picasso painted

Nun before a Mirror what would her reflection be? God frowning? Or offering His fingertip to touch?

This cement square is a popular spot to consider what you're giving up—your little girl? Your vows? Your home?

Just like Gone Mom, Evangeline made an *appointment* with the future that did not include the ropes and roots of the past.

Chapter 15

Elliot James paces the art room, combing his hair with his fingers. He glances over when I come in. We both know my detentions are over now, that I only come here to look at the Picasso poster and talk with Mr. Howard.

Whatever his upsetness is about, it is very dramatic and includes huffing and clenched fists. I hope he doesn't plan to cut off his ear.

Out of my mouth pops this question: "What's bothering you?" He just stands there silent, supertall with no pencil or paintbrush, no handful of clay. "Well, *okay*. Why don't you *draw* what's bothering you?" I say. I like the idea, but I hate how I *sound*. I have a let's-get-this-over-with tone that's just like my mother.

Elliot shakes his head. *I know, I know. Everything I say is stupid, Elliot.* He bumps the door open, heads out to the track, and runs. If I drew *him* he'd be a sprinting, tongue-tied stick figure with floppy hair. Drawing him would not help me understand him one bit better—one minute he's calling me stupid and the next he's drawing my portrait.

Mr. Howard comes in. He nods to me and once again rearranges the still life. "If kids have trouble drawing that thing I know why. It's boring as hell," he says. "Plus, life doesn't stay still." In his peripheral vision he catches Elliot running, gives me a puzzled look.

"I have no idea what's going on. It might not surprise you to know that he didn't tell me."

"He's not big on small talk. He either talks *big* or nothing. He could use a bit of coaching in repartee, but the two of us *have* tiptoed into some interesting subject matter lately." Mr. Howard smiles, then turns to the Picasso poster. "How's our girl with the mirror?"

"Busy," I say, "trying to figure out who's staring back. Is it herself in the future, maybe, or her past or what?"

Mr. Howard studies the poster, his hands stacked on his broom handle. "Look there." He points. "She's not just looking, she's *holding* that mirror."

I squint. I'd missed it before, but Mr. Howard's right. The girl has both arms raised, hands gripping the frame. "So you think she's reaching out for her mother, maybe?"

He gives me a wide-eyed look, shakes his head. "Maybe. I knew *mine*, but I wouldn't know my father if he spit in my face. I can't be ashamed of it. I had nothing to do with it."

A nervous hum starts in me that turns into these words. "M . . . m . . . my parents were Chinese. I remember my mother, but not my birth father. He's a *phantom*."

"Phantom," Mr. Howard says. "Phan Tom. Sounds kinda Chinese, doesn't it?"

I smile. "Yeah, I guess. But Phan Tom was rotten no matter what I call him. He could have been a crook or a bum or the emperor of China or . . ."

"You ever try to locate him?"

"Never."

"You think he might be deceased?" Mr. Howard says softly.

"He is to me."

"We're alike then. We will never know the blood men who made us. Trying to be who you are, when you don't *know* who you are, is a hard go," he adds. "But I do know some nice Chinese folks. I work for them evenings at the House of Chow."

Air forms a boulder in my throat. I glance out at Elliot starting his second round of the track. "You know Mr. and Mrs. Chow?"

"I work there weekend nights. I love Chinese food! Don't you?"

"Well, I have eaten one-fourth of a fortune cookie, and

I've had hot tea, which is Chinese, or maybe it's Japanese . . . and then, uh . . ." *I have the worldly intelligence of a wart.*

"The Chows live with prejudice every day," Mr. Howard says. "They turned it into energy. They turned their Chinese heritage into a business. For Chinese New Year they serve long noodles for a long life and dumplings that look like little money pockets with pennies hidden inside for prosperity." He shakes his head and smiles. "And of course there are the fresh dragon eggs." Mr. Howard squats. "The mother dragon sits right on 'em in her nest in the kitchen. Tricky business collecting those eggs." He goes back to sweeping the spot he just finished cleaning.

I think how my mother can turn any conversation into a ball of barbed wire and how Mr. Howard turns a loaded, tense topic like our birth fathers into fun. We watch Elliot circling the track. "He told me I was stupid for walking out of class that day, you know, when I got the detention. But *you* saluted me!"

Mr. Howard smiles, rubs his chin. "Yup. But I'm not so sure Elliot was calling you stupid, Miss Firestone. Maybe he was referring to the class."

"Hmm . . ."

"Why don't you ask him?" Mr. Howard says. "It's real easy to start imagining things in other people."

"But."

"No. Hear me out. I know you weren't imagining what

happened in class. I saw it! I'm just saying that it is easy to make assumptions that everybody is against you when maybe they're not. But prejudice you internalize, turn against yourself, is the worst. It can get you so sunk inside you're unwilling to take a risk. Leaves you kinda"—he shrugs—"*cold* acting toward other people."

"Unwilling to take what risk?"

"Caring about somebody else and letting it show. Feeling like you have something worth giving."

We are quiet a long moment. "What do you tell your kids? Don't they get, you know, bothered by people who . . ."

"I hope they learn by watching my wife and me." He turns. I see the exact moment it dawns on him that I don't have an example. All I feel is the weight of Donald Firestone on one shoulder and Vivian Firestone hooked to the other.

Elliot barges in the door steamy and panting. He waves to Mr. Howard. "Hey! How you doing?"

"Hungry. We're talking Chinese food. Chopsticks. Eel. That sort of thing. Lily says she likes her dragon eggs scrambled with a side of soy sauce."

"Me too," Elliot says. The track has absorbed all his angst or headache or diaper rash or whatever put him on edge.

"When you go to the House of Chow, Miss Firestone, check out the friendly Chinese fish and try the dim sum," Mr. Howard says. "Lights you up on the inside."

"I sure will," I mumble. My lips feel stuck to my teeth.

With Elliot's agitation problem over and the fact that Mr. Howard and I have ceased discussing how prejudice can make a person disown herself, we move on to the fact that Chinese people never eat alone, but always in groups, family groups, around a lazy Susan with all the trimmings. They do not sit alone chasing Cheerios around a bowl of chocolate milk like Ralph does. They share wontons and dim sum—whatever that is—and turn their families into a circle of lighted lanterns.

This is not talk of the bloody Red Peril. This is about good luck and chopping cabbage and families and tanks of friendly, non-Communist fish and their nice owners.

For the first time being Chinese does not sound like a crime against humanity.

It's Saturday. I review my plans on the bus. I will enter the gift shop and purchase a fan or chopsticks and look for a wrist rest and a Martian slipper like mine. I will walk out if I start to panic. Why would I panic in the House of Chow? If Mrs. Chow is Gone Mom, if my father comes in, if anybody recognizes me, if someone asks about my past, if I start crying, if I am forced to eat eel.

I am coming here because I am not a stuffed animal. I am a human with research to do. Mr. Howard and Ralph and everybody else flies in and out of the House of Chow free as pigeons. Why not me? I want to meet Asian fish. And if Mother finds out I came, I will say that the Future Homemakers of America are learning the art of fortune-cookie baking without singeing the fortune.

It's three thirty, an off time, restaurant-wise. I enter the reception area. Straight ahead is a huge, empty red-and-black dining room. The sharp scent of ginger and scallions shoots me right back to Chinatown. I am perched on Gone Mom's bent arm by a food cart with hubbub all around.

I sink down on a seat by the cash register, hold my little-girl self, wipe my cheeks.

Paper lanterns with gold tassels hang from the light fixtures. Panels carved with flowers and birds divide the booths from the round tables. The aquarium hums and bubbles, casting watery light across the reception area. Water sliding over stone dragons in a fountain enhances the carving and accents the details of Abraham Lincoln's copper profile on the pennies tossed in the lighted pool below.

All of China seems packed in here. I walk into the gift shop and step right on Mrs. Chow seated cross-legged on the floor unpacking a carton.

"Oh, God, I'm sorry!" *Oh, God. Oh, God.*

I grab her arm as she struggles to stand up. "Fine. Fine. No worry. No problem." She taps her foot to demonstrate it's working. "I think you Mr. Chow, not customer. Sorry not get up."

I am at least a full head taller than she is. We give each other the once-over—me discreetly, she overtly. She glances off, clears her throat. She has a mole above her lip, gray streaks in her bun, and glasses. I have pinkish lips, thick hair loose over my shoulders, and wide-set eyes. Mrs. Chow wears black Keds and a bright apron decorated with orange and red barbecue tools. I wear penny loafers and hose, a pale blue sweater and skirt, and a white blouse. Her middle is round. Mine is not. Her hands look strong and scarred. Mine are pale and untouched. She starts to say something, then doesn't. She smiles. So do I. She is not Gone Mom. I like her instantly.

She sweeps her hand. "You want something special?" Her voice rockets out of her mouth, probably from years of commandeering a kitchen over the sizzling stove and dirty dish sprayer.

"No, ma'am, I just dropped by. I'm uh . . . a friend of Mr. Howard, who cleans here."

"Mr. Howard? Ah!" Her hands fly up. She gives me a bow. "Mr. Howard best *chef* anywhere. Even China."

Chef? "But . . ." My words catch on the net of assumptions I have made about Mr. Howard. My face burns. I scramble for a way out of my mess. "Yes, h—he mentioned his dim sum and the long-life New Year's noodles."

Mrs. Chow nods as though she can taste them this minute. I tell her my name is Lily and—thank you, God—she does not ask any questions. I scan the crowded displays. Back scratchers, fans, cloisonné mirrors, ashtrays, and shiny wrist rests with the calligraphy sets. Of course, there's no bootie to match mine. Just black cloth slippers with straps like Gone Mom wore. I spot a carved box like mine—bright red with sticks of incense lined up like cigarettes.

"Lacquer," Mrs. Chow remarks. "Sap lacquer tree, dry, and carve. Very strong."

My incense box is better, with sharper carving and clearer layers of color *and* it contains the few remaining perfumed flakes of Gone Mom.

"You know Mr. Howard in school?" Mrs. Chow asks, her dark eyes round and bright.

"Yes."

She tilts her head. "You only Chinese person there?"

"Yes."

"That hard. You brave girl. No Chinese sister, no brother?"

This sentence comes out without my permission. "I have a brother but he isn't Chinese."

Mrs. Chow pauses a minute, thinking. She nods to herself and resumes unpacking a box of cutesy Chinese dolls wearing bright jackets and painted-on sandals. The faces are all identical. The girl dolls have thick bangs and shiny black braids with tight bows at the bottom. Mrs. Chow flaps her hand at me. "Take time. Look."

"Okay. Thank you."

"Touch! Touch!" She blows a wooden flute, points to a calligraphy set, and pushes a ceramic dragon labeled QUI toward me. "Qui *baby* dragon. Say *chew*, like ah . . . *choo*! Best Chinese stuff anywhere. Touch China here. Taste China here. Better than big art museum. *Pffff*" She waves away an imaginary museum, then rubs her hands together. "Can't *touch* China in art museum. All antique."

I read the labels on a shelf of small sculptures. BUDDHA— AWAKENED SPIRITUAL TEACHER, PHOENIX AND DRAGON— ANCIENT MYTHICAL SYMBOLS, CHIMERA—GUARDIANS AGAINST EVIL SPIRITS, and BODHISATTVA. I recognize the word from my fortune cookie. Some figures are painted gold. Others are bronze with fancy necklaces and scarves. The description of the bodhisattva is simple and confusing: "An enlightenment being." *Enlightenment being?* "Person who shows compassion for others without judgment." I pick up a bodhisattva. It is surprisingly heavy. I balance it on my hands, raise it high. The face is serene with a slight smile. The fingers are bent in what looks to be Chinese sign language. Mrs. Chow points to the crystal embedded in the forehead. "Called *urna*—the bodhisattva's *wisdom eye*. Can see right to heart." She motions to an alcove in the wall behind the front counter. On it sits a large statue with candles and incense sticks. "Bodhisattva a person of good spirit who bring people together. Very earthy."

"I got a cookie fortune once that said, 'Bodhisattvas surround you.'"

Mrs. Chow smiles, pats her heart. "Mr. Howard *my* bodhisattva." She claps her hands. "And he good cook!" Her laugh winds around her front teeth. She gives me a deep look, as if my face is a map she's reading. "You very pretty, Lily." I touch my cheek. The aquarium bubbles. The fish circle. A shadow crosses Mrs. Chow's face. "But China hard for girl like you—no chance!" Her tone turns bitter. "China hard place *any* girl." She jabs her finger at me. "You thank mother who bring you here. She save your life." She raises her chin. "We happy. Our son in Michigan Medical School."

Mrs. Chow stands, dusts off her apron, and announces, "Tea!" She heads to the kitchen. I examine the shelves of toothpick holders, jolly Buddhas, and wind chimes. Minutes later Mrs. Chow returns and sets a wooden tray on the floor. It contains three cups and a steaming pot. Mr. Chow shuffles in behind her. The cups are small with no handles. She pours all three. He gives me my cup with both hands. "Always two hand," Mrs. Chow explains. "Do this." She taps her index and middle fingers on the table. *"Thank you."*

I put my cup down, tap two burning-hot fingertips on the table, and say, "Thank you."

"No speak. Just tap."

"Okay." I tap and nod.

Mr. Chow grins at me. There's a fleck of tea leaf stuck to his mouth but his wife doesn't bother him about it. It just hangs there. I think of Mother having a conniption at dinner when Dad has a crumb on his lip. And that's not all she'll have a fit about if she learns that two out of four Firestones have traversed the forbidden Bamboo Curtain into the House of Chow.

"Okay," I say when our tea is over. "Thank you. Nice to meet you." I bend over and nod, then straighten up quick. *Did I just bow?* I head out the door empty-handed and quickly turn around. "I'm sorry. I forgot. I w—would like to buy one of the dolls. A girl."

Mrs. Chow holds one in each fist. "Color?"

I scan the rainbow of China dolls with perfect cheeks and unblinking eyes. *Choose me, Lily. No! Pick me.*

"Pink," I croak. "I'd like the pink clothes."

I dig for my coin purse but Mrs. Chow holds up a hand. "No *buy*. Give."

She fixes a small cardboard box with a bed of tissue paper and places my pink girl and the little satin pillow she's supposed to sit on inside. Mrs. Chow's fingers are short but nimble. She has a simple silver wedding band, and a world of calluses and old burn scars up and down her arms.

She sees me watching, examines herself a moment. "I

hate laundry work. No more iron." She pretends to wipe decades-old sweat from her forehead, turns to her husband. "Ha! We steam dumpling now, not shirt!"

I smile.

Mrs. Chow nods, pats her chest. "You call me Auntie Chow."

I bow again. "Thank you, Auntie Chow." And I walk out the door.

Chapter 16

Oh no. Ahead of me down the corridor, strolling like royalty, come Anita and her boyfriend, Steve, who is the all-time school-champion sidestepper of the chink. He is also Neil Bradford's best friend. Steve's and Anita's hearts pump liquid Red Hots.

Anita spots me coming. Her eyes dart like scared roaches. The hall is narrow and empty with no shuffling crowd to buffer us. I slow way down, eyes on her, my stomach churning as they approach. *So, Anita, when Steve does his typical enemy sidestep, what're you gonna do? Look at me, or not? Sidestep too? Don't sidestep? Ignore Steve? Turn around? Start coughing, sneezing, choking? Gaze into thin air? Go blind?*

Anita slides around behind Steve and switches places so he's by the wall. She shifts her books to her left arm and slides the right through his bent elbow. Parked a distance ahead of them, right in their path, is one of Mr. Howard's rolling utility cans full of trash. Anita looks up at me in a complicated *help!* kind of way. I square my shoulders and let my feet steer me across the *centerline* so they will have to either slow way down or bump into the trash. I have them, for a split second, *trapped.*

They stop. Steve makes a slight *I smell garbage* sniff. I look right at him and sniff back. Anita looks down. I glide past them all the way to my locker, my insides buzzing. *Ha!* I twirl the lock but I can't remember my combination. No matter. For once, I do not want to crawl in it.

I hug my books, staring at the vents in the chipped metal door, and try to calm down. I wonder what they would have done if I was walking with Elliot James. *Hmm* . . . battle won. But, ugh. A victory, I guess. But it doesn't feel like one.

Elliot never would have stooped so low. Neither would Mr. Howard.

Sorry, everybody. I acted as pathetic as them.

While the rest of the world continues to obsess over Valentine's, just two days away, I am lining my bathroom sink with a towel and running my weird bootie under the faucet. A web of hairline cracks appears on the surface, plus faint flecks of gold on the toe. I set it next to my new Chinese doll, which is so gaudy compared to this serious little slipper.

Next I rinse the broken jade piece. Detailed cuts of a

scaly tail show up. I hold it to the light. A lizard has been hiding inside it all along.

Maybe if I take a bath it will reveal the true me under my skin.

Ralph is in his room. He is making Valentines for his sixth-grade party on Wednesday, but the Valentines aren't about girls. They're about getting the Art merit badge. He read the requirements from his *Handbook for Boys* at the dinner table. "Part A: Make a sketch of some Scout equipment grouped together. Part B: Design a decoration for some article of your own. Part C: Tell how your artwork would be reproduced using the *half-tone* process."

"What's that?" Dad had asked, swiping his mouth.

"Half of the full-tone process," Ralph answered, dry as a bone.

"Yes, Ralph," I said. "Hearts will burst when people view your Valentines with still-life renderings of athlete's foot powder and pellet guns in a latrine trench."

My parents are cohosting a party Wednesday night at their friends' house. Cupid is discriminating against the Chinese this year. My love life is as interesting as saliva.

It's hard to imagine where Elliot James will be, since his heart pumps India ink. He and his tall, blond, sculpture-perfect girlfriend will probably reenact those immortally sweaty lovers in the backseat of his car.

Mr. Howard has been hounding me about the special

Valentine's dinner at the House of Chow. He says he could use my help and the Chows are all for it. "I need you to fold napkins, scoop out the fish heads, chase the frogs' legs, tie up the eels, choke the chickens, stir the bird's nest soup . . . unless you are already busy. It'll be an adventure."

I finally promised him I'd come. I told my parents that the Red Cross Club was having a Valentine's Day gathering at the soda fountain at Cooper's Drugs. It definitely sounded strange, but also social and safe and *American*.

Only Ralph knows what I am really doing—going to the House of Chow, something social and safe and *Chinese*. Thank God he isn't bugging me to come. He's got a date with his candy hearts.

Early Wednesday evening Mother is all girdled in and made up—painted rosy red with dark undertones. She drops her fancy gold compact and lipstick into her beaded purse as Dad escorts her to the car. He has stuffed a red handkerchief in his suit coat pocket.

I race up to the bathroom, stare in the mirror, and splash my face, which is light tannish with pink undertones. In a minute I am on the streetcar headed to the House of Chow.

Auntie Chow waves a meat cleaver in greeting. I hurry past a big bowl of chocolate marshmallow hearts wrapped in red foil. Mr. Howard gives me a quick tour. This exotic kitchen is on a different planet from the Firestone kitchen, with its offerings of watery canned pears served at room temperature and suffocated lima beans. My mother uses a recipe for everything, even ice cubes. This kitchen is *alive* with plucked chickens and gutted fish on huge chopping blocks made from slices of tree trunk. The surfaces are infinite crosscuts. Mrs. Chow pours boiling tea over one to clean it after filleting a fish. "Oolong best," she says, her glasses fogged. She guides me around baskets of seaweed, racks of stockpots, strainers, knives, and whisks. Rounded cooking pans called "woks" balance over the burners on collars called "rings of fire." The kitchen is a controlled explosion, like an art room for food—cluttered and creative. No wonder Mr. Howard likes it.

"No Minute Rice here. No bleach!" Auntie Chow says this at honking-goose volume while standing over the rice cooker. She sticks out her tongue. "American Chinese food different than Chinese Chinese. American like fragrant and predictable. Real Chinese *pungent*! Fried oyster pancake, coriander, chive, garlic, ginger pull out tear and joy."

Auntie Chow's face is pungent—etched by steam and onions and garlic sizzled in hot chili oil.

My job is to fill bud vases with water and artfully insert a trimmed, golden chrysanthemum. The mums are pungent too, and gorgeous.

Shock of shocks, Elliot James walks in through the kitchen door off the alley. Alone. "Greetings, my man," Mr. Howard says, giving Elliot a tight little Chinese bow. Mr. Howard wears an apron and a flat, pleated chef's hat.

My man?

Elliot takes off his coat and scarf. Mrs. Chow stuffs a dumpling in his mouth. Mr. Chow claps him on the back. His wife brags about Elliot's calligraphy skills and lists the signs they need for tonight's buffet. Mrs. Chow pours a cup of plum wine for each of us and toasts, "Happy Valentine Day." Her eyes shift from Elliot to me. "You two *sticky?*" she asks, raising her cup to us. Oh, my God. I shoot Mr. Howard a desperate look, but he just shrugs, drains his wine, and seasons his wok full of lotus root.

I steal a glance at Elliot, who is pushing up the sleeves of his wrinkled navy-blue shirt. The only part of us reacting to "sticky" is our hair. His is curling every which way in the steamy heat and mine has wilted straight as a broomstick.

Mrs. Chow stuffs more bites in our mouths. I try egg rolls and pot stickers with pork and plum sauce. This kitchen seems like the only island in the universe where different colors of people are *dancing* together—stirring, laughing, sniffing, chopping, sharing. And that's just in the kitchen!

The dining room fills up. Valentine's toasts float through the kitchen door. We run our legs off. Time races away. "I've got to go!" I tell Mr. Howard suddenly, dashing to get my coat. What I don't say is that I have to take a shower and wash my hair, get rid of the *pungent* on me before my parents get home. Auntie Chow shoves a paper sack in my hand at the door. In it is a fish head—a dead-eyed, chopped-off fish head. "Old Chinese tradition for good luck! Prosperity!"

Oh yes, I will attract many Valentine's suitors with my guillotined carp head.

"Take home," she insists. And I will, because it's the perfect Valentine for Ralph. I stand in the streetcar shelter. Mr. Chow stands under the front awning, waving four hundred thousand times.

But it's not the streetcar that stops. It's Elliot in his car. He leans across the seat, cranks the window down. "I'll take ya."

I clutch my fish head. "B—but don't they need you in there?"

"I'll go back. Get in."

So I do. His car smells like turpentine, which masks the dead carp. There are rags and tablets, and a big tackle box on the backseat. Not a good spot for the make-out session I had envisioned. I crack the window.

My voice sounds like a flock of birds has flown from my mouth. "I live off Oxford Road on . . ."

"I know," Elliot says.

"Oh, of course, you brought my books over."

Elliot punches the car radio. Every station is in the

"mood for romance"—Perry Como, Nat King Cole. No war news.

"Chinese . . . uh, calligraphy must take loads of practice," I say.

"Yeah. I copy paintings at the museum," he says. "The brushwork is amazing." We sit at a stoplight. Anita and Steve and another couple stop right beside us. She looks over, superdazzled, as if she's witnessing a miracle. *Ha! Ha! HA!* Elliot doesn't notice. He just stares at the red light, then turns to me and says, "I like Chinese stuff."

What?

Heatstroke.

Mind smoke.

I wrap my arms around my waist and stare at the baby-blue diaper pin that he uses for a key chain. The whole universe has caught fire at his use of the word "stuff." Is he referring to paper umbrellas or soy sauce or humans?

"The Chows are gonna cater a big event there pretty soon," Elliot says.

I turn and sputter, "A big event *where?*"

"At the *art* museum. They're dedicating the Buddhist temple. It's been redone. I'm gonna go." All I can imagine is Mrs. Chow yakking so loud *The Thinker* will plug his ears.

As we pull up I check my parents' upstairs bedroom window. No light. *Thank you, God.* Elliot turns the car off, turns to me, runs his hand through his hair. But before

he can speak, I do. "Bye." I yank the door handle—
"Thanks"—hop out and race up the walk, picturing Dad's
car wheeling up the driveway any second. I fumble with
the house key and stop right inside the entry hall, my fist
pressed against my lips. Chinese *stuff*? I peek out the side
window. His taillights flash. *Bye, Elliot.* . . . I hear him shifting gears: first, second . . .

I plod up to the bathroom and scrub myself into an all-
American Minute Rice girl. Pungent gone. Flame doused.

Ralph is tickled pink with the fish head. Pigeon fuel.
I almost have him convinced that they served bird's nest
soup. "It's made from nests that flicker birds build in Chinese caves using their own spit. It dries hard as cement and
then they boil it in soup."

Ralph stuffs a handful of Neccos in his mouth. "Why
don't they just have the birds spit in the soup pot?"

I climb into bed with a stomachache—oyster pancake
and marshmallow heartburn. I mean, what else *would* I
have? A headache?

A heartache?

Chapter 17

We cannot stop listening. A rare moment of togetherness for the Firestones. The radio announcer sounds
grave. *"Mind control" is being practiced by the Red Chinese in
Korea. American POWs are exposed to torture, sleep deprivation,
starvation, and harassment. In their weakened state they are fed
Communist indoctrination. The advantage of their captors' position is repeated. Their brains are being programmed with enemy
propaganda. The thought reform may be permanent. Only time
will tell.*

Yes, America, we have entered the era of brainwashing. *Tomorrow night—Communist Chinese atrocities on the island of Formosa.
U.S. protection proposed.*

We don't say a word. Mother sits with her elbows on the
table, her head in her hands, holding her brain so the commies won't get to it.

Dad's face says that the world has wobbled off its axis and rolled down the drain. He reaches over, pulls Mother's hand onto the table, and covers it with his.

All I can do is picture Neil Bradford's brother, Tom, suffering this very torture, this very minute. Can brainwashers really make people erase the past—their wives and their mothers and children and homes and dogs—and replace it with Communism?

What's next? Commies terrorizing America? A nightmare scene of bright red Communism soaking our cornfields, flowing down the Rocky Mountains, and staining the oceans comes to my mind, with good U.S. citizens clambering into bomb shelters with their pets and batteries.

On Sunday I head upstairs at the art museum. I need to see a shelf of nice, old, peaceful Chinese art, if they have such a thing. My stomach groans. I stifle a yawn, my legs stinging from three flights of stairs. I catch my breath. The air smells old and polished by time. There's something familiar about it.

I look around. They don't have just a shelf up here. The Chinese galleries take up most of the second floor. Down a long corridor lined with display cases is a room called the Chinese Scholar's Studio. I stop at the velvet rope across the opening. It's a re-creation of the "workroom of an educated, cultured Chinese gentleman who lived in the 1600s—a place to study, paint, meditate, and write poetry."

I spot an antique wrist rest that's exactly like mine on the scholar's massive desk. It even has a radish carved into it! I step back, my hands and face tingling. What was Gone Mom doing with one? I wheel around as if expecting somebody to walk up with the answer, but I am alone in the hall. I turn back to the museum label by the doorway and read how the scholar used it to prop his forearm and keep his ink brush at the perfect painting angle, just the way Ralph demonstrated on my vanity.

Ceramic pots hold fat brushes with fine-pointed tips. I gaze at water droppers, carved jade paperweights, a stringed instrument called a zither, and a fairy-tale rock so twisted and full of holes it looks like Mother Nature used an egg-beater to make it.

Hanging flower scrolls and fancy shelves with porcelain rabbits and teapots are described as sources of scholarly inspiration. Mother's favorite quality—*refined*—comes to mind. A true gentleman-scholar was accomplished in all the fine arts.

I step back thinking that Donald Firestone would completely disagree with this definition of "gentleman."

The only thing missing here is the scholar. There's just a trace of him—a colorful embroidered robe and matching silk slippers by the door, as if he's about to step out to his imaginary garden and complete his peach blossom poem.

Elliot would make a perfect Chinese scholar-artist. He

could live alone in a room like this, only messier, with his dented coffee thermos on the desk, his forearm propped on a towel roll, and rarely talk to anybody. Mr. Howard says he cares about his brush and pencil strokes more than any artist who has ever lived. He's probably right, but the *gentleman* part doesn't exactly fit. Elliot's hair would never make a neat topknot.

These old men cultivated their brains. They loved nature. How can people who once made porcelain bunnies and painted bamboo branches have turned so ruthless?

I hear hammering around the corner, and voices. I walk over and stop at folding screens blocking entry to a gallery. Except for the workers behind the partitions, I am the only visitor around. I peek into a large, unlighted room—the Main Chinese Gallery, filled with stacks of wooden crates and carts. Beyond it is a smaller, brightly lit room with construction workers and museum people wearing lab coats. One man on scaffolding adjusts a spotlight. The beam sweeps the walls and flashes on something hanging from the ceiling—a shiny gold globe on a chain.

My stomach jolts.

I hold my breath, cover one eye, and look again.

The next thing I know, I have slipped around the partition into the darkened gallery. I tiptoe behind a crate, sneak around toolboxes and tarps, and crouch down, my eyes fixed on the glowing ball in the next room. I see nine dragons—*gau luhng*—playing on the ceiling. I gaze at the very same dragon pearl I tried to catch with Gone Mom.

This was where we came together. Right here! I sit back on my heels, imagining the pressure of her hand molded against my backbone. Her soft laugh rattles like wind chimes inside me. The workman shifts his light. Our pearl winks out, but I have retrieved our memory—alive and vivid and full of heartache.

A ladder rattles in the temple. The light man is coming down. I snag my petticoat on a nail as I sneak out of the room. I stop, feeling along the nylon net to unhook it, until finally I just yank, leaving a jagged lace dragon tail behind. I slip silently into the hall, my revelation exploding inside. Leaning against the wall, eyes shut, heart thumping, I let my mind tumble back and I am little, reaching with both arms to hug Mamá around the neck. I pull in a deep breath. She still smells like sandalwood.

I find my way downstairs to the fainting couch in the bathroom. A mother is in there feeding her baby boy a bottle. Did Gone Mom ever feed me in here? The baby stops sucking when I sit down and burst out crying. They both look over. Without a word the mother hands me a folded diaper to wipe my face.

My eyes are a mess and I'm still shuddering when I leave the ladies' room, praying I won't run into Elliot. I make a beeline back upstairs to peek once more between the folding screens. A security guard walks up to me. *Uh-oh.* His glasses are smudgy. He wears a badge, a gray uniform, and thick black shoes.

"They're redoing both of these galleries—the Main Chinese and our Buddhist temple," he says, adjusting the screen. "Just conservators and the construction crew allowed."

"I used to come here . . . with my m—mother," I say.

He smiles. "That's nice. Well, it's getting all spiffed up. Come back for the opening. They invited Buddha himself, and he's *coming*!"

Ralph points at my eyes. "You're all puffy."

"So are you," I say, pointing to his butt.

Ralph grabs the seat of his new pants. "I know. Mom. She always gets them too big. But so what?" He gives me a look. "You've been crying."

"Yes, as a matter of fact, I have." I tell him about the dragon pearl and Gone Mom and me and the wrist rest and how I sneaked into the gallery.

"Were you crying *while* you were creeping around in there?" he asks.

"No, in the women's bathroom."

"You were creeping around in the women's bathroom?"

"*No.* In the gallery."

Ralph shuts up. He is petrified of what girls my age do in the bathroom. He looks over at me, eyes wide. "You could have been arrested for trespassing! I could be visiting you in the penitentiary."

"This isn't *Dragnet*. I wasn't planning to *steal* something; I was just looking around." I shake my head. "Maybe we went there because Gone Mom was homesick for China."

"Or maybe *she* was an art thief," Ralph says. "I can't wait to see that dragon ball."

Catty Piddle, formerly known as Patty Kittle, telephones me out of the blue. There's lots of phony, superficial talk, but I know she's going to get to something eventually. She cannot truly care how I liked reading *Jane Eyre* or whether I had a fun Valentine's Day. I hear about how she hates geometry and gym. *So . . . nausea. Questioning the point of this phone call, Catty. Insincerity practice? Need to borrow my diary?*

"A *friend* of mine"—she says the word almost apologetically—"likes *Elliot James*."

Nerves sizzle in my stomach. Dead silence from my mouth.

"And since you *know* him, we're wondering if you know if he already has a girlfriend. He's so *mysterious* and all."

Since I have swallowed my tongue, it takes a moment to respond. Answering would also be easier if I *had* an answer, which I don't. "Uh . . ." Through the phone I hear another really faint conversation; wires are crossed somewhere. Real girls are yakking it up and laughing. It sounds nice.

"Yes, he does," I say with quick authority. *"Sorry."*

"But . . ."

I know Catty wants more info, like *who?* Of course I don't have this information either, but she doesn't need to know that I don't. "See ya," I say with a *ching-chong* lilt. I hang up. Clunk! Flunk! Junk! I shake my hand, getting Catty's pure, transparent *nerve* off of me.

I sit back in Dad's cigarette chair, the one Ralph calls "Old Smoky." Dad's sandbag ashtray and the evening paper are on his ottoman. I heave a deep sigh and imagine Elliot James in an embroidered robe, with his scholarly forehead knit and a branch of ink bamboo growing from his brush onto rice paper. I see his steamy hair in the Chows' kitchen, and his profile flashing under the streetlights when he drove me home, and him pounding his problems into the track at school. I picture him *embracing* the naked lovers with his charcoal pencils. I see him every which way, except with Catty Piddle.

"Sorry, George Washington," I say to his picture on the front page of the newspaper. "I know today's your birthday, but I lied anyway." I glance at the telephone. Sigh. And if Patty had asked me if *I* have any girlfriends, I would have lied twice and said: yes, I do.

Chapter 18

It's small and scary. I should have seen it coming—the new political cartoon pinned to Miss Arth's bulletin board.

A Chinese guy with a shaggy Fu Manchu mustache holds a shower nozzle and a scrub brush. He aims the stream of water down into a U.S. GI whose head has been sliced off above the eyebrows. The Chinese guy's face looks robotic. The caption reads: "China's Red masters brainwash our boys."

Neil Bradford comes in, stops to absorb the cartoon, and announces, "My brother would *never* fall for that."

The class gives Neil *you bet!* nods, but they're not convincing. Everyone's edgy. Another cunning chink tactic. Another atrocity. The idea of Reds scouring the brains of our soldiers and filling them with Communism is horrid. And if we lose the Korean War, the Red Horde will wash our American minds too. Resisters will be blown away by atomic bombs, except the few underground survivors lucky enough to have fallout shelters.

Fear lives in our peanut butter jars, parks and baseball fields, barbershops and beauty salons. If you look up a pole, the American flag can only momentarily block the atom bomb on its way.

Miss Arth shows us a newsreel of the "concussion," the aftermath of the atomic bomb President Truman dropped on Hiroshima, Japan, in 1945. In a flash the city was transformed into flat nothing with agony on top. There's a picture of what remains of the "little man Jap"—a ghostly sidewalk imprint after his encounter with heat at the speed of light.

What *is* to stop the Communists from turning the USA into a giant photographic negative?

Brainwashing. Bombs. Brainwashing. Bombs.

Where can a sane person go?

Underground?

Art room?

Crazy?

After school I turn on the art room lights and take a deep breath. It smells good—wet clay, oil paint, and shellac. The sink drips its rusty recital. Mr. Howard's prisms hanging in the windows spray the spectrum everywhere. He calls them his "reminders of miracles."

I wander over to Elliot's stool and sit down, hook my feet around the legs the way he does, and stretch my arms across his drawing table. Elliot could never be brainwashed. He seems totally untouched by what other people think. Maybe being a genius just takes care of that.

The Art 3-D class has made sculptures. They sit on racks across the room in varying stages of dryness. The surfaces have distracting polka dots of lighter gray clay, so it's hard to tell how they are going to look. They're free-form. Creating something out of the clear blue, with no anchor in the real world, seems impossible, just squishing your guts into a wad of clay with the chance it will turn out looking like throw up. As Mrs. Van Zant says, express what's inside you!

I walk over, hold a chunk of wet clay, and balance its cool weight in my hands. I feel the details of the Gone Mom *sculpture* inside me accumulating. I've got her incense smell and the sound of her laugh. I've decided coriander is her flavor, since pungent pulls tears from our eyes. I can touch what she touched—the wrist rest and the bootie—and I have our memory now anchored in the art museum. But her sculpture is still hollow.

Even though I remember her face, it is the woman reflected in Picasso's mirror I see when I picture her *now*—empty inside, ghostly, shrunken from life, with a hard tear scarring her eye. Not good. It matches my feeling that she's *gone*, not just from me, but also from the earth—sucked behind the mirror of time.

But gone or not, I'm still shoved around by her.

She is powerful. She's everywhere. She's changing me.

People who have lost something—a dream, a soldier son, their country, a baby—can go backward and then go forward. Sister Evangeline and Mr. Howard and Picasso and the Chows are proof of it. They are reaching out, figuring things out. They are so different from my mother. The hint of something painful stops Vivian Firestone dead. Fear shoves her around. It makes her slam doors and twist the locks inside. *Do not live in reverse! Wash, starch, and iron the past away. Brainwash yourself. Use bleach to remove every trace.*

But Picasso's *Girl before a Mirror* reaches out, touches her hurt.

My mother says, *Hands off! Don't go backward.*

But I say, *Sorry, Mother, it's too late.*

Chapter 19

Mr. Howard's response is "Phooey" when I unload my brainwashing and atom bomb fears on him.

"Isn't that kind of an *understatement?*"

"Brainwashing will never work." He sits on the edge of Mrs. Van Zant's desk. "When I was stationed in Okinawa, we hated the Japanese, and the Chinese were our allies. Now, with the Korean War, we hate the Chinese and befriend the Japanese. Minds can change fast."

"It makes everyone crazy. All Oriental people are stirred together into one big enemy."

"Fear thwarts thinking." Mr. Howard shakes his head.

"I feel like the enemy all the time."

"Yeah. That's real hard. Real unfair. What does your family say?"

"Nothing. My mother is *adverse* to my past." I look off a moment. "She's also adverse to my present."

Mr. Howard's eyes narrow. He stops his next question before it exits his mouth. "She's scared *for* you, you know, protective. Mine sure was."

Mentioning Mother flares her up in me. I can't stand that she believes she really knows me. She thinks she's so right and worldly with her timid little brain, all shampooed and shaped and shellacked with hairspray.

Mr. Howard heaves the art room trash can and dumps it into the container on his cart. "It's hard to keep a whole group of people your enemy if you get to know one or two of them personally. Challenges your mind. Do you think my relationship with the Chows happened overnight? Very tricky territory at first, but so worthwhile." I think of Sister Evangeline's theory about important changes requiring a gestation period. Mr. Howard starts to wheel his cart out of the room, turns, and says, "I remind you, Miss Firestone, it's real easy to start believing in your own inferiority. Disowning yourself. It's the biggest battle of all."

Mr. Howard leaves. I check out the window. Elliot's usual parking spot by the track is empty. A rainbow dances on the drawing pad he has left on his desk. Elliot's *diary*. About half the pages look drawn on. Okay, I will look at only one. I flop the cover back, leaf through, and stop at Meleager's strong, beautifully foreshortened arm reaching right out to me.

It's Sunday and I'm waiting for Ralph, who is taking forever getting ready for our visit to the museum. He's jammed something from Mother's dressing table into his Scout pack along with binoculars and gum.

I hold my little slipper on a blank notebook page and try a new tactic, tracing around it in the hope of understanding it better, which is ridiculous. I have decided against trying to draw the gory pictures and the lizard tail and the camels. It takes me several tries to get all the way around the shoe without my pencil slipping. I hold the outline up, study it from every angle. The toe is the strangest part, the way it's bent straight up. But tracing it makes me wonder if it's just my imagination or if the sole of the bootie is ever so slightly curved.

My heart flips. I sit back, stare at the paper, chew my pencil. Of course, it's half of a pair. I've learned something new. But I don't understand a thing.

After visiting the wrist rest in the Scholar's Studio, Ralph and I stand by the opening to the Main Chinese Gallery, still blocked by screens. The Buddhist temple beyond is brightly lit. Wall painters are working on Sunday. Ralph sets his pack on the floor, pulls out his compass, and turns it, whispering to himself, "North, where's true north?"

"Don't you mean east? Isn't China east?" I say. "Plus what good's a compass in *here*?" A *shut up* look comes in my direction. Ralph scratches his behind, wipes his hands on his pants. He's wearing the Scout neckerchief slide he carved to look like a matchstick. I take his shoulders and turn him toward the screen. "Look, in the far room, beyond the ladders. The dragon pearl's hanging right there."

He stands on tiptoes, cranes his neck, breathing through the crack. He turns; his eyes are lanterns. "Whoa!" He peeks again, his cheek pressed against the screen. "God. Lily. Look on the table back there." We trade places. I focus on a folding table draped with white cloth. On it sits a sculpted hand cut off above the wrist. It's pale golden-brown and has a wide band of carved gold bracelets. "That's the hand in your picture," Ralph says. "I swear."

I look again. The severed hand is balanced right there with the fingers spread.

"Wow! I bet the rest of the body parts are under that tablecloth," Ralph says.

There's static where my voice should be. A dark-haired lady has walked into the temple through a door hidden in the wall. She stands by the table with her hands on her hips. She lifts the hand, examines it. "A lady just picked it up," I whisper.

I fix my eyes on her, freeze. Animal instinct. The museum shrinks to a closet containing only her and me. Tears roll.

"God! Ralph!" I screech in a whisper. "It's Gone Mom. I swear. She just walked in and walked out. It's her. She went to the other end of the room. I can't see her now!"

Ralph nudges into my place, looks, turns, shakes his head. "Damn. I need Mom's compact!" He paws through his pack.

"What? You have her *compact*?"

"Yup."

Ralph lifts it out, presses a tiny bar on the side, and snaps it open.

Without a word he slides the screen and slips his chubby self through far enough to plant the compact on a tall crate, with the mirror angled toward the temple.

He returns, slides the screen back into place, bumps me, and says, "Jeez, give me some room. I'm on business. You're making me jittery. It is not a crime to look in a mirror. Why, a person can stand anywhere on earth all easy-breezy and spy just fine using strategic mirror placement. Using strategic mirror placement, one can catch the odd angle, peer around corners. Why don't you go distract the guard or something?" He looks through the crack. "Besides, she just walked out through a hidden door in the wall. You want me to ask somebody if she's really Lien Loo?" Ralph says, his voice softer now.

"No! I'll just stand here wondering why you aren't on a leash." The ceiling lights buzz. My chest cracks down the middle. "God. It really could be her!" Suddenly I'm running downstairs, across the main hall, and out the front doors onto the steps. I hear Ralph huffing behind me.

I wheel around. "What if she has been living behind that wall in the very same town as me for thirteen years? And all this time I worried she'd gone to hell!" Gone Mom turns into something small and hard. Forget her. I will *never* go in there again. Didn't she think she might run into me someday? Did she care? Does she care? No, she does not.

It is hours and an endless stomachache later—long after I have exhausted the Gone Mom possibilities and the fact that the hand is wooden, not stiff, dead enemy flesh— that I remember we have left Mother's precious, mono- grammed, family-heirloom, ultrapolished compact on a crate in no-man's-land.

When I knock on Ralph's door to tell him, he waves me off. "I know. It's closed tomorrow. I'll have to wait till Tues- day. Can Mom survive that long without her face goop?" He rubs his cheeks, imitating her.

"It's not the goo, it's the *container*—her most prized pos- session of her whole life, and that includes *you*!"

On Tuesday Ralph comes into my room right before dinner looking all serious and smug except for one thing. He does not have Mother's compact.

"What happened?" I say.

"I sneaked in to get it. . . ."

"How?"

He points to his moccasins. "These. I employed Indian ways. And also these." He holds up binoculars.

"But you didn't *find* it?"

"No wampum, but I bring news." He gives me a careful look, says slowly, "The lady you thought was Gone Mom, isn't."

The room absorbs this revelation. I lie back on the floor, eyes locked on the dead bugs in my ceiling light.

"I used my binoculars and I saw her point-blank. She isn't a Chinese person at all. And then she walked right past me in the hall and I asked her about the hand and she said it was a secret, part of the big grand-reopening event, so I got you one of these on my way out." He hands me a fancy flyer with Chinese figures on the front.

Grand Reopening and Dedication
Chinese Temple
Nelson-Atkins Museum of Art

Friday, March 9, 1951
6:00 p.m.
Lecture and reception
Chinese buffet and cocktails

"Mr. Howard, if you had the chance to learn something, you know, about your birth father, would you do it?"

"Nope." He pops the *p* sound as we stand on the curb in front of school. It's windy and humid with an edge of spring.

I look up, shield my eyes from the sun. "Because?"

He turns to me, taps the side of his head. "I'm *good*. I've got him where I want him, squared away. If that man's soul got restless to seek me out one day, my advice to his soul would be: go chase your tail."

"Yeah, but what if you had a chance to learn something new or see his face?"

"I put myself and everybody else through hell finally getting my feet on the ground." He turns to me. "I can make a perfect Peking duck. I can spoil my wife, whack a baseball, play the flute, pick my way through a crapload of prejudice, and tickle my kids' funny bones. I'm glad he abandoned me. I never would have learned those life *essentials* from him. Let him be." Mr. Howard waves a fist at his invisible father. "Bye-bye, ol' buddy."

"But you yourself said things change, that life doesn't stay still."

Mr. Howard nods. "Yep. Sounds good. Sounds right. But I admit I don't want him meeting my kids—their *grandfather*. Sheesh. But don't you believe I haven't *thought* of it a million times." Mr. Howard pauses, gives me a puzzled look. "I'm more than a little curious why you're asking, Miss Firestone? Did you happen to run across my birth father?"

We stand there, me knowing I've swirled up the dust inside him. "Sorry, Mr. Howard."

"No. That man did me a favor letting me figure my own self out." Mr. Howard looks off and says slowly, "On the other side, think what *his* life has been like. Leaving your baby boy must feel raw right up to the day you pass. Maybe especially on that day."

Misty is how I would describe Mr. Howard's face. He doesn't try to hide it. Seems he has bruises under his eyes. I wonder, if I have the chance to see Gone Mom and I don't take it, if I'll regret it every day until I pass.

Cars and buses slide by us. I am already late for first hour. "Okay," Mr. Howard says, "why *are* you asking? You got something?"

And from my mouth spills the legend of my box, my stupid museum-lady mistake, the slipper, the dragon pearl, the photos, and the teeny chance that Gone Mom might be at the celebration at the art museum. I am shaking by the end.

Mr. Howard throws up his hands. "Oh, is *that* all?" He raises his eyebrows, whistles, and says, "Well, fear ends when you do what you fear." He looks off, thinking. "I'll be there stirring the bird's nest soup. Elliot's coming. The mayor's coming too and museum bigwigs, archaeologists, Chinese art types." He looks at me—eyes wide. "I can get you a ticket."

Chapter 20

Lantern light washes the museum entrance in Chinese red. Wind chimes chatter. A huge, bug-eyed dragon coiled over the doors warns—enter at your own risk. I have a ticket and six pictures in my purse and fear shredding my stomach. I need the "do what you fear" flame in me. It's not.

I review my plan: sit in a chair in the back row, locate the exit, bolt if I see someone I know, do not get in a picture, do not leave my purse under the chair, stay incognito, and watch the clock. I have until at least ten to get home. Dad is being honored by the chamber of commerce for his real estate developments and innovations in Kansas City. My parents left the house in a twit, all bow-tied and *girdled* with not one question to me or to Ralphie about our plans for tonight.

I will also avoid Auntie Chow and her jade-shattering voice—HA! LILY FIRESTONE! WHY YOU HERE?

I am searching for my birth mother, Gone Mom.

Fur coats sweep up the steps, their owners all dolled up and in high spirits. I stand in a stone column's thick shadow, shivering.

Limousines slide around the circular drive. Their shiny black sides swim along the icy water of the lighted reflecting pool. Valets swing car doors open. Passengers slip out. Clustered momentarily, they exclaim over the huge, billowing dragon and the spills of knotted red silk streamers, then waltz inside.

Hours ago in social studies we learned of the USS *Essex*'s ability to handle atom-bomb-carrying planes and how "in civil-defense news, cities gird for attack as war crimes soar and truce talks stall." I walked out of class tasting jellied gasoline napalm, a mushroom clouding my mind, scared for our civilized world, wondering if war is "just" or just organized violence.

I walk inside, hand over my ticket, and head straight to the restroom, astounded that so many have come to celebrate the artwork of the enemy. I pick at a threadbare place in the fainting couch upholstery, wondering what Gone Mom and I will do if we meet. I will show her my pictures—the proof that I am her daughter—and then what? Exchange hugs? Tears? Telephone numbers? Or not. Surely lots of girls like me have fainted here before going upstairs to meet their birth mothers.

I creep out of the bathroom, stop at the drinking fountain without swallowing a sip, and go upstairs.

I skirt the Main Chinese Gallery, which is filled with people, not crates. No remnant of my ripped petticoat, either, just glowing gorgeousness everywhere—polished wood, a floor-to-ceiling green-and-gold-tiled walkthrough, and towering open-cut screens that divide the ceiling light into snowflakes dusting us all. Flashbulbs bounce off display cases full of jade and porcelain. I hop around a photographer and spot Mr. Howard in his chef's hat. He raises a wooden spoon in greeting, shakes his head slightly as if to say he won't tell the Chows I'm here.

A gong sounds and everybody finds a seat in the Buddhist temple. I head down a row of folding chairs to the back corner. I have dropped my program somewhere, but I am not about to get up now. I put my purse on the floor, wrap my feet around the chair legs, and try to swallow my heart, which is lodged in my throat.

I spot the hidden door in the wall by the stage, just a rectangle of molding with a keyhole. I have imagined Gone Mom coming through that door and stepping up onstage a thousand times. Will she look out and recognize me instantly? Will I run to her or turn away? Will we look alike? Or will we gaze up at the dragon pearl—our starting point or ending point—together?

One whole wall is a painting of Buddha. The platform at the front has a tall red curtain on wheels. There's a slide projector, a podium, a table with the wooden body parts hidden under a tasseled red cloth, a vase of chrysanthemums, candles, scrolls with rows of calligraphy, a bowl of sand, and an old Chinese fellow playing a skinny, high-pitched instrument. His strumming calms everyone's voices. The man in front of me whispers—*zither*—to the lady he's with. She wears a heavy armor of Chanel N°5 perfume. Mother's favorite. Ralph swears that if our mother ever once perspired, she'd sweat Chanel.

Somebody tests the microphone and dims the lights. The overflow crowd settles down in the Main Chinese Gallery. Blood rushes from my hands and feet. I straighten my face and look ahead.

Mayor Taylor welcomes everybody, thanks a million people, and says, "A well-publicized stranger has come to town, and I don't mean our special guest speaker." *Ha-ha-ha.* "I am referring to the treasure behind this curtain." *Ooh . . . aah . . .*

The director of the Nelson-Atkins Museum speaks next. He will introduce the guest speaker. He has white hair and a crimson necktie. I scan the audience. There are lots of Chinese people—distinguished-looking scholar types and couples, the men in tuxedos, the women in slim silk dresses. None are carrying bayonets. None of them are Gone Mom. They are black-haired and elegant. I am unelegant in my swing skirt and blue cardigan. In their beaded purses I imagine silver combs and cigarette holders. My purse contains Chiclets, my compact, a comb, Tangee, and six grainy photographs.

"We've waited fifteen years for this evening . . . Dr. Benton molded our Chinese collection . . . a mecca of Oriental antiquities right here in the Midwest . . . painstaking . . . searching and piecing together . . . fakes and halos . . . sixth sense . . ." We learn that the featured speaker's credentials and talents are too vast to be contained in one institution. He and his colleagues will stay in Kansas City for several weeks.

Now the crowd laughs. The museum director has said something funny, but I don't care what. It feels like nothing is happening *outside* of me tonight.

The audience stands, so I do too. Dr. Michael Benton walks onstage to huge applause and begins his remarks. His American face and Chinese coat and pants are an odd mix. "*Jin wan xie xie ni men lai. Wo hen rong xing he ni men zai yi qi.* Thank you so very much for coming this evening. I am so honored to be with you." He's the expert, the head of the archaeological team, the one everybody but me is waiting to see. He thanks the museum for sponsoring the work of his team in China.

He explains he has *come home* to tell a Chinese fairy tale. He lights incense sticks, pokes them into the sand, and steps back with his hands folded. We watch the smoke rise.

"Smoke carries our deepest desires and gratitude to the ancestors," he says.

Sandalwood curls to the back of the room, mixes with the Chanel N°5. Gone Mom combined with Mother. Tears spring down my face. No warning. No stopping them. I turn toward the wall, use my sleeve for Kleenex. Why didn't I bring some? Why didn't I *think*?

The expert shows slides of artworks in our museum— sculptures of pharaohs and martyrs, busts of Roman emperors, statues of Hercules, Shiva, Buddha, stained- glass images of Mary and Jesus, the beaded throne of an African king.

"An art museum is the perfect place to experience diver- sity. No wars allowed in here. Rulers and kings, gods and goddesses, mummies, and saints live peacefully under one roof!" He smiles, extends his arms in a wide circle to include the audience, Buddha, the guardian lions, and dragons all around.

The audience claps and cheers.

"And it is in this spirit that we gather tonight to dedicate our Chinese Buddhist temple and to celebrate an object of unparalleled merit, an object that exemplifies heavenly peace and compassion for all. But let us first hear the tale of its discovery."

His voice fades. I check my watch. I try to figure out which of the lumps under the red cloth is my wooden hand, which is the head. "Our team's search began here in Shanxi." The expert points to a slide of China. *Shanxi.* His next picture is tethered camels and a bonfire and rubble.

I lean forward, squint, my stomach a pincushion. *I know these camels.* I have their picture in my purse.

He slides the cloth away, but instead of the hand and toes there are piles of rocks, a scale, a magnifying glass, and logbooks. He undoes a leather tool roll and explains the painstaking process of excavating "the hidden strata below China" using hand shovels, trowels, picks, and paintbrushes.

I recognize the bamboo brushes. I own two just like them.

"We were an international mix of archaeologists, art historians, locals, guides, camels, and grooms. We each contributed our expertise and passion to the search. China in the 1930s was a country in collapse, a victim of endless political turmoil, unequipped to maintain and restore its own treasures. But fortunately, we were able to uncover and preserve those treasures and bring them into the present."

A slide comes on. Everyone gasps, including me. He walks us through the unearthing of a dead man's hand. It's a close-up of the tips of stiff fingers poking out of the dirt, like five thick plant shoots. "When we unearthed this wooden beauty, we knew we were *there*. The elegant fingers pointing to *nirvana*."

Each photograph shows more of the hand—*my hand*—

as it is dug out of the ground. The next slide is a profile picture of a kneeling woman with a snowy hat pressing the sculpted fingers to her cheek.

I have touched that same cheek with my fingers.

Mamá.

I suck in air and hold it. The crowd falls away. I see the two perfect folds in her eyelid, her soft ear, and the side of her nose—the same view I had when she carried me into this very room.

I touch my own cheek, breathe sandalwood smoke, and stare at the pearl.

A tall lady sitting several rows ahead turns and looks right at me. I look away. I don't know her.

"A school had been built over the ruins of the Buddhist temple that once housed our bodhisattva. But not all our *digging* was done in the ground. We scoured flea markets, grottoes, and ransacked ruins." He shows the slide of the snow-dusted head with crystal eyes and a hole in the forehead. Another shows pieces of the flame-shaped halo. "Before being researched and labeled, these random artifacts are gambles, intriguing finds, nothing more.

"But here is our *find*, our masterpiece, today! The bodhisattva." The expert rolls the curtain away, revealing a radiant towering *person* dressed in green and gold scarves and ribbons, with polished skin, elegant hands, wrists wrapped in bracelets, a soaring flowered crown, and crystal eyes. A golden starburst halo shoots out all around it.

He waits for the crowd to quiet. "Bodhisattvas are spiritual beings who offer compassion to all people. But in this case, the bodhisattva needed *our* help. It lay broken and scattered for a thousand years, waiting to be made whole again—the head, toes, hands, halo, and torso reassembled. Fortunately, bodhisattvas are patient by nature.

"Bo-dee-satt-va," he repeats, encouraging the audience to say it. I roll it through my mind. I know the word. I have it in the fortune taped in my notebook:

Bodhisattvas surround you.

"Viewing a bodhisattva is like smelling salts, awakening us. The figure is made of wood, but *we* aren't. It enlivens our capacity for love and compassion. I know because bringing these broken pieces together transformed everyone on our team. Please notice the indentation called an *urna*, or heavenly wisdom eye, in the forehead."

He shows a new slide—the group I thought were gypsies in my picture. The speaker points to a Chinese man with a heavy coat and boots. "Meet Chun Loo, our brilliant archaeologist and Asian art historian from Peking University, and his daughter and apprentice, Lien Loo."

Chun Loo . . . Lien Loo.

Chun Loo—my grandfather.

He stands next to his daughter, my mother, in the picture. They look alike. They smile alike. I stare at his hand resting on her shoulder. Father-daughter. One glimpse—the camera capturing their connection. Father and daughter. Gone. Past. I weave my fingers, focused on my lap, guarding my heart.

Dr. Benton names everyone else in the photograph—each assistant, guide, and groom. Then he folds his hands and rocks side to side, absorbing the picture. "We walked northern China together examining ruins on top of ruins, armed with our tools, our bargaining skills, our money, our passion, and our cameras." He announces that the Chinese Temple is dedicated to his former colleagues, the "finding team" in China.

I hold my breath, arms wrapping my waist. Now the secret door will open and they'll step onstage. I am twisted so tight I'm numb. The expert clears his throat and explains in a voice mechanical and sad that they lost contact with Chun Loo after their collaboration and that his daughter, Lien Loo, who had planned to come study in the U.S., remained in China.

I cover my mouth. *WHAT?*

The tall redheaded woman twirls around again, her eyes locked on me. The speaker fades. I look from Gone Mom on the screen to the dragon pearl and back. *Why is he saying that?* Tears leak down my cheeks. I clutch my

purse, shrunk to nothing, heartsick, confused, and . . .
relieved.

"If you think a bodhisattva is a strange *heathen* from
across the sea," Dr. Benton says, "think again. Bodhisattvas represent what is best in us. They are beginning points
and ending points too, like the miracle of this evening." The
speaker holds his hand the way a crossing guard would stop
traffic. "This hand gesture is called a *mudra.*" He turns to the
bodhisattva, matches palms. "It means 'go in peace.' What
better message could we hear tonight?"

Happy ending point? Really? I could walk up there, open
my purse . . .

I'm startled by strains of zither music and the scrape of
chairs. Everyone is inching to the front to congratulate the
speaker and view the bodhisattva up close, except the lady
who is heading back to me.

Sister Evangeline!

Chapter 21

Evangeline has switched from black and white to color! She wears a gold necklace and green plaid dress with a scoop neck. Her purse sways as she sits on the edge of the chair next to mine. The nun is gone, but not her voice.

"I hoped you would come tonight," she says.

Really? I don't say that she is the last person I expected to see. She is the last person I expected to see ever again!

Evangeline looks at the bodhisattva, then turns to me. She reaches to my cheek, then curls her fingers back. Nun training. Most of the audience has moved into the main room now. The expert, Dr. Benton, converses with Mr. Chow in Chinese.

"My birth mother used to bring me here to look at this dragon pearl," I say, pointing up. "It must have reminded her of home."

Evangeline raises her eyebrows. Nods. I cannot take my eyes from the matching curves of her collarbones, the elegant upward sweep of her neck. We each sit waiting, it seems, for the other one to talk.

"She was the Chinese archaeologist's daughter." My voice is raspy. I clear my throat. "Did you know that?"

"Adoption records are sealed."

"The speaker said Lien Loo never came to America. Why would he say that? It's a lie." A tunnel of silence stretches between us.

"Perhaps you should ask him," Evangeline says.

I glance at the dragon pearl collecting candlelight. "I thought the pictures in that box were clues to help me find her, that she might be here and I could show them to her and, if not, I could at least show them to someone." I take a deep breath, knit my hands. "Idiotic. After all this time, but . . ."

She glances at my purse. "Did you bring the slipper?"

"No! It's too fragile, and I don't know . . . I . . ." I fiddle with my purse strap, glance up at her. "I came back the next day. I needed to talk to you."

She looks off. "There are restrictions for sisters who leave. I couldn't . . ."

What restrictions? "Joy took me on a tour. Sister Immaculata can't hear. Joy's food was dried out, her water was frozen, and the new nun is allergic to cats. Joy was curled up on your bed when I left."

Evangeline lowers her head. I wish I hadn't said it. I wish I had Kleenex. "I'm sorry, Lily. Leaving was terribly difficult." She stares at her lap. "I grew up there."

"You *did*?"

She straightens her back and chin. "Yes."

"But . . ."

"I became one in the stream of souls going out the door."

"Y . . . you left that day, after the shed, didn't you?"

"It was time. My work was finished. The Mercy Home saved all our lives—yours, mine, my mother's, and both of your mothers'."

I sit back, picturing my mothers. So strange to think Evangeline actually knew both of them. The Sisters of Mercy saved Mother?

"How did it save my adoptive mother?" I ask.

Evangeline looks puzzled, as if this is something I should already know. "Maybe you should talk to *her* about it."

Is she crazy? My mother is the last person I could talk to. I check my watch. Eight thirty. An hour to get home. I say the dumbest out-of-the-blue thing. "So you're just plain *Evangeline* now?"

Her cheeks crinkle. "Just plain." She stands. "I understand the art experts will be here for a few weeks. Their story is certainly a fascinating and important one." She gives me a serious look. "Good evening, Lily." Evangeline weaves out of the temple opening and through the reception crowd, catlike, mysterious.

I sit with my head tilted back. "I came," I whisper to Gone Mom, "and even Sister Evangeline came. Where in the world are you?"

Beyond the rows of empty chairs the bodhisattva glows on its lotus flower throne. Its smile is calm and simple. Its scratched crystal eyes remind me of Evangeline's somehow—with every bit of life they've witnessed leaving a mark.

The bodhisattva's raised finger catches the candlelight. How has it not been broken in a thousand years? I weave through chairs, pulled to the front of the room, and stand so it is pointing right at me. I reach up and touch fingertips with the bodhisattva.

God and Girl.

Lien and Lily.

I dodge the photographers and Elliot James and exit the museum petrified that a picture of my fingertip will be on the front page of the Sunday paper. I cross the lawn and sit down by *The Thinker*. The full moon has washed his bronze face in milky light.

Sometimes things come together and sometimes they don't. I came for Gone Mom and I left with a lie. And what did Evangeline mean about the orphanage saving all of us?

"Mr. Howard said you might be out here."

I whip around, nerves unzipped.

Elliot!

"God! What're you doing? You scared me to death!"

"Sorry." I can't see his face, just his flappy horse blanket of a coat.

I hear car engines in the circle. Voices. Horns. Elliot and I stare at the other member of our trio—*The Thinker*, the only one of us without clothes.

He sits, asks why I came tonight. Garbled words rush from my mouth—I have become interested in various aspects of Chinese culture because I don't know very much and I . . . that my *brother* is doing a Boy Scout merit badge and tried some interesting mirror angles to see the Chinese artifacts that . . . bodhisattvas are good inspiration and . . .

This would be the perfect time for Elliot to rescue me, acknowledge that something is painful and weird and help out by changing the subject. But when he's not holding a pencil or paintbrush, Elliot's personality can shred down to nothing.

"*The Thinker* and the bodhisattva are opposites," he says finally. "*The Thinker*'s all clenched, wanting answers to everything, and the bodhisattva's just calm, like he knows there aren't answers."

I unclench my jaw, drop my shoulders, breathe, breathe

again, and for a tiny moment unhook from the world. It feels heavenly.

"Two statues," Elliot says. "Same size. Same museum. Opposite message."

"Yeah."

"So do you need a ride?"

"Did you drive your car?" *Stupid. Stupid.*

"No. A camel."

I turn, debate his offer, and while I debate his offer, Elliot leans over and kisses me. No warning. Just boom! Lips on . . . lips off.

Instant heart attack. Inability to speak. Wobbly world.

He stands and stretches. Since my brain is blank, I stand also, *wobble wobble*, and follow him like a tethered camel to his turpentine car parallel parked by the curb. The rusty door squeals open—*squeeeeek! Leeleeeian got keeessed!*

During the drive my purse comes alive on my lap. It has responded to *the call*. It has provided a focus, an activity to get through the next few immensely awkward minutes. The flap flips up, and the purse flips over and spills itself into the murky never-never land on the floor of his car. I hear my lipstick roll under the seat.

We stop under a streetlight in front of my house. By instinct I glance at my parents' bedroom window. Not home yet, but Ralph's light is on.

Elliot leans toward me. I lean toward the car door. The

top of his head is a tangle of curly brown hair. He swipes his hand over the floor mat, fishing for my stuff. I move my feet. I don't dare bend down.

He has hooked a few Chiclets and a photograph—the one of the camels and grooms. He looks from the picture to me. "What's this?"

I blink. Twice. Three times, scrounging for an explanation. Instead I give him a *look*. A steely *none of your business* type of look, which I mastered from my mother, and pluck the picture from his hand.

Elliot holds the steering wheel. He stares through the windshield. I cannot look at his face. "That was undimensional," he remarks, the way you'd judge a flat, old, dull work of art.

"What was undimensional?" And before I can suck the words back in, I know what he's referring to—*the kiss*.

I yank the handle and leap out of the car, my purse tucked up in my armpit. I don't even say thanks. Thanks for what—the ride or the insult?

I go straight to Ralph's room. He's sitting on the floor in his winter coat. "It's gonna take nine lives to figure out my life!" I say.

Ralph looks over, his face screwed up. "Is this a cat riddle?"

"God!" I cringe at the reflection of my pathetic lips in

his dresser mirror and swipe my mouth. I march over and bounce on his bed. "She wasn't there."

"Yeah."

"Gone Mom was the big Chinese archaeologist's daughter! Part of the team. She was supposed to come to America as a student, but the guy said she bailed out and stayed in China. That's a lie."

"Yeah."

"She was in the slides, though. You shoulda seen them."

"I did."

"No, I mean tonight, on the screen. She was there with the bodhisattva's hand against her cheek. You shoulda been there."

"I *was*!" Ralph shakes his hands, palms up.

"What?"

"I helped the Chows carry some stuff in and I sorta stayed. I just got home. On my bike! Stealth. Last requirement on my *stalker* merit badge—check!" He gives me a grin.

My mind leaps off wondering if he witnessed my undimensional disaster. "So the game of Gone Mom Clue is over without a winner," I say.

"Who was that tall lady?" Ralph asks.

"Sister Evangeline, from the orphanage. She helped me get adopted."

"She's a *nun*?"

"She's an un-nun. She gave me that bootie and then she left."

"Wow! Nuns rarely get fired."

"She didn't get *fired.* She quit!"

"So maybe she couldn't quit until she gave you that shoe."

"No way."

"Well, why was she there?" Ralph says.

"I, uh, didn't ask her. I was so surprised and . . ."

Ralph gives me a look. "Well, you still can."

"Can't. All I know is her name—Evangeline Wilkerson. I have no idea where she lives."

"I do," he says. "I followed her home, which took about a second because she went into an apartment house on Warwick Boulevard a half block away from the museum." He raises his pointer finger. "*And* I saw her in the window when she flicked on a light on the second floor, left-hand corner on the front."

"God. Did she *see* you?"

"Nope." Ralph claws a pudgy hand through his hair. "Piece of cake." He sighs. "I'm gonna be an archaeologist someday."

"When'd you decide?"

"Just now," Ralph says. "You know, all the tools, the sextants, and detective work, and art deals and ancient camel dung."

"Well, you already know how to *lose* tools," I say, "like Mom's compact. That's a start." I feel rotten about her stupid compact. She's been frantic. We have both lied, saying we haven't seen it, which Ralph pointed out technically wasn't lying because we truly haven't seen it lately.

Ralph pours out a million details about shipping problems in China and the trials of reassembling the bodhisattva—dowel rods and special glues and matching paint samples and how it took years to find the pieces of the carved wooden throne in flea markets and pawn shops.

"How did you know all that?" I ask.

"The guy, Dr. Benton, explained it. Weren't you *there*?"

"Hmm . . . I was *distracted*, Ralph." I get the pictures out of my purse. I want to review them and match them up with the statue. But when I lay them out, my blood freezes. The bodhisattva's head is missing. I know exactly where it is. I got into Elliot's car with six pictures and out of his car with five.

Chapter 22

My head is on the pillow, my eyes are shut, but my ears are on duty listening for the phone in case Elliot calls about the photo, and listening out the window in case he leaves it by the front door in the middle of the night.

I reenact, for the thousandth time, the kiss fiasco. How could I have seen it coming? *What were you doing? Maybe you're just like a pigeon, a pigeon that sees a bit of Chinese stuff in front of himself, and whether he's hungry or not he can't help it—he swoops down and pecks it. Animal instinct.*

I sit up, blinking in the dark, return to my folding chair in the Buddhist temple. "*. . . his daughter, Lien Loo, who planned to come study in the U.S., remained in China.*" Gone Mom caught behind Dr. Benton's myth. What should I do? Just leave her there or what?

The Thinker jumps to his feet, looms furious at the side

of my bed. *What kind of idiot are you? Show him your pictures. Get answers.*

Jesus preaches, *Seek ye the whole truth.*

The *Girl before a Mirror* says, *Reach out.*

The bodhisattva smiles, touches my fingertip.

They will all sleep better than me tonight.

Sunday morning the newspaper carries a big headline: "The Sublime Side of China," with a front-page photograph of Dr. Michael Benton face-to-face with the bodhisattva. Dr. Benton stands with his hands in his pockets looking up like they are dear, old friends. I read his quote. "Our bodhisattva was the victim of a thousand-year wreck, the result of China's political collapse, religious turmoil, chronic warfare. It was neglected, abused, and scattered. Our team saved this sacred sculpture from oblivion."

I search for the continued story inside, praying I won't be in a picture, but instead, right there in clear, full view is the whole finding team, *the gypsies*, in China, including the camels and my smiling first mother front row, center. It is the same picture he showed us Friday night.

Lien Loo, close up, right here at our kitchen table.

I stare down between my elbows at the squiggles in the tabletop and cry a little bit. She is closer and farther away every minute. Other photos show additional "finds": a pair of Ming Dynasty vases, guardian lions called chimeras, a famous carved jade disk, and a long shot of the audience that includes the back of Evangeline's head.

Dr. Michael Benton's quotes continue. "But all we brought together in China fell apart during shipping. We thought we'd have our bodhisattva in Kansas City a decade ago. Some things are simply worth waiting for."

Floorboards creak upstairs. The toilet flushes. Dad will be down in a minute in his blue plaid robe and slipper socks.

The percolator waits for him. I fold the paper together and replace the rubber band. My hands are sweaty. My stomach is Jell-O.

"Morning, Lily," Dad says with a flip of his wrist.

"Hi."

He stands at the counter, opens the Folgers can, sniffs it—*"ahh . . ."*—before he measures. He walks to the refrigerator for the ritual look inside. He always does this. It drives Mother nuts. *Don't just stand there with the door open!* But she's not in here, so he's free to cool the whole downstairs if he wants.

He sits across from me, pulls his ashtray over, and lights a Lucky Strike. The match smells good. The percolator talks coffee. He gives the front page the once-over, shakes his head, and says in his crazy-ol'-world way, "What the heck? What'll they think of next?"

Huh? Do you mean the bodhisattva? China? Newspapers? Is it just the shock of seeing something that's Chinese and decent and peaceful?

"What?" I sound sharp.

"The Chows." He points to the background of the front-page picture, where you can see them by their buffet table. He shakes his head. "My tenants. Those two don't miss a trick, I'll tell you that. A Chinese cafeteria in a museum!"

"What's wrong with Chinese food? Have you ever tried it?" I snap.

Dad turns, eyebrows raised as if to query, *Have you?* He pours coffee that sloshes onto his saucer. The coffee smell reminds me of Elliot. One and a half cigarettes later he comes to the inside page with more photos. I rub my thumb along the chrome table edge. Mother would die to know toast crumbs live between the rim and Formica.

Dad scans the pictures of Chinese vases and jade. He stops. His eyes tighten on the photo with Gone Mom. A tiny ripple seems to cross his face.

Do you know her? Did you hide my box in the attic? Did you look in it? Does her face ring a bell?

My heart is in the freezer, but my mouth can't stand the silence. "It's about art they found from old China."

My father sniffs, scratches his thigh, sets his drippy cup right on the print as he reads.

"Java's ready!" he announces, instantly abandoning the article when he hears Mother. He refolds the front section and turns it facedown as she enters in her sateen scuffs and nylon mesh Sure Set Slumber Net. Dad gives her a peck and carries his coffee refill and the sports page to the living room.

I cannot sit here one more second anticipating her looking at Gone Mom. And I cannot get up for the very same reason.

"Hey," Ralph says, coming in. He flips open the paper and glances at me. He assesses the situation, eyes darting from the bodhisattva photo to Mother to me. *What gives?*

He pours a glass of orange juice and plops onto a chair. I fan my nose. "God, go brush your teeth."

"I did already." He puffs into his palm, then turns it to me. "See?" Ralph leans across the table to study the bodhisattva picture. "Wow! Neat!" He holds it up for Mother. "Bo-dee-satt-vah, continued on page five."

The roller coaster careens forward. I sit strapped in my seat.

Ralph scans the inside pictures. He's checking page five for a problem picture of one of us. He flicks me a look and points to the group picture. "Hey, Mom, these people—archaeologists and stuff—found this amazing statue from *China* and . . ."

Mother steps over, wiping her hands on the apron tied over her robe. She peers down. It's clear she doesn't register she's seeing my birth mother. "Beautiful," she remarks, pointing to the pair of matching vases, "They'd be perfect in our front windows." She adjusts the bobby pin in her left pin curl. "They're exotic."

Ralph reads aloud that Dr. Michael Benton will work for several days in Kansas City researching artworks in our collection and updating their labels. "*Provenance* is everything," he is quoted as saying. "The accurate history of an artwork is key. Meaning and identity are often revealed in layers."

Ralph slides me the funny paper. Dad turns on the radio in the living room. Mother fills the toaster. And Gone Mom lies flat on her back on the kitchen table, smiling up at all of us.

Ralph is talking fast up in my room. "I checked it out first. I *saw* we weren't in the pictures before I showed Mom. If one of us *was* in a picture, I would have spilled my orange juice on it. I mean, didn't you want to know what she'd do when she saw the picture, if she recognized it?"

I release my hands from around his neck.

"She doesn't know about them," he croaks. "I could tell."

"Or she conveniently forgot." I tilt my head. "But *Dad* acted weird." Ralph looks up as if this is not news. "He was nervous the minute Mom came in. Folded the paper, turned it over."

"Yep. He's always on *Vivian Firestone alert*."

"What're you gonna do?" Ralph asks.

"Move to China."

"Seriously."

"Continue bulldozing piles of problems from my past and shoving them into today."

Ralph looks at me as if this is a good thing, spreads his arms. "Your past is a thousand times more mysterious and interesting than your *now*."

"Yeah. Whether I want it or not, my past *is* now."

Chapter 23

Monday after class I head down to the art room praying Elliot will be there. I will wait a second and see if he looks up from his drawing table and mentions finding my picture. If he doesn't, then I'll say I left my lipstick in his car and is it locked and can I borrow the keys so I can go out and get it, blah blah blah.

I will act as if life has not become surreal since our pigeon kiss.

But Catty Piddle is sitting on a stool by Elliot. He looks flattered by whatever she's saying, even though she's really not that cute—horse teeth, stubby neck, and that lumpy pageboy. Or at least he doesn't look miserable. He writes something down. Probably the time and date of some sorority beauty contest she's asking him to judge.

Gag. "Hi, Patty," I say.

She gathers her books. "Oh, hi. How are you?" Her

smile looks pulled up with marionette strings.

We dangle there a second, then she waves at Elliot, mouths *Thank you!*, and leaves.

Elliot's cheeks are splotchy red. He looks down, twirls his pencil on the table. As usual, when he needs to fill in an awkward silence, he doesn't. "I . . . I left something in your car," I say. My voice sounds like it's *his* fault.

"Yeah. Sorry."

Sorry?

"I didn't bring it over. The picture." He takes the bodhisattva's head out of his tablet. "And here's a sketch of it I did." He gives me a puzzled look and hands them over. "It's the bodhisattva at the museum, right?"

I nod and stare at his perfect little ink drawing. Now it's my turn to fill in the blank. I don't. The faucet drips.

"Why'd ya have that?" he asks, glancing at my purse. "What about the other ones? Can I see them?"

My stomach drops. I clutch my purse. "I don't have them today. I . . ." I am one million degrees. I check the clock. "Oh, gosh! Wow! I'm late for an appointment." I grab my books and sprint to the door, turn back a split second and wave the sketch at him. "Thanks."

"But, hey! Lily . . ."

I spend the next half hour, the entire bus ride to the Sisters of Mercy Home, playing out the scene of actually showing

Elliot everything in my Gone Mom box. He would go nuts, ask a zillion questions. The thought grows as fast as a weed in my garden of bad ideas.

I won't. I can't. But what if I did?

I step off the bus at the Sisters of Mercy Home for my *appointment* with Joy. Actually, I intend to kidnap her. I dash across the street and up the orphanage steps. Her water dish is ice. In seconds she is meowing around my feet. I pick her up and whisper, "What're you doin' out here, featherweight? It's too cold."

She is little and perfectly built to transport. Her magnificent green-gold eyes stare up at me without blinking.

"This is an adoption," I say as I dart back across the street to the bus stop with her inside my coat. "*Your* adoption. I know somebody who needs you."

In a few minutes we step onto the bus, which strictly prohibits animal passengers. I feel illegal, but I can live with it.

We get off a few blocks from the art museum and, after a little walk, enter the lobby of Evangeline's apartment house. I find her name on a mailbox next to a sign that reads:

ABSOLUTELY
NO SOLICITORS
NO PETS

Damn. Joy squirms up as if she wants to chat. I rub her little black neck feeling thunked on the head. What to do? "You can't live inside my coat forever. So we can either go back to Sister Immaculata or to the art room or *home* home. That's about it."

The art room's *out*—unless Mr. Howard would take her. She can't live at the House of Chow, with its fishy kitchen and aquarium. I can't stand the thought of the Sisters of Mercy Home—returned orphans feel permanently sunk on life.

I open my coat to give her more room. She seems to be asleep, trusting fate—which is *me*. I wrap one arm under her, balancing my books and purse in the other, and walk the entire way home with that *you did the right thing* flame burning inside.

Mother's here, in the kitchen. I hear the Mixmaster. I head straight to our *immaculata* basement and unbutton my coat. Joy jumps down and runs right behind the furnace where it's warm. I brush black hairs off my parka. It will take no time for Mother to sense something new in the house. I might as well have ushered a camel down the basement steps.

I head back up imagining Joy's little kitten prints all over the divan and dining room table. "Mother," I say over the beaters. Mother flips it off, turns to me in her navy-blue apron. I plant my feet, hold the counter edge. "I found a cat, a kitty, who needs a home."

She waves her spoon. "Well, put a sign at the grocery store. Is it diseased or pregnant?"

"No!" I lower my voice. "It's not *diseased*." *Are all orphans diseased? And what's wrong if she is pregnant, I'd like to know? Cats don't need penance.*

Mother's eyes narrow. "Where has it *been*?" *She's been living in an orphanage. Is there something wrong with that?*

"It's a *she*," I say, "and some *nuns* were taking care of her and they can't anymore." I know that nuns will sound good to my mother. Better than a junkyard cat.

"Where is it?"

"In the basement."

"Seriously, Lily."

"Seriously, she's in our basement," I say, pointing down the hall toward the closed door. "She has black fur. Her name is Joy."

My mother looks puzzled.

"She's just *black*, plain black. There's nothing wrong with that. People who don't want black cats are just superstitious." I force myself to look right at my mother. "People step around them, don't want them crossing their path, but not me." Usually I can sniff her mood, but I can't figure it out at the moment. Either she doesn't believe me, or she's starting her silent treatment, or maybe, for once, she is trying to figure *me* out. *Ha!*

I open the refrigerator, get the milk, and pour a dish,

giving my mother plenty of time to—*almost hoping* she'll—say something offensive about black cats. Besides Ralph's secret pigeons there has never been a pet in our house.

"You want to meet her?" I ask. Mother's eyebrows arch. "I'm not kidding. She's really here." My mother tilts her head—left, right. It either means "okay" or that her head is falling off.

I go to the basement. "C'mon, Joy." She gives me a wary look. "Time to meet my mother." I carry her upstairs. She immediately jumps from my arms, sniffs the kitchen, cleans her nose, and sniffs some more. Mother stares at this wild creature from outer space. Joy does figure eights around her feet, dusting Mother's house shoes with her tail.

Mother jiggles her foot. Joy pounces on the bow on her slipper. Mother jiggles again. Joy pounces again. This goes on awhile. "Does it have a name?" she asks.

"Yes. I already told you, her name's Joy."

"You say sisters kept her? Where? At your old school?"

I lean down and pat Joy's back. "Uh . . . she was a nun's cat. So was her mother . . . well, or a cat-nun with kittens!" I know I'm not making any sense, but fortunately Mother isn't listening. She turns to me and says something unbelievable. "I used to have a kitty." She looks off, her mouth moving silently as if she's listening to a memory. "Pazooie Pazaza."

Watching my mother's lips say the name is astounding.

The way her mouth hangs open a bit after the last *za* . . . "Was that really its name?" I say.

"*Her* name." Mother kneels down and rolls her knuckles over Joy's little head. "Pa-zoo-ie Pa-za-za."

Joy meows, turns a circle, and curls up—a purring black puddle in front of my mother's Frigidaire.

"Cats shape themselves around the habits of the people who feed them," Dad says later between sneezes. He's obviously allergic to Joy but not admitting it. He looks at Ralph and me across the dinner table, points to the kitchen door, and whispers behind his napkin, "If your mother wants to keep that *cat*, then so do I—so do *we*, right?" He sips his bourbon, rattles the ice, and adds, "That animal's gonna have *her* on a leash the way your mother will follow it around with the sweeper. I say, save a step and vacuum the cat!"

Joy follows Mother into the dining room. Mother sets her sausage-and-green-bean casserole on a trivet and says, "I heard that comment about the leash, Don, and I'll have you know that my first cat, Pa-zoo-ie Pa-za-za, was black, just like Joy, and she raised her tail like a skunk."

Ralph and Dad share a glance. Mother sits down and lets Joy hop onto her lap.

"Well, how-dee-do," Dad says. We all sit, hypnotized, smelling that old, skunky cat of hers. He nods at Mother.

"Joy will elevate your vacuum to family-member status. At least sweepers are cheap to feed!"

It feels good to laugh. Drowns out the siren that's been going off inside me since Friday night.

"Wasn't Joy supposed to be *yours*?" Ralph asks me later in my room. "I mean, since you couldn't leave her with that nun, Evangeline."

"Yeah. Her being *mine* didn't last a minute. She's a professional orphanage cat. She knows what she's doing, filling the lap of the loneliest." I instantly feel a pang. I need to tell Evangeline what happened, how I adopted Joy for her, and that I'm sorry she can't have her.

"What do you mean?" Ralph says. "Do you think Mom's lap is *lonely*?"

I shrug. "I don't know. But Joy does."

Chapter 24

Sidestep it or step *in* it.

Which?

If I step *in*, go back to the museum and hunt down the world-renowned mythmaker Dr. Michael Benton, I will need to take my box and the pictures, which means lugging them to school first. Ugh.

If I sidestep, I can be *done* right now. No more brave flame of truth, but less pain. Maybe.

I sink down in my bubble bath. Joy sits on my towel taking a cat bath. This is a rare appearance. Since the moment they met, Joy became Mother's guardian shadow. I pile up bubble mountains like I did as a little girl, with Ivory soap for a boat.

Gone Mom traveled alone all the way from China for a reason. So why can't I travel a few miles to the museum?

Simple. It would explode our family. I sit up. My bubbles slosh. On the other hand, there is no one on earth but me who *can* do it.

It's my trip to the truth now.

I shiver, my mind twisting into a new curiosity about Lien Loo. Not about what she did to *me*, but about her as a young woman probably not much older than I am. Was she truly planning to go to school here? Why? Her father was famous. They had archaeology school in China.

I can't blow out the flame—or is it fury?—in me. As I dry off I realize I have made a two-step plan—first confront my parents with my box, then Michael Benton.

"Ralph, I am warning you, I've decided to show them the case." He looks up with a stricken expression. "I'll show them everything but the pictures and the slipper."

"*Why?* They're going to blame me for snooping around up there. They're going to discover the pigeons and—"

"No they won't. Not unless you tell them. It's just going to be the truth about how you found the box in the attic like any kid would. . . ." Ralph gives me an expression that says *I'm not any kid.*

"Right!" I say. "Sorry. You are only disguised as a normal person. But anyway, looking around in your very own attic isn't a crime. I am going to do it. So you might want to go on an extended campout . . . or not. It's going to be a *test*. I'm going to put the box in plain sight and see if either of them shows a glimmer of recognition."

"Well, one of them *has* to because I wasn't born yet and *you* didn't hide it under a dirty tarp in the attic, so . . ." Ralph gives me the Boy Scout sign. His voice hops octaves. "My pigeons and I accept the challenge. I will witness the test and help interpret results."

Ralph is the coolest uncool brother on earth.

So right after dinner, while Dad is in the kitchen helping dish up butterscotch pudding, I put Gone Mom's box, closed, in the middle of the table by the dessert spoons. With the evidence right there, Dad can't ho-hum it away.

They don't notice it for a second. Ralph sits hunched in his chair, his stalker skills in high gear. I grip my napkin, on the verge of exploding.

"What's this doing on the table?" Mother asks. Ralph and I share a minute glance. Dad inhales sharply, pats the cigarette pack in his pocket, and shoots a look toward the ceiling. Ralph and I say nothing. The air closes in. The radiators gurgle and spasm. Joy weaves through the chair legs, meows at Mother.

"Don?" Mother insists. "Is it something from work? Blueprints? Invoices?"

Ralph's eyes shift: Mom—Dad—Mom.

"So, hmm . . . I don't know." My father wipes his mouth, screws up his forehead, without looking at me. "Actually, I believe this is from the *home*, Vivian," he says, packing a pillow around every word. "It was given to us when we picked up Lily."

"But you . . ." Mother snaps her mouth shut; her eyes finish the sentence—*you said you got rid of it.*

"I . . . uh, just stuck it in the attic. I'd forgotten all about it." Dad gets busy distributing the pudding and spoons.

"You hid it in the attic under an old tarp," I say too loudly.

"Did you look in Lily's box, Dad?" Ralph asks with a slightly phony tone of little-boy enthusiasm.

My father examines the ceiling molding. "I maybe remember shaking it, and yes . . . there were scraps of wood, as I recall, and sticks and rocks and rubble. Nothing much."

"It was only *nothing* to you," I say.

Mother's eyes are trained on my box. I know she is already finding fault with it.

I reach out, slide the case over, and open it. One at a time I put everything on the table. I even turn the box upside down and tap a cornerful of dust onto the tablecloth. *There!* Mother leans in, looks over the wrist rest, the incense box, the dusty brushes and broken jade bit. Under the table Joy claws her chair leg. Mother reaches down and places her on her lap.

"These things were left to me . . . from my life *before* I came there," I say. "Before" silently screams *from my birth mother.*

Mother looks from me to her husband. "But . . . ?"

My father bites his lip.

"This *rubble* is mine," I repeat. "It's from my life before the sisters. Did the nuns tell you that the regular protocol was to bring it home and hide it from me? Or did they advise you to tell me I had no belongings from my past even though I did?"

Dad chimes in. "Lily! It would have only confused you. We were so ecstatic to have you, to move forward and start a family. What would have been the point?"

"But you said it didn't exist when you knew that it did. I believed you, even the other night when you said everything was gotten rid of. Why live in reverse?"

I wave my hand at Mother's fancy cabinet of crystal glasses. "You inherited all this stuff from *your* mother. What if somebody had lied and told you it didn't exist or had just hidden it under a dirty old tarp or had even thrown it away?"

The misery on my mother's face stops me cold. She looks shrunk into a little girl.

Ralph digs furiously into his pudding.

"It's my fault," says Dad in a raspy, tired voice. "I thought it was best for everyone."

My mother straightens her back, picks up the jade, puts it down, and waves her hand. "Well, I can't make heads or tails of it." She picks up a paintbrush, drops it back in the box. Rage flashes in me. It takes everything I have not to blurt out about Gone Mom and the art museum. I sweep my things back into my box. I don't want her to touch any of it, to spout her puny two-cents'-worth assessment of things that are priceless to me. This was an awful idea, putting my heart on the dissecting table. They won't see it again. But now I know one important fact—it was Dad who hid it from Mother and me.

"Were you crawling in the attic, Lily?" Dad asks.

Ralph chimes in. "*I* was, you know, in the attic because I am doing the Pigeon Raising merit badge." Mother looks repulsed. Ralph looks pleased. He's chosen to hit them while they're down, a one-two punch. "It seemed easy to raise pigeons if they are already on the premises and don't actually need *raising*, so . . ." Ralph takes a breath. "I found this box that we figured out belongs to Lily and—"

Mother slices through Ralph's explanation. "*Pigeons?* Where are your birds now?"

"In the attic," Ralph answers, "like I said." He and I turn to our father.

"About those birds . . . ," my father says, shooting his wife a look. "We need to talk, son. They carry disease."

"They're supposed to carry *messages*, but they're not speedy learners."

"We need a screen on that window," Mother says as she stands and heads up to her room with Joy in her arms.

Minutes later Ralph and I do the dishes. "Wow! Team-work!" Ralph gives me a Scout salute.

Twirling the dishrag, I figure out why Mother wasn't more upset, why she didn't seem threatened by these parts of my broken past—one, because my things looked like random bits of *heathen* nothing, and two, they are contained *inside* our family. This has not become a public embarrass-ment like my detention, so it doesn't count. It's just *me*. So what? Sure enough, Dad pops through the kitchen door and says, "Hey, Lily and Ralph, let's just keep this box busi-ness in the family." He tilts his head in the direction of the stairs. "Easier for everyone that way."

"Dad?" I say.

"Not all memories are good ones. Dredging up bits and pieces of a person's . . ."

"Past?"

"Yes. Parts of a person's past can be difficult," he says.

"Don't you think I know that already? Plus, I'm not 'a person,' I'm *me*. You act like we're talking about somebody else."

My father doesn't say it, but his look does—*we are*. . . .

The door swings shut. I squeeze the dishrag and listen to bubbles popping in the sink. Funny how the fact that they hid my Gone Mom things makes the things more impor-tant. Pushing her away makes her closer.

*   *   *

On Wednesday after school, my purse and I enter the museum. "Are the Chinese experts here today?" I ask, sounding nonchalant in a panicked sort of way. The woman at the information desk looks at me funny. Maybe she can tell I need her to hold my hand. She tells me to check upstairs.

I pass the Scholar's Studio. The wrist rest still sits on the desk. It's good to see it there, doing its job of doing nothing. I clutch my purse and head around the corner to the Main Chinese Gallery. No ginger and scallion steam, no whining zither today, just Dr. Benton by a display case with its wide glass front swung open. He wears white gloves and is examining what looks to be a collection of tiny tea sets.

My mouth tastes like metal. I cannot just walk over and interrupt him. My mind sparks a million warnings, especially this one: *You are about to make misery.* So I fiddle around pretending to be interested in this and that and check my watch. One hour until closing. I stare into a case full of ancient jade pieces. Prongs hold them up at a viewing angle—part of a crouched tiger, a broken knife hilt as big as my hand, and the flat carved disk Dr. Benton showed us, the exact same greenish-tan color as the broken lizard tail in my purse. The label says the disk is called a *bi,* and that it represents the universe with two dragons dancing on the edge. A *bi* was buried with the emperor because jade ensured immortality.

I slip past the gates into the Buddhist temple and sit on a bench, my heart a hummingbird. I swear the bodhisattva has grown. They have added a display of fragile silk prayer scrolls and bits of broken mirror found inside cavities in the head and back, left by devotees a thousand years ago.

Showing Dr. Benton my jade will be an easier place to start than the photographs. I take a breath and begin the impossible trek back over to him in the Main Chinese Gallery. He is crouched on one knee, angling his huge camera lens at miniature teaspoons made of clay.

"Sir?" He turns. Light bounces off his horn-rimmed glasses. "Excuse me," I croak.

He sighs, lowers his camera. He looks windswept, sculpted, Hollywood handsome with thick coppery hair.

"I've got something here. . . ." I fumble my purse open and lift out a folded Kleenex. He glances at it and gives me a questioning once-over. My nerves leap and scream, reminding the rest of me that my next move can never be reversed. I hold up the jade.

He sets his camera on the floor, stands up. His fingers clench and stretch as if he's lost his pockets. I see his reflection in the display case glass. An odd thought comes to me—Elliot would have an easy time drawing a caricature of him, with his strong jaw, straight nose, and wavy hair.

"May I?" He turns the piece to catch the light. He clears his throat, gives me a look of immense puzzlement, or maybe it's immense wonderment. "Where did you get this, miss?" he whispers.

I look through the opening into the temple. The bodhi-sattva looks back. "From a relative of mine, a person who was a part of your team in China."

He gives the piece back to me. His hand trembles a bit, or maybe I'm trembling. I *know* I'm trembling. He takes off his gloves.

There's noise in the hall—museum visitors. They walk past the door. Dr. Benton pauses a moment, then motions me into the temple. "Do you have anything else from your relative?"

"I do."

He does not ask my relative's name. He is clearly more interested in art than people. I remove the red lacquer box. "Ming Dynasty," he says, turning it in his hand. He points to an animal carved on the lid. "This is a *qilin*. It has the scales of a dragon and hooves of a deer. The peony sym-bolizes that one's sons have great character and success. It is the wish for the birth of sons."

It didn't work, I think. Gone Mom didn't give birth to sons, at least as far as I know. "I . . . I also have pictures."

"Would you mind my seeing them?" he asks. His eyes are pale blue, deep set, and nervous. I would be too if I were him, wondering how he'd been so careless as to leave these things behind. Of course, he lost track of a whole person, Gone Mom, so who knows?

He takes a long breath and sorts through my pictures. He

drops one and snatches it off the floor. He drops another one. "Sorry, miss." I point to the group picture. "Although it's hard to see her in my photo, that young lady is Lien Loo," I say, pointing. "You talked about her . . . saying she didn't come to America."

He nods.

"But she *did*."

He folds his arms across his chest, steps back. He's obviously not used to being corrected. "Excuse me?"

"Lien Loo. I stood in this room with her before the bodhisattva was in here and after *she came to America*."

His face is impossible to read. "When exactly was that?"

"I was born on December twentieth, 1934, in San Francisco. It was a few years after that." He says nothing. I glance around the room thinking he must not believe me. "Would one of the other experts know more about her?"

Dr. Benton straightens his shoulders. "I can ask," he says. "Yes. I will surely do that. Consult my colleagues. What year did you say you were here with her? It might clear up a discrepancy."

Discrepancy?

He is definitely a date person. It goes with being an archaeologist, I guess. "I'm not sure—in 1937, maybe. I was around three." I half expect him to ask my height and weight, what I'm made of, and how I was created—the facts for my *label*. He'll probably want to take my picture.

"Did you say Lien Loo was your distant relative?"

"Not *distant*. She was my mother." The syllables vibrate in my ears, my bones. *She was my mother. She is my mother. She is one of my mothers. She was once my mother.*

"I see." He takes off his glasses, rubs his eyes, and fumbles with his handkerchief. "As I said, we lost track of her and her father. It was a great loss. W—where is she now?"

"I thought maybe you would know. You said she didn't come here, but she did. She placed me in the Sisters of Mercy Children's Home when I was three, and after a while I was adopted." My words sound strong, true, and terrible.

He glances around as if looking for something, maybe the hidden door to disappear through. "So how is it you have these pictures and the jade?"

"She left them for me."

"Where?"

"At the orphanage."

"Are there more?"

". . . yes."

"I see." He nods. Works his hands. His cheeks have a shadow of whiskers. It's a strong face, one that could be famous—*is* famous, I guess, in the world of antique art, anyway. "Might you come back with those things? I am most interested. I need to do a bit of research. This is quite a revelation, to say the least. Saturday at ten o'clock?" He looks anxious, ready for me to leave.

"All right. Saturday morning," I say, as if I'm making plans to sort canned goods for the Future Homemakers of America Club.

He turns and asks, "Your name?"

"Lillian," I say, and snap my mouth shut before "Firestone" escapes.

Chapter 25

Armed with my truth pin, I am about to burst the next Firestone balloon.

While guilt can motivate a person to do many fantastic and insincere things, anger and resolve—maybe even a bit of fiery Gone Mom–ness—can motivate many fantastic and sincere ones. Mr. and Mrs. Donald Firestone hid Gone Mom in the attic. They don't think it's a big deal. Just ho-hum, la-di-da. I know what Mother would do if I tried to tell her that her mother and grandmother, the legendary women who handed down her sacred crystal and currently lost compact, were not real members on her family tree. She'd start growling. Or what if Dad found out that his father—who died in his prime after supposedly handing down his formidable business brains—was really an imposter? No ho-humming that away. No, sir.

The radio is off. Dad is fidgety even while ensconced in

"Old Smoky." My brother acts like he's waiting for a horror movie to start. He has already scarfed half a bowl of popcorn in the living room, a Firestone felony. Mother, outfitted in her house shoes, is not saying a word about the popcorn. She sits in the companion chair to Dad's, looking scared of my box, which is making its second appearance on my lap. She should be.

Joy is on her lap asleep or playing possum. I wish she weighed a thousand pounds so Mother can't get up, something she will do any second now.

My hands are frozen to the lid of my case. My tongue is dry. My heart is turned off. My nerves switched on high.

Outside, snow dusts our lawn—lazy flakes that won't live long. I imagine Ralph's pigeons gathered, eavesdropping at the top of the attic stairs, ready to spread my message around the world.

Dad crosses his legs. He jiggles one loafer off the toes of his right foot. "So, Lily, I see that you've brought *that* out again."

Ralph stops chomping and fixes me with a look of encouragement. I clear my throat and open my mouth, looking right at Mother. "This box contains some things that the *lady who gave birth to me* wanted me to have." I inhale so sharply I cough. Joy stretches and repositions herself on Mother.

My mother changes from looking scared to mildly bored—*we already know about this, Lillian.*

"Some of these things"—I open the box and hold up the brush and the little metal stake with a string attached—"are left over from an archaeological dig in northern China in 1934."

Dad stops shaking his foot, leans in for a quick look. "How would you possibly know that, Lily?"

I lift out one photograph of the dig site with the camels and crew in the background. It's way too small for my parents to see. Ralph leaps off the couch and walks it over to Mother. He does the same with Dad. "It shows the place where she worked with her father, who was an archaeologist in China."

Ralph then walks all the pictures of the sculpture parts around. "These are pictures of pieces of a Chinese Buddhist sculpture," I say. "They eventually found all the parts and put it back together."

My mother's lips are sewn shut.

Dad gives the pictures a glance. "And . . . how do we know *this*?" he asks with a mock lawyer tone.

"The statue is all put back together now in the art museum. Ralph and I saw it. Remember the big newspaper article?"

Dad sits back as if the mention of *art* has blown him into the safety of his armchair, but I can see the wheels turning in my mother's head. "You and *Ralph*?" She gives my brother an imploring once-over. I know exactly what this is about. She's going to use Ralph as a side door, a way out

of this moment. *How did you get to the museum without an adult?*
What eleven-year-old would be interested in this*? Why, you've been*
sneaking around behind our backs!

But Ralph keeps his eyes riveted to me.

"The other things that I showed you at dinner are connected to the art museum," I say.

"Which museum?" Dad says.

"The Nelson-Atkins Museum here in town," I bark.
Where'd you think?

Silent questions bounce between us. "I was brought to
the orphanage here because the lady who had me had con-
nections to the art museum."

There! Said! I am outside of my skin, untouchable. I glare
at my lap.

Silence.

I halt a colossal urge to try to explain Gone Mom,
defend her for helping me to not die a slave in China. More
silence builds around our huge, stifling togetherness. The
living room walls cave. The air dies. Time sucks into a drain
in the carpet. And still we sit, lassoed.

Why? Because, miracle of miracles, for once, Mother is
still here. She has not stood up. She hasn't marched to her
room.

But Dad is twitching. He coaxes Mother with his eyes.
Please, Vivian, go on upstairs and get us out from under this. I'm
surprised he doesn't get up and carry her.

She stays put.

"This *lady* . . . ?" she says, staring at the box with X-ray vision. "Where is she now?"

I shake my head and swallow the word. "Gone."

She sniffs. "Gone *where*?"

"China." *Or dead.* But I feel her right here, right now, helping me, gutsy and unafraid, doing the extremely difficult and right thing. Relief floods from my eyes.

Mother slumps in her chair, elbow on the armrest, cradles her forehead in her hand. What in the world is holding her here? I know she has Kleenex—perfectly folded—in her apron pocket, but she doesn't hand one to me. It must be too much of an acknowledgment, a "giving in" to feelings about my past. But I do the strangest thing—I lay the bodhisattva's hand photo on Joy's little back.

The snow picks up its pace. Ralph points to the fireplace and announces, "Hey, Dad, I'm gonna build a fire."

Dad hops up. "*I'll* do it!"

Ralph turns to him. "I'm the Scout, remember?" They head out the kitchen door to the woodpile on our screened porch. Cold air curls into the living room.

I stand, propped upright on the rug in front of my mother. This is what Mr. Howard would call a "prism moment," one that shines light, reveals what's been hidden. Right now my mother is a prism revealing a rare bit of a mystery inside her.

Or maybe the rhythm of Joy's respiration is instructing her—
stay put . . . don't go . . . stay put . . . don't go . . .

The log arranging, flue checking, newspaper stuffing,
and flame fanning take over the living room. Ralph and
Dad exit to the kitchen. Next comes the rattle of more
popcorn kernels into a pan and soon a burst of popping
and shaking.

Mother and I do not talk. The bodhisattva's hand rises
and falls with Joy's breathing.

"So . . . you've known about *this* for a while?" Mother says.
I nod.

My father may wear the pants in the family, but Mother
wears the *perfume*—her mood reigns, soaks everything, rules
the day, the night, and everything in between. But at this
moment I cannot sniff her mood.

She stares out the window. I pick up the photo and find
my way back to the sofa. The streetlights are on now. Snow
coats our front walk, the bare elm trees, and the cars parked
along the street. Dad huffs into the room, leaves the popcorn bowl, and announces he's going to shovel. I shoot
Ralph a warning glance, but he's already figured out he's not
offering to do it. Dad needs *out.*

Mother, incredibly, amazingly, breathtakingly, plunges
her Revlon Where's the Fire? fingernails into the bowl and
grabs a handful of popcorn. Joy hops down and bats pieces
fallen on the carpet.

Ralph and Mother and I sit munching and listening to Dad's shovel. A million beginnings or a million endings sit between us in the room. I cannot figure out which.

My mother looks right at me and says, "You cannot change the past!"

I force my eyes to meet hers. "Yeah, but you can conceal it. You can cover it up with a tarp." I take a deep breath. My voice quavers. I gather my box under my arm and stand up. "What if we had moved from this house? What then? Would you have just left my things for the new owners to inherit?"

The fire pops, shoots sparks against the screen. Mother leans over and examines the carpet in front of the hearth for cinders. Ralph pokes the logs, then heads to the kitchen.

Without an answer from Mother, I march upstairs. I am shaking so hard I can't cry. I sit on the top step listening to Dad scrape stripes in the driveway snow. My parents' bedroom door at the end of the hall is gaped open, the empty room sunk in twilight. I hear Mother rustle downstairs. Clear her throat. There's a faint *tap-tap*, and the click of Dad's lighter. After a moment the scent of cigarette smoke winds up the stairs to me.

Out of the blue at breakfast the next morning, Dad announces he is taking the afternoon off to teach Mother to drive, even in this weather. We all know he is making the supreme sacrifice, creating a colossal distraction, the ultimate filler-inner to keep the subject of Gone Mom swept under the rug, to keep her from creeping back from China.

"Who knew you'd have a lead foot?" he says later, giving Mother a pat on the rear after their first outing. He actually seems proud of her. "We need to go car shopping!"

"God! Gag. Everything feels fake now," I say to Ralphie while we do the dishes. My head is on fire after our especially inane, trivial, feigned interest in boring nothing conversation at dinner—Mother: *I'm switching to Bon Ami. I'm fed up with Ajax.* Dad: *There's a hide-a-bed sale at Levitt's this weekend.* Mother: *The milkman is out of small-curd cottage cheese. Why can't cows make adequate amounts of all the curd sizes?* Dad: *I'm sick of the trials and tribulations of the Dionne quints, aren't you?*

Ralph gives me a *duh* look and says, "Why do we need a hide-a-bed? Nobody ever visits us."

"So you notice the weirdness?"

"Of course I notice it. After he's done with Mom, Dad's gonna put my pigeons behind the wheel."

Chapter 26

I wake up Saturday wondering where I've been all night. Archaeologists have been digging in my dreams, but they weren't neat and professional. They left piles of my unprotected roots and nerve endings exposed. Nobody, including Ralph, knows that in a few minutes I will be in the Nelson-Atkins Museum of Art. I haven't even told Joy. I wish she was with me.

I scan the area for Elliot's car, the same thing I do walking into school every morning—a habit that started up all by itself.

I will walk into the Main Chinese Gallery and Dr. Benton will be waiting there, maybe with some other art experts. I will show them my things and they will ooh and aah and ask questions I can't answer. And I will ask them questions they won't answer, until there will come a horridly deep moment when Dr. Benton will blurt out the real truth about the Lien Loo cover-up. He will reveal that she's dead or that she turned bad or that she lives right here in town and has a family full of people she actually loves.

The wrist rest, jade piece, and slipper box are in my book bag, wrapped in a hand towel inside another towel. Dr. Benton was so clumsy with my pictures, I'm nervous he'll drop the slipper.

I'm early, which means freezing on the steps. The wind whips up my coat. I hear a rattle as the metal accordion gates behind the front doors slide open. Guards unlock each set and the museum is ready for business.

An idea jolts me off course the moment I step inside. What if Dr. Benton contacted Gone Mom and she's in here waiting for me? He could have.

Shut up, imagination. Just shut up.

I glance in the Sculpture Hall. No Elliot easel. I take the elevator instead of the stairs. I can't run away in the middle of an elevator ride. I force my feet toward the Oriental art expecting to hear voices in the Main Chinese Gallery, but I don't; only the closing swoosh of the elevator and the rhythm of my saddle shoes.

I am a bundle of sparking nerves. My bag feels impossibly bulky. What if a security guard stops and asks to check inside it? Why wouldn't he think I'd stolen my things right off the shelf? He'd insist on knowing my full name and take my fingerprints.

I'm turning into Ralph.

Nobody is in the gallery. I recheck my watch: 10:05.

"Miss?"

The voice comes from the temple. I walk over. Dr. Benton is seated on a bench along the wall, alone except for the bodhisattva. He's wearing an all-American wool shirt and corduroy pants. *Where are the colleagues he said would be here?* I glance above him at the polished dragon pearl, glowing gold. I take two steps in and stop. "Sir?"

"Would you mind accompanying me up to the Conservation Department on the top floor?" He points to the hidden door, the door I expected Gone Mom to walk through. "The lighting is excellent. We do much of our work up there, especially with the most rare and precious artifacts." He sounds stiff and official and very different from his public personality.

How would he know I've brought something rare and precious?

I glance around. "But . . ."

Dr. Benton motions to the security guard. "Roy, would you be so kind as to accompany us up to Conservation?"

The guard nods officially, throws me a questioning look, sorts his keys, and unlocks the door. He acts torn to be following orders that seem wrong.

Gone Mom is not waiting on the other side of the door.

It's just a huge utility closet full of brooms and ladders and feather dusters. There are also wide freight elevator doors and a steep metal staircase with a narrow railing. The stairwell walls are scuffed and gouged. Roy stays downstairs. I don't blame him. I clutch my bag and follow the expert to the top floor. He does not look back to see if I'm coming. He does not say a word. He just trudges up and up, more slowly with each step—twenty-one altogether.

At the landing Dr. Benton pushes open a heavy door labeled CONSERVATION. I squint into a big, sunny space on the roof with skylights and windows all around. It smells like the art room, but it's not messy, more like a laboratory or an operating room. Gone Mom is not sitting on a stool. I have no idea what's happening.

Dr. Benton motions for me to put my bag on the table. He seems preoccupied. No doubt he's got better things to do today. "Conservation is a hospital for broken art," he says. "Conservators do their best repair work using natural light. But, of course, overexposure can damage the very objects we endeavor to protect."

Across from us, attached to a tilted easel, is a big canvas with a painting of a smiling young girl playing a tambourine. It looks old. The frame has been removed.

Dr. Benton motions me over. "Look closely. The canvas on her upper lip is ripped. The art *doctors* are stitching and repainting it, plastic surgery so to speak. With something as intimate as her smile, the repair has to be perfect. The smallest difference makes all the difference." He looks at me. "We suspect there's another painting underneath. Another face beneath the face."

I clasp my hands behind my back, lean over a large magnifying glass on a movable arm, and study the little spot that needs fixing. There's a tray of dentist-type tools and brushes that look like a miniature set of archaeologist equipment.

"The conservator's task is to uncover the layers: hidden underpainting, mealy bugs in the wood glue, fingerprints, cigar ashes, staples in the impasto—all the clues to an artwork's creation and creator. Stories lurk under every surface."

Chunks of white marble hang on a contraption of slings and pulleys. Dr. Benton rubs one of the biggest pieces. "In 325 BC this was a lion. We suspect an earthquake near Athens 'killed' it. He's getting a steel skeleton. They're reconstructing him from the inside out. Still looks pitiful now, but not for long."

The entry door pops open. Dr. Benton jumps. I twirl around. A lady in a white coat starts in, sees Dr. Benton, waves *I'm so sorry*, and backs right out. It is the same woman I thought was Gone Mom.

My heart pounds. Cloud shadows roll over us. Dr. Benton walks to the door and turns the lock from the inside. He takes a long breath, sweeps his hand.

"Artworks are like people—fragile and complex. They migrate up here for different reasons." He pats two stone busts positioned face-to-face. One is a pharaoh with huge ears and the other has a wavy beard and mean eyes. One is missing his nose, the other's jaw is broken. "These two would have been mortal enemies in real life, but it's never too late. After five thousand years they're learning to get along in here." He pats one head. "With no fancy label, no pedigree, it's just you and your flaws. To me, Conservation is the most fascinating *gallery* in every museum I consult."

There's an awkward pause. Dr. Benton stuffs his hands in his pockets, looks at his shoes. His profile is all shadow except a stripe of white light down his nose from the skylight. I think of Sister Evangeline in the shed, standing so straight and determined under the dusty lightbulb. Dr. Benton doesn't look determined. He seems to have lost track of the reason we're here.

"Was the bodhisattva put back together in this room?" I ask.

He clears his throat, looks up. "Ultimately, yes. The reuniting of it was a miracle almost sixteen years in the making." Dr. Benton turns, rests his hands on the back of a metal stool, very formal and businesslike. "So what did you bring today, Lillian?"

I step over, undo the latch on my bag, and take out the

towel hoping Dr. Benton knows my things aren't for sale. He bites his lip and watches me unroll the wrist rest. "It's got a radish carved on one side," I say, turning it over. I can tell he recognizes it. "Like the one in the Scholar's Studio."

"May I?" He runs his fingers over the carving. "It's well used. Imagine the ink masterworks this helped produce."

"But what has it got to do with my mother?" I say. "Why did she have it?"

"I remember we purchased this from a vendor in Peking. Chun Loo was a brilliant archaeologist. He had a sixth sense about finding *gems*, sometimes thirty centuries old, buried in junk shops. He was my mentor. Lien Loo was like her father—smart, impulsive, intuitive, unafraid of challenges, a fine artist in her own right. Unusual qualities for a young Chinese woman, but she was well educated and had traveled with her father."

I have no place to put these revelations—unless, of course, he's making them up. *Impulsive? Unafraid?* "So she and her father traveled with you and the others for a long time?"

"Yes. . . . We worked together, explored, trusting our wits, bewitched by it all. With her father's encouragement, before I returned to America, I arranged for Lien Loo to study here." Dr. Benton shuts his eyes a long moment, shakes his head.

A million questions hang between us.

"She did come," I say. "But she didn't go to school; she had me instead."

He nods, looks away. "Yes. I understand that now. But since we had lost contact, I didn't know until you told me. Her father had either become ill or was killed. We don't know. Communication within China became impossible."

Dr. Benton walks to a folded pad spread on another table. "Did you bring the broken jade piece you showed me the other day?" I take it from my bag as he uncovers the *bi*, the disk of immortality with two dragons slinking on the rim that was displayed in the case downstairs. I rub my thumb over the rough edge of my lizard tail. He points, then folds his hands, waiting. I know what to do. I slide my little piece into one dragon's broken tail. Not a tiny chip is missing. A perfect match.

Dr. Benton closes his eyes. I imagine he's connecting a thousand dots in his mind: which emperor owned it and was buried with it on his chest, where they found it or bought it, its age, its cost, how it was made, the seller's face, the bargaining, everything.

I step back. I don't know what to do—leave my piece there or pull it apart?

"An artwork, out in *the wild*, without documentation of its provenance, is a gamble. But we were convinced by the workmanship that this piece was priceless, one of a kind."

"What's 'provenance'?"

"Provenance is an object's *life story*, its history. In the art world it means who made it, where and when, why it was made, who bought it, owned it, used it, hid it, sold it, repaired it. Every detail of an object's past constitutes its provenance. It separates the real from the fake."

We leave the dragon whole. I reach for my bag. "I brought something else." I retrieve the box with the slipper. I hear Dr. Benton's breathing and the faint sound of his hands moving in his pockets. I take the lid off, separate the cotton fluff, and lift the bundle. I roll the shoe onto the pile of powder-blue silk. "I think it's for the right foot," I say stupidly, as if any creature could ever wear it. The bent toe casts a sharp upright shadow. Dr. Benton picks it up, cups it in both hands. "The cloud slipper," he says simply.

"Gone Mom gave it to me. . . ."

He turns. *"Gone Mom?"*

"My first mother. You called her Lien. I call her Gone Mom, because that is what she is."

He tilts his head, nods slightly, and says, "What do you call your first father?"

I shake my head, stare at the table. "The *phantom*, Phan Tom, because it sounds Chinese. Actually, I never call him anything. I don't think about him. All I know is that he stayed in China, if he is anywhere at all."

"How do you know that?"

"My parents told me. That's all they know about him.

Anyway, he didn't want us, I guess. Maybe that's why she left there." Dr. Benton rubs his mouth. He reminds me of Elliot—his long legs, his brooding way of turning in on himself.

I look up at Dr. Benton and ask, "You traveled together. D . . . did you ever meet him?" Dr. Benton doesn't answer, just stares silently ahead. "Well, I will never know *that man*," I say.

The slipper sits on the wide table. "Why is it this odd shape?" I ask. "What's a cloud slipper?" He doesn't answer, walks to a stack of file drawers, and opens one. He slides folders forward and reaches behind. He brings a cloth box tied with twine to the table and slowly unwraps it. Wind rattles the frames of the skylights. Birds swoop over the roof.

In a moment a matching slipper appears on his palm. He gives me a strange, almost apologetic look. "Here's the *mate*."

My stomach drops. My eyes shift between slippers. The pair.

His eyes are deep blue, welling with tears. "The phantom is not in China, Lillian. He is in Kansas City. I am *that man*."

Chapter 27

Chisel strike. Panic. No air. No place to look.

Silence.

I move to the window and stare at the massive museum roof. It's slate, with pigeons, like at home. The sound of Dr. Benton clearing his throat creeps up my spine. I cross my arms and shiver, turned inside out. It is impossible to be alive in the same room as him. Hot tears roll down my cheeks. My brain spins and sputters. He's not Chinese. He's not in China. He is an American man.

My parents lied to me.

His voice is low, matter-of-fact. "I did not abandon you, Lillian. I did not *know* about you. I did not know that Lien came to America. She never contacted me. She must have been expecting you when she arrived. That's why she never enrolled in school." He pauses a moment. "I've had some days to think about this and you haven't. Lien and I had traveled together a long while. We fell in love. Based on your birthday and so forth, I have figured and refigured it and I am absolutely sure that I am your father."

"You cannot tell a *soul*," I say. "Ever! Gone Mom didn't tell you she was in America because it would have been terrible for you to have a baby without . . . It *is* terrible for you . . . and for me. She knew I'd ruin your life, your reputation."

We must keep the true and evil Lillian a secret.

"I loved Lien. That much is true, no matter what you think or how it turned out." We are quiet with the sun washing over us and the slippers and the broken art.

He points to a room connected to this one. "I am going to sit in that office and leave you alone for now. If you want to talk, just knock." He turns to me. "If you wish to leave, I will understand that, too. I promise I will not contact you. I do not know your last name and I will not seek to know it."

The phantom stands. I glance at his jaw, the cleft in his chin. "We will be leaving soon, then back here at the end of the month." And the next moment he disappears into the office and shuts the door.

It's quiet except for the pigeons and the wind. I look from the doorknob to the pharaoh to the lion to the girl with her silent tambourine—all off their pedestals, out of their frames, in pieces, exposed.

I study the slipper mates nestled in a powder-blue cloud,

tiny birds that will fly off if I move too suddenly. I think of the deep look Mrs. Chow gave me the first time we met, the way she scrutinized my face. She must have seen it then— the mix in me.

Dr. Benton is many wrong things, but he is not a liar. The facts add up. I know what he says is true. I shudder, stare at nothing, teeth clenched, unable to cry.

No sound from the office. No light under the door. Is there a window in there? Is he straining to hear my next move? Is he asleep? What are we doing? The world has stopped. It's waiting for me. My whole self is waiting for me.

I pack up the wrist rest and dragon tail piece and stand, careful not to scrape the stool. I take my coat, slowly turn the lock, nudge the door, and walk out. If I stay silent, this is less real.

I descend the stairs.

I found him, Gone Mom. I finished your journey.

I exit the museum horribly unhooked from the world.

Chapter 28

On Saturday night I sit at the vanity studying the *girl before a mirror*—the cleft in my chin, my jaw and triangle nose, and the auburn in my hair. Him. I get my notebook, straighten my backbone, pencil ready, but instead of a drawing, a poem appears.

The Lie
by Lily Firestone

When I was four I swallowed a lie.
It sunk inside me, grew a shell, stayed hidden.
But the lie became restless.
It broke into bits and surfaced so I could not ignore it anymore.
The lie dissolved into truth and
showed up in the mirror.

It's not perfect, but it's finished. My first *Chinese-scholar* poem. The whole truth is better than half believing a lie.

I sit back, take a breath, wrap myself in my arms, eyes shut, waiting, aching for all the pieces of me—the lone rice-face high school girl and the pagan baby, and the little Jap monkey girl I didn't love and protect enough. I hug the orphan riding her witch's broom, and the innocent believer in dragon pearls, and the unborn baby rocked in the boat from China.

I find the tracing of Gone Mom's cloud slipper in my notebook and add the left shoe—Michael Benton. It's tricky to fit it with the right, but eventually, they look less like suffocated lima beans and more like a pair. Mates. My first parents were bewitched with each other. They had a love affair all across China, a burning secret—impossible, incredible, irresistible. I bite my lip against what I think next: *I* want that someday. Not the baby part, but the real romance. I want more than thinking in circles and hearing ugly things and feeling shame, and swallowing slurs and hiding in my locker.

And I want more than *undimensional*, Elliot. I do.

The idea glimmers bright in my mind that once upon a time Gone Mom was anything but undimensional. She had a flame too. She was strong willed and inspired and in love. She was determined to move all the way here to be with him until *I* ruined it.

* * *

Dad's cigarette smoke floats upstairs. He and Ralph are listening to *Dragnet*. When it's over the newspaper will slide off Dad's lap and he'll start snoring in the chair.

I remember Mother describing how scared I was of him when I first came here. "You thought he was a dragon in his bright red bathrobe, shooting smoke from his nose." I was supposed to act like he was my daddy, but what was *that*? How was I to tame a dragon with a huge, blustery laugh? The only men I knew were priests in black robes or barbers and doctors in white arriving for our haircuts and checkups. Their hair never stuck out. They didn't have morning whiskers and bare ankles. They didn't play poker and smoke and swear at the radio.

Mother, in her way, was cuddly back then, hopeful, trying to tame us into a family.

I taught her how Nancy braided my hair and which side my cowlick was on. Mother taught me how to fold sheets and towels *her* way. Every day she folded me closer to her, and it was bliss. We took care of each other. I was the curiously cute center of her whole world and she was the center of mine.

But during all this folding and braiding, the myth of my preadoption life was manufactured. My Firestone future required re-creating my past, especially the tale of the phantom. *He's a Chinese man still in China. Gone forever.* I knew he was a million miles away. And all the while, clues to the contrary sat as a perch for pigeons in our attic.

Is Michael Benton still sitting in that office, hoping I'll knock, or praying I won't? Are the slippers still on the table? I want mine back just as much as I want them to be together forever.

I picture Michael Benton sliding them until they touch. I imagine him matching them sole to sole, touching them to his cheeks. I imagine Michael Benton rewrapping them. Did he put them in two boxes or one?

I rub my face, press my fingers on my eyes. Do I remember it, or am I dreaming it? A gold band on his ring finger. Was he or was he not wearing a ring—a thin band with etching?

A wedding ring . . .

I shut my notebook. I break my pencil and hurl it into the wastebasket.

I knock at Evangeline's apartment door, nervous, knowing I will shock her. But I have questions about Gone Mom and the phantom that standing alone at an ironing board won't answer. And since she's not a sister now, maybe she can *talk*. Plus I need to explain my trying to adopt Joy for her, and the crazy way it turned out.

She opens the door of her tiny apartment. A wind seems to blow her back. She motions for me to come in. I look at the mess. Do I have the right room? Do I have the right Evangeline?

She moves patterns to make a perch for me on the edge of the bed and sweeps her hand. "My new enterprise! Dressmaking and alterations."

There are stacks of books, a lamp with a rosy pink scarf draped over the shade, a radio, a dresser, a sink, and a hot plate. She runs her hand through her curls, sits across from me on her sewing chair. "So, you found me!"

I tell about my attempt to adopt Joy for her and how Sister Immaculata was terrible at taking care of her and how Joy has adopted my mother now.

Evangeline clasps her hands and says softly, "Immaculata took very good care of *me*. . . . She raised me."

"Oh, I'm sorry, I didn't mean to insult . . . I'm so stupid, she just seems so . . ."

"Everything changes. She knew me much better than I knew her. I remember Mrs. Firestone, quite well. Joy will take good care of her. What a marvelous idea you had."

We turn to her dressmaker's dummy fitted in a rainbow of fabric swatches. "Color is such a joy!" Evangeline says.

I am struck speechless. *I definitely have the wrong Evangeline.*

"Everyone has favorites. And, of course, everybody knows that little girls like bright pink. At the Mercy Home I encouraged would-be mothers who wanted to adopt little girls to wear *pink* when they visited." She stops, as if she'd like to swallow this revelation. Her secret pink adoption weapon fills the moment.

Very sneaky. Sister Evangeline was a *plotter*.

"Did it work?" I ask.

"Sometimes." Evangeline looks off.

"Did you tell people who wanted to adopt boys to wear cowboy hats and spurs?" She smiles. "Did you advise my mother to wear bright pink the day she came to find a little girl?"

"Yes. It was an unusual encounter." Evangeline knits her fingers, looks down. She must sense the problems my mother and I are having now.

"So how is it since you left the sisters?" I ask, although it's none of my business.

"I had lived there for forty years."

My mind tumbles. "But . . . ?"

"I'm an ancient orphan, Lily. Never chosen. I was placed as an infant, went to Catholic school, became a 'little maid' in the eighth grade, and at eighteen entered the convent." She speaks in a singsong way, as if sweeping up her past. "And now . . . here I am!" She flashes a smile that instantly dissolves. "I had never lived alone until now. It's difficult."

"What's a little maid?"

"At fourteen we were farmed out to families who paid our expenses in exchange for housekeeping and child care." She straightens her spine and says bluntly, "I preferred the orphanage. I did not create my fate. I adapted. We all do."

A revelation stirs in me. Without Evangeline's intuition and plotting, I might have become a nun or . . . who knows? I might be a little maid right now! Evangeline and the Firestones created *my* fate—as simple and impossible as that.

"Do you remember your first mother?" I ask.

"No. But I have a brother—a half brother . . . or I *had* one. We were separated. I intend to find him." She looks right at me. "I will learn the whole truth about him even if he is dead. Even knowing *that* will still make him more alive in me. I am going to bring him into my life, love him, reclaim him. That's one reason I left. God and I are having regular conversations now. Arguments, actually."

I look around Evangeline's tiny studio apartment. It's like the Conservation Department—everything undone, exposed, before coming together.

"I learned the whole truth about myself," I say. "Both slippers."

Evangeline inhales and holds it. She turns the full power of her gaze on me. "Oh, Lily . . . the other *slipper?*"

"Yes."

The impact of this revelation holds the moment.

"Dr. Michael Benton has the other one. The mate."

Evangeline sits, composed and nunlike, while I fall apart. "He's more unreal now that he's real," I say between sobs. She steps toward me. I lower my head and cry and cry until a tiny miracle happens. Evangeline, the human pillar, sits down beside me, slides her arms around me, and hugs me.

"D . . . did my birth mother mention him or the art museum when she left me with you?"

"Only that her father was ill and she needed to return to China. She said she could not, would not take you. Life in China for girls was unbearable, and for a mixed-race girl even worse. You know, Lily, there are rules in many states, including Missouri, laws that prevent people of different races from getting married. They say it's an attempt to keep the races pure."

So the slippers fit together in my notebook, but not in real life.

I feel Gone Mom is here with us. I imagine Sister Evangeline struggling to comfort her the day she left me. I imagine Sister Evangeline trying to do the same with three-year-old me minutes later.

We are quiet a long while.

"So you took the slipper out of my box? Kept it separate?"

"Lien asked me to, so it would be safe, unbroken."

"Did you suspect her connection to the museum?"

"I was curious. I've spent quite a bit of time there. I knew of Dr. Benton's legendary travels in China. And, yes, I saw the mate in the Chinese collection and began to suspect." She pauses, looks off. "Have you told anyone about him?"

"No! Just you. I can't tell anyone, ever. Neither can you. What if I hadn't come back to the orphanage? Would you have just kept my slipper forever?"

"No! When you turned eighteen I'd have figured out a way to give it to you." Evangeline pauses and shakes her head. "That little slipper has created a powerful dilemma in me over the years. I knew that if I had given it to your parents it could have gotten broken or discarded. And I knew how critical it was to Lien that you have it."

"Do you believe she wanted me to find him?"

"Yes."

I sit, my mind running in circles. I imagine the huge responsibility Evangeline felt trying to do the right and honest thing. I am sure I am not the only child who arrived there with complicated secrets left to her safekeeping.

"Actually I've just started a part-time job at the museum information desk. All the color! Inspiration!" She taps the side of her head. "I can already match visitors with the art they'll like the moment they arrive."

"So do you direct little girls to paintings with lots of pink?"

"Yes, I do. Pissarro. O'Keeffe. Monet. Cassatt." She smiles, raises and twists her fist like she's holding a rein. "And now, after your helpful suggestion, I will direct little boys to Remington."

"Remington?"

"Western scenes. Cowboys and Indians," she says. "Oh, and by the way, the Chinese art expert will ride back into town in the middle of April."

I let this fact slide right through my head. I glance at her nightstand. *Jane Eyre* is on top, with fabric scraps used as bookmarks. "I'm reading this too, for English extra credit," I say.

Evangeline reaches down for the book, thumbs through it. "So many quotes I like. This is my favorite at the moment." She glances up at me and reads. "'If you knew it, you are peculiarly situated: very near happiness; yes, within reach of it. The materials are all prepared; there only wants a movement to combine them. Chance laid them somewhat apart; let them be once approached and bliss results.'"

She gets paper and pen. I leave with the quote in my pocket.

Chapter 29

"You should have heard Mrs. Chow," I say to Mr. Howard. "I went by their shop to find an early birthday present for my brother. She was really wound up. I think that the stories about the hard lives girls have in China are not something she has just *read* about; she's *lived* it. If I told her my whole story she'd say *pfft!* and put me to work chopping cabbage. She's carved out a new life for herself and her family in Kansas City. Plus they have their son in Michigan they are so proud of."

Mr. Howard grimaces, hoists the tall art room waste can, and dumps it into a bag on his janitor cart. I know he and his family have had their own outrages to bear. He leans on his broom. "Sounds like you've really been doin' some *research* with Auntie Chow."

"A little."

Mr. Howard says, "The Chows' son, the medical student who hung the moon, is planning to marry a white woman, and in some states that's against the law. And even as open-minded as they are, they will still struggle to chisel her name on the *ancestral tablets*."

The door bangs open. Elliot comes in, puts his art folder on the table, and shoots me a furious look. I step back, glance at Mr. Howard and back to Elliot. The air sizzles. "Somebody in this school thinks I like you," he growls.

Mr. Howard gulps. "Say what?"

Elliot's fuming. "Somebody knows I like Lily."

Well . . . wow.

Mr. Howard steps up, stops Elliot with a look that screams, *Good, it's about time!* He taps the air with his index finger, his eyes flashing. "I don't get it. What's wrong with having the whole world know it? *I* know it. Am I the party you are speaking of? I knew you liked Lily before *you* knew it. Although at this moment I am quite sure Lily doesn't know it."

"It's not *that*." Elliot braces himself. "Okay . . . I like Lily," he states again, as if I am not floating two feet away. "And someone, besides me and *you*, knows it too."

"Yeah, yeah, you already *said* that," Mr. Howard remarks, as if this is the continuation of a normal conversation, which it is not.

Elliot pulls the charcoal-and-chalk drawing he did for

the Fine Arts Showcase from his portfolio. It's Atalanta and Meleager of the sweaty, twisted bodies. Their perfectly shaded arms and legs are entwined, wrapped in drapery. It's beautiful, muscley. It is a world apart from what anybody else in our school could do, and it has a blue ribbon.

Elliot points to the woman, Atalanta. Mr. Howard leans in, straightens up fast, sparks shooting from his eyes. *"Shit!"*

I look. Someone has drawn a droopy, Fu Manchu mustache on Atalanta in blue ink. I understand it instantly. Elliot James likes a *chink*.

The insult pokes tears right out of my eyes. I cover my face.

"Weapons come in all shapes, from mustaches to machine guns," Mr. Howard says.

"I'm sorry," I whisper.

Mr. Howard holds up his hand. "Stop the music! For what?" he snaps. He turns to me, his voice softens. "Why in all of heaven and earth should *you* be sorry, Lily? Don't think I don't see all that you go through every day at this school. Are you apologizing for being *liked*?"

"Yes. No. I don't *know*. . . ." *For my whole mixed-up-ness. For triggering this awfulness.*

Mr. Howard points. "As I've said before, the worst war, the worst discrimination, is what we feel against ourselves. Do not draw a mustache on your own face, Miss Firestone."

Elliot looks grim. He stares out the window, his fingers twitching. He is seeing something Mr. Howard and I don't.

Mr. Howard swipes his hand in front of Elliot's face. "Excuse me, Mr. James, but let us pause a moment here before you go shooting off with your pencil loaded. Since you purportedly *like* somebody in our immediate vicinity"—he flips his hand in my direction—"who has just been party to this repulsive act of discrimination—which only disgraces the person who did it, by the way—you might offer a bit of a touch to her, a consolation, a drip of the sweet nectar of humanity." He points first to the defaced drawing, then to me. "*That* is a drawing, Elliot; *this* is a person."

Elliot turns to me and says slowly, "It's not the drawing I care about."

Flutter. Float. "Okay . . ."

Elliot squeezes his fists. "I've gotta go now, Lily. Bye." And he bolts out of the room, pulled by a plan only he knows.

Mr. Howard and I exchange a long look. No doubt we're thinking the same thing—imagining someone walking past, checking the scene, grabbing a pen, and in a split second swiping the drawing. Someone all charged up, maybe even with an audience. "It was probably Neil Bradford or his friend Steve," I say. I remember the day I trapped Anita and Steve in the hall and how stupid I felt afterward.

Mr. Howard isn't buying it. "You don't *know* that. It could be anybody . . . somebody you least expect . . . even Miss Arth." He straddles a stool. Elliot's drawing lies on the table beside us. "He's a genius *artwise*, I've gotta admit it. How could *anybody* mark on this?" Mr. Howard turns, nails me with a look. "Do *not* let the mark get on *you*."

I nod, but Mr. Howard and I both know the truth—it already has.

I sit down. His gaze stays on me, strong and direct. Silence. Tears come, and then this stunning gush of stored-up awfulness out of my mouth. "Lots of the time here I feel like a yellow locker creature. Everybody sidesteps me. I was so dumb, I thought geisha girls were Chinese, for God's sake. The whole world knows I'm adopted. Hard feelings are piling up at home. I've got a rice face. Not once has any guy even shown one ounce of interest in me." I wave my hand at Elliot's drawing. "And now this!"

I cover my cheeks and sob. Mr. Howard sits. The clock ticks in reverse.

"Are you finished?" he asks finally.

"I guess."

"So, according to you, Elliot's pretty dumb to like you." Silence.

Mr. Howard rubs his whiskers. "Does he have any idea if you like *him*?"

I slump on the stool, shake my head. "I don't know. . . . No! I've never . . ."

"So . . . you've got your guard up. Getting sunk inside can make a person kinda . . ."

"Clammed up," I say.

"Exactly." He pats his heart. "It can cut a person off right here."

We sit quietly for a long moment, then Mr. Howard motions for me to stand up. We face each other. His expression says he is viewing something glorious. He raises an invisible torch in his fist. I know exactly what he's doing— saluting the flame in me.

Friday night. Joy sleeps on the foot of my bed. Why? Mother is in Wichita for the weekend visiting her great-aunt, who is ill again. She did not want to go. She never wants to go there. Ralph says it feels like the house has taken its girdle off for three whole days. *Ahh . . .*

The doorbell rings. I check the clock. Almost eight. Ralph nearly knocks himself out racing downstairs to answer it. A male voice—then Dad's. My nerves chatter. Stomach somersaults. "Come in."

Oh, God . . . oh, God . . . Is it Michael Benton?

Ralph yells, "*LILY!*" loud enough to start the neighborhood dogs barking.

God! My *fathers* are chitchatting.

I cannot go down there. I will climb to the attic and hide under the tarp. Ralph runs upstairs. "Lily! It's the guy, you know, the . . ."

"*Michael Benton!*" I screech. "Oh, God." I burst into tears.

Ralph's mouth hangs open. Blink. Blink. "Who? That guy from the museum?"

"Dr. Benton!"

"No! Are you crazy? Yes, you are crazy. It's what's-his-name . . . Michelangelo."

I gasp. I sink onto the edge of my bed, my nerves out of gas.

Elliot.

Ralph raises his eyebrows. "He brought his drawing stuff."

Elliot sitting in Old Smoky in our living room! Elliot and my father talking. God. What on earth can Elliot be saying? I kick slippers off. Pull socks up. Select loafers. Apply Tangee. Remove Tangee. Pinch. Pat. Lick lips. Descend.

He's three feet taller than my father, or maybe it's his electric hair. "I wasn't sure you'd be home. I came by about the cartoon," Elliot says.

Dad's expression reads, *Cartoon?*

"Wow" cannot work its way out of my mouth. Nothing works its way from my mouth except a silent squeak.

"I have an idea for it," he says.

Dad does one of his meaningless "ho-ho-ho" laughs. I assume it's supposed to convey a crazy-teenager tone, and for the first time in recorded history I am actually grateful for his filling the moment with something . . . anything.

Ralphie springs into action. "Hey, Dad, I need your help

with this Scout thingy, upstairs, it's a *construction materials quiz.*"

We all know it's a cheat. Ralph to the rescue.

"Have you had your turn for current events yet?" Elliot asks, his hands in his pockets. He is standing in front of a photograph of me holding my newborn brother in a blanket. I have a toothy grin and two huge hair bows that look like crushed antlers.

"No," I say, remembering I have legs. We walk into the kitchen and sit at the table.

Ralph darts in. "Sorry!" He yanks the freezer open, shakes two Eskimo Pies from a box, and runs out.

"D . . . do you want something? Coke?"

"Coffee would be good."

Coffee. Coffee . . . of course he'd want the thing I can't . . . Shut up. Just get the percolator and . . . God. Put coffee scoops in the basket, water, lid, plug in. Pray.

Elliot unloads his newsprint pad onto the kitchen table and slides a paper out. I find the bottle opener, carry my Coke and his coffee mug to the table, and glance down at Neil Bradford's horrible current events cartoon of the Chinese tank crushing the United Nations. "I got it off the bulletin board," Elliot says.

I stand with a hand over my mouth, my face burning, my eyes shifting between the cartoon and Elliot. I step back. "Why'd you bring this? Is it supposed to be a joke?"

"No! Wait." He pats the cartoon. "You'll see, Lily. Really!"

I stand, fist around my bottle. Elliot squints at me. Grabs his pencil. "Okay, Lily, that's perfect. Exactly what I need. Now raise the Coke and look up like you're carrying a torch. Turn so I can get your profile, straighten your spine, twist a little, and step forward. Now freeze!"

"What's going on?" I say with my eyes fixed on the Aunt Jemima box on top of the refrigerator.

"Just do it, for God's sake. Please?"

He sketches, rips the page off, and starts over. His whole body is drawing. Elliot and his art locked together, entwined at my kitchen table. Ticking clock. Ralph and Dad laughing upstairs. Refrigerator clicks on, shudders off.

He sits back. Rubs his eyes. Stretches. "Can I see it?" I ask.

"Not yet. Not until it's all finished." He looks at me, almost smiles, his voice low. "I wish I could draw it in color. Your hair's got gold and auburn tints in it."

I swipe my head, as if I'll feel it shimmering. Heat rises up my neck. "W—what's this for?"

"You'll see. You'll *know*." Elliot closes his drawing pad, steps over to me, and tilts my chin up. I am washed through by something—liquid lightning?

Dad or Ralph or a herd of camels chooses this moment to clomp across the ceiling. Elliot looks up, then at me. He brushes his fingers over my cheeks and lips as if erasing the awful ink marks once and for all. He gathers his supplies. "Good night, Lily Firestone." And he's out the front door.

I have waved Elliot James good-bye, vowed to never wash my face, and fainted on my bed. If somebody asked me to describe him at this very second, I'd say: totally unpredictable, tall, messy-cute, art genius, awkward but not *that* awkward, and not like anybody else. I used to believe he was pure egomaniac with stuck-up tendencies, but now he's creating something mysterious for me, which is a million times more than I've done for him.

Snap judgments can snap you back.

Elliot James has also temporarily rescued me from obsessing over the other tall art person—Dr. Michael Benton. Even though the phantom has left Kansas City he's everywhere—coming up our front walk in the form of the postman, driving the car beside us at a red light, seated next to Ralph at the barbershop. Crazy, crazy.

Ralph is, of course, saying the inevitable. "So, your weird mood and all . . . is 'cause of Elliot what's-his-name, isn't it?" Or yesterday when I brought him a fresh fish head from the Chows, he popped his face into the space at the top of the attic stairs and said in a fake Chinese accent, "Oh . . . you speak? Hau yu? So glad you return to long-lost brother. Pigeons fussy, worry about honorable sister who all kissy now. Lowly ignored pigeons need good luck too. You go Chow House? Fishy date? You and honored boyfriend play kissy-kissy egg-roll lip all time now?"

I say good! Let Ralph believe I'm all kissy-moody-whatever. I can't talk to him about Elliot and I am not ready to talk to anyone about the phantom and how I'm exploding inside out.

When Mother got home Dad didn't mention Elliot's visit. I think Ralph gets credit for that move. And my mother is so carefully attended by her kitty godmother, she does not yet detect the secret intruders from my past.

I thumb through my notebook, past my recipe for bird's nest soup and *Jane Eyre* quotes, and find a blank page. I am going to draw my family tree, intruders and all, using an original code of initials Ralph would envy. I start with a branch for infant me born to Michael Benton and Lien Loo. I add some bamboo shoots that look weird and erase them. On another branch I draw toddler me with Evangeline Wilkerson as my mother and my older *sister* Nancy beside me. I leave a bunch of unnamed leaves on this branch for my other Mercy orphan sisters in the dorm. Above Evangeline's initials are two blank branches for her birth mother and father and another official branch for the *mother* who raised her: Sister Immaculata. Next to Evangeline is a leaf named "½" for her currently missing half brother. Another whole branch is for the almost-inkindergarten me, adopted daughter of Donald and Vivian. Ralph is beside me. I add our four-legged child, Joy. And on still another branch is high school me with a twig connected to my new Auntie Chow. I'm not sure where the pagan babies I helped adopt in grade school fit, so I draw a bunch of little unidentified, baptized angels, except one I specifically got to name in the third grade: Rita Marie.

I close my notebook, realizing I've left out Mother's great-aunt in Wichita. Oh well. . . .

In my mind I see Michael Benton's ghosty finger with its ghosty wedding ring pointing to an empty spot beside him. I shudder. Enemy intruders on every branch.

Chapter 30

April 2, 1951
Dear Dr. Benton,
I will be in the Buddhist temple at 3:45 p.m. on Friday, April
13. I need to retrieve my belonging. You can leave it on the bench by
the bodhisattva.
Thank you.

I slip the letter out of Dad's typewriter. No signature. Not even an initial.

Mother drones in my head—*Don't live in reverse.* But my slipper is part of that "reverse," and I want it back. The thought of Evangeline keeping her word to Gone Mom and saving it for me all these years makes me stand up. Literally.

I write the envelope in care of the Nelson-Atkins

Museum with no return address, stamp it, and walk it to the mailbox before I lose my nerve. Spies and undercover agents and even nuns who plot adoptions must feel the way I do now—just walking down the sidewalk, all nonchalant and simple on the surface.

I listen to the note slide and hit the other letters. Out of my hands it instantly grows to dragon size, exhaling smoke through the slot.

"Where are we going?" I ask Elliot in the car on Friday night.

"Art room."

He must sleep there, shave, and take baths in the sink.

I have not seen him since our kitchen table encounter. He has picked me up at the bus stop down the block. We follow his flashlight beam from the side street by school to the building. Mist swirls in the cone of light. He shoves the clunky door open. No key needed. It's cold. The light sweeps over a table with lots of candles. Elliot lights a match, lights them, flips though a big newsprint pad, and pulls out a drawing slid between the pages. He smooths it onto the table. Shines his flashlight. I lean down.

It's a cartoon, a takeoff on Neil Bradford's political cartoon. Now I know why Elliot had me pose, pretending to walk with my fist raised. It's drawn in the Chinese style—simple ink strokes on paper. It shows a girl who looks like me in a crosswalk. There's a tank about to smash her. But instead of demon Chinese soldiers, this tank is packed with kids who are labeled "Wilson High School." They point machine guns at me. But instead of spraying bullets, the guns spray words—*chink, monkey girl, Jap, slant-eye, ching-chong, rice girl, commie* . . .

The caption is: "War casualties at home."

One of Elliot's ink strokes jumps out at me. It is the one that forms my backbone—*straighten your spine, Lily, twist a little, hold up the Coke bottle*—a strong, perfect upward sweep of ink. Other lines capture the swing of my arm and my hair flying back as I march ahead. My other fist is raised as if I hold an invisible victory banner.

It's ingenious. He's twisted the old defeat into a triumph, *my* triumph, with just a few ink marks. I can't talk. I wipe my eyes—afraid they'll drip and smear the drawing. I can't look at Elliot.

"You like it?" he asks, scrutinizing his work. "It took practice to get the feeling, the *force* of you right. You could use it for your current event—you know, twist it on them. . . . It'd take guts to do it."

I stare at the Lily in the cartoon. Elliot has captured that flame in me—the feeling I had walking out of class that day and when I touched fingers with the bodhisattva and when I adopted Joy.

"It's amazing," I whisper.

"Here's the old cartoon." Elliot stuffs into my coat pocket a copy of the original newspaper cutout—or as Mr. Howard now calls it, the cartoon that was the catalyst for my new career as a real person.

He's right. It was the starting point for everything—my detention, my acquaintance with *The Thinker* and the *Girl before a Mirror* and Mr. Howard and Elliot and the bodhisattva and the Chows and Evangeline and even the phantom.

Hmm . . . We stand silent, watching the crosswalk girl lifting her self-respect like a torch.

"If you want to understand a tricky situation—draw it. Right?" Elliot says. He reaches over and tucks my hair behind my ear. "Do you know that you are a golden-tea color and your hair is iridescent in this light?" Jitters. I look away. "In case you were wondering . . . you're brave and also smart and funny." His cheeks are splotchy pink. I can almost hear Mr. Howard coaching him.

He puts his hands on my shoulders. "So here we are in the third dimension, which some humans *prefer* to other, more uncomfortable dimensions such as: un-, first, and second. It's easier to move around in the third dimension."

I smile. So does Elliot.

"By the way, I think the *un*dimension is a *point*, a starting point, a beginning. Every artwork starts with one."

Hmm . . .

He takes his scarf off, wraps it around me, and pulls

me closer. It feels as though he's re-creating the mythological lovers sculpture. Elliot sighs, looks down. "Okay. Try reaching out and holding my arms."

I follow his instructions by cupping his elbows in my hands. His coat is scratchy. Elliot leans down and kisses me. Our coat buttons clack on each other. I hear the scarf fall on the floor. He takes a deep breath and repeats the kiss, puts his arms around me. Gives me another kiss and pulls back.

I bite my lip, look down.

Elliot runs both hands through his hair.

"Kiss me *back*, Lily."

. . . *Kiss back?*

My face is 1,000 degrees. "I guess I don't . . . I . . . I'm not very good at . . ." I stare at the floor.

"What's the matter?"

Wobbly world. Scary territory. "The cartoon is perfect, Elliot, but I've gotta go now." I stop short of saying I'll walk. I want to run.

Elliot grabs his scarf and car keys. "Okay. *Fine!*"

There's not a word between us in the car, just Elliot and the gutless, *golden-tea-colored girl with the iridescent hair* he liked until she froze.

Elliot stops in front of my house. I wipe my eyes and climb out. He grips the gearshift like he can't wait to get going.

"I'm . . . sorry, Elliot."

"Me too."

*   *   *

I stand in my bedroom panting, my new current event in hand, staring down at my shadow—a motionless bar of gray locked onto the carpet. It reminds me of Mother. I acted just like her. I abandoned the golden girl in Elliot's cartoon crosswalk.

I flip the light off, go to my window, and look down. My stomach drops. Elliot's still parked down there and I'm parked up here—both of us in the dark.

Gone Mom struts into my mind. I need her help right now. I have no doubt what she would do. *You'd race right back down there and fix this with Elliot, wouldn't you? But then, you'd never be in this spot. You knew how to kiss back. . . .*

And I don't.

Chapter 31

On April 13 at 3:45 p.m., two people sit in the Chinese Temple: the bodhisattva on its lotus throne and me on a hard wooden bench. There may be three if the phantom actually received my letter and cares enough to come.

It's good to have Evangeline downstairs at the information desk, sitting in her blue tweed jacket and skirt as if she's about to have her portrait painted. We waved. She must wonder why I'm here.

Shadows surround the golden bodhisattva. I have rehearsed and re-rehearsed what I will and will not do. I will check his ring finger first. I will not look him in the face. I will receive the box and walk out. *I have a nicely starched wall built around me today, Dr. Michael Benton, and you are on the outside.*

The dragon pearl appears to spin, although it can't really

be. There is no air moving in here, unless the bodhisattva's breathing. I know I'm not.

Footsteps approach from the Main Chinese Gallery. If I had Mother's lost compact I could angle it for a view around the gates.

Michael Benton appears, carrying two wooden posts on stands. He positions them on either side of the opening with a velvet rope stretched between that blocks the entry.

"Hello, Lillian," he says softly. "I thought we might need privacy." He glances toward the bodhisattva, bows, and hands me my box. "I put *my* slipper back in the display case of *ming qi*—objects placed in ancient tombs to be used by the spirit in the afterlife. *Ming qi* assure immortality." He gestures out to the Main Chinese Gallery. "That's where it had been all these years, until I removed it for our meeting in Conservation."

I study my shoes.

Dr. Benton sits on the floor in front of me, looks up. "May we talk for a minute?"

I turn and study the hidden door across the room. I cannot look at his ring finger.

"There's an ancient Sanskrit term called *rasa*," he says. "It refers to the feelings an object evokes. The bodhisattva is made of wood and paint, but it can tap real urges in us of compassion and understanding. I am so glad you picked to meet here today."

Dr. Benton must know I don't know Sanskrit, but I understand the idea. "I used to come in here with Gone Mom . . . to look at the dragon pearl," I say before I can stop it. "I thought it was a memory from Chinatown in San Francisco but it wasn't."

I look down. I do not know why I broke my rule—why I am talking to him. Illumination through the carved gates casts petals of light across the floor. I follow the pattern toward the bodhisattva, let my eyes adjust, and out of the deep shadows a pair of shoes appears—women's shoes with straps, shoes on the floor, attached to ankles, attached to a person sitting on the far bench.

A strangled shriek whips out of my mouth. I rock back. *"Mamá?"*

Dr. Benton leans forward, grabs my arm. "No! Lillian, it's not Lien . . . it's my *wife*." He takes a deep breath, another, breathing for both of us.

"Your *wife*?" I grab my box and try to get up, but Dr. Benton holds on.

"Yes. Her name is Iris. Iris Benton." His tone is like a soft sash encircling her.

I shrink down to no one. Nowhere. I set the slipper on the bench, afraid I'll drop it. I cover my face with my hands.

"She knows all about Lien," he says. "She knew before we got married."

Fear and panic knock these words out of me. "So . . ."

I whisper through my fingers. "She has already told people about me, hasn't she?" I shiver. "She'll tell everybody and . . . and . . ."

"I assure you she has *not*."

Silence. The silence before the storm. I imagine her disgust at me—the evil spirit who is ruining her life. And her rage at him, slapped flat by the shame of it all. I glance over. A few feet in front of Iris Benton's dim profile are the bodhisattva's elegant, polished fingers, lighted from above. I follow them up the palm and wrist and arm to its shoulder and face. The crystal eyes seem illuminated. They return my gaze. They dissolve the panic in me.

After a moment Mrs. Benton stands, walks over. She is tall and moves quietly on the floor. "Hello, Lillian. I do not want to upset you, but I must admit I wanted to see you. I have heard so much about Lien and her talent, of her importance in my husband's life, his love for her and his pain at losing her."

She sits on the other end of the bench. Dr. Benton looks up at us as if he is witnessing a miracle. "Michael and I met in Chicago," she says after a minute. "I was a graduate student at the university there. He was consulting at the art institute. We married in 1936 in Kansas City. I grew up in Atchison, Kansas but I have extended family here."

I can tell she has memorized and rehearsed these lines.

Iris Benton doesn't seem crazy or angry or shattered. She's not throwing things or clamming up. She is beautiful, actually, with creamy skin, wavy brown hair, and deep, greenish-gold eyes.

"I have my own reality to face about this," she says, turning to him. "But I am not upset with anyone."

Dr. Benton says, "Since we last met, Lillian, I researched Lien's U.S. entrance records and learned she came through Angel Island in July 1934, several months after I left China, a whole year before we had planned. I imagine her father's influence facilitated her quick departure. But she did not enroll in art school. She entered a Christian mission house for unwed mothers in San Francisco. She did not contact me. I had no idea she was here. I suppose she did not want to be found. I think I now understand her reason."

Me.

"So why did she come?" I ask.

"I believe when Lien discovered she was expecting a baby, she left China immediately, so you would be born in America. So you would have a chance. In China"—he shakes his head—"neither Lien nor you—a baby of mixed race—would have had a prayer."

I knot my fingers.

He glances at Iris and continues. "Lien adored her father. He educated her, showed her the world. As a little girl she lived with him for a time in Washington, D.C., when he consulted there."

"She didn't contact you because of *me*. I ruined your chance to be together," I say.

Dr. Benton looks so sad, lost in his scattered past. "After many years and no contact, I met Iris, or rather she captivated me, and she still does." He takes her hand; his voice is husky and unashamed. He turns to me. I look back, eye to eye. In his expression I read how much I must look like Lien.

"She must have learned of my marriage and, since she had to return to China, placed you with the Sisters of Mercy. Knowing Chinese custom, and knowing Lien, she was determined to go back. A daughter's duty would be to return if her father is ill or dying, to pick parent over child."

"Why would she come to Kansas City at all?" I ask.

"Our bodhisattva project, no doubt. She thought I would be here."

"So she left me the pictures and cloud slipper hoping I might find you."

He tilts his head. "Yes. Probably. It's not all logical . . . life isn't."

"I was told you were an unknown man who lived in China. All along I thought I was looking for *her*."

"Yes. I understand that now. Lien knew the power

of objects to motivate us and the importance of provenance." Dr. Benton starts to say something more, but his face crumples. He lowers his head and starts crying. Sobbing. Shaking. Iris puts her hand on his shoulder. I can tell she will sit here until he is through. So I do too. It feels like Gone Mom is here. At this moment I understand her and Michael Benton and Iris and even myself a little.

Dr. Benton heaves a huge sigh. "There is something else, Lillian." He looks from his wife to me. "Iris and I have a daughter. Her name is Julia."

Julia.

"She's nine."

Julia Benton. My half sister. My mind darts to Evangeline and her lost half brother. "Does she know about me?" I whisper.

"No."

"Are you going to tell her the truth?" I look away. Bite my lip, feel the heat crawl up my neck. *The enemy and the innocent daughter.*

"We needed to tell you first while we had the chance."

"Is she here?" I ask.

"No, she's at home in Chicago."

Home. Julia's home. The Benton family home.

I picture it. I picture the ballerina prints on Julia's bedroom wall and her bookshelves filled with stuffed animals and her Cinderella birthday cake with nine candles. I wave it all away. I can't think. I am a scattered pile of pieces from different puzzles.

We look up at the dragon pearl. Gone Mom's gift to me. I don't move. None of us does. I know why. Because when we separate, it will be for good.

Chapter 32

A whole week has passed. Even though Michael and Iris Benton are back at home in Chicago, the truth about them is a growing pressure in me, like held breath. I sit outside by *The Thinker* after a long visit with Atalanta and Meleager in the museum. The real-life *Meleager* is avoiding me totally, not that I blame Elliot one bit. He's probably started dating Catty. Kissing a partially phony, partially real person like her is much better than kissing me.

The mythical Atalanta has such a creamy, marble complexion. No ink mustache, just polished perfection, so completely different from *The Thinker*'s bronze skin, which holds Rodin's fingerprints—the trails of his touch. I remember Elliot explaining that artists can turn anything into skin—paper and chalk, marble, wood, glass, paint, charcoal, crayons, clay, granite. Oil-painted skin is a maze of layered colors. Watercolor skin, he says, always has the texture of the paper.

I imagine that the Bentons' daughter Julia's complexion is creamy like Atalanta's. What if she someday stumbles upon the existence of me? Will she feel permanently betrayed, the way I do by my parents?

I sit back, sigh. And what about Ralph? If I don't tell him, he will eventually discover it anyway. He will feel betrayed by me. If I keep the truth hidden, I am also betraying myself.

An unused backbone gets weak.

The *Girl before a Mirror* and Jesus would definitely vote for the whole truth.

The Thinker would too—*If you don't tell them the truth, Lily, it will be impossible to kiss back and have it mean anything, because your heart will always feel clammed up and phony. You need to go further than Gone Mom, who never did reveal her secret to the people who mattered most.*

"But I am terrified to tell the truth."

Tell your brother. Try it out on Ralph. See how it goes.

"Okay, I will tell Ralph about Michael Benton. I will try out the truth on Ralphie and see how it goes."

Ralph and I assemble his early birthday present—a dragon kite—in his room on Saturday morning. I got myself one too so we could spend the day together. No one on earth has worse knot-tying fingernails than my brother. They are chewed down to nothing and dirty.

It's a warm day. No coats. Blue sky with a few clouds whipped by the breeze. Sun. My kite trips across the Sculpture Park lawn—lift, crash, lift. But Ralph's kite carries the blessing of "auspicious good luck" that Mrs. Chow bestowed when I bought it. Ralph twists and runs like an authority on kite loft and trajectory with dog doo on his shoes and pink jug ears. He gets both kites airborne.

Mud patches, tree roots, and buckled sidewalks do not stop our kite runs. With the controls in our hands, they dip and soar, chains of color smacking the wind.

Ralph is full of pointers. There's a trace of Dad in his voice. He's going to change so fast, so soon. It's already started. But for now he is *set* with the Boy Scouts, his school buddies, his pigeons, and his brains. He's winning the Clue game of his life.

"Your pick," I say when our kites are exhausted.

"Chocolate Coke," he says. Ralph also picks the huge corner booth in the drugstore, the Cupcake Corral. It's also the booth old guys use for their morning coffee talk. "You can keep both kites," I say.

Ralph looks up with his straw in his mouth. His eyes narrow. "Okay, what're you buttering me up for? This is weird. My birthday is not until summer."

"I know that."

"So what is it? Do I need to act like Mom on the phone again, or to help you sneak out, or stalk the nun, or what?"

"Yes."

"Then I'll have another Coke," he says. "No, a Coke float."

I get him a Coke float, which he eats delicately, dissecting every bubble. I order coffee.

"What? COFFEE? For real?"

"Don't have a conniption."

Ralph peers at my cup. "Is it black? Ugh. Since when did you start—"

"Since when will you stop asking two million questions and start shutting up?"

Ralph shudders. "So . . . okay. What do you want me to do? Be Mom?" He rubs his throat, cranes his neck, and squawks, "Why, hello, Vice Principal Thorp, yes, our Lillian has dropped high school and become a member of a Chinese opium den. She is also a coffee fiend. We are so proud of her."

"Opium?"

Ralph shakes his head. "Yeah. It grows in *dens*, or something."

"Very cute, but what I really need you to do is hold on to your underpants . . ." Ralph rolls his eyes. "While I tell you something that you must lock and swallow until I say it can be known out in the real world, which it never will be."

Ralph burps and chews his thumbnail.

"God, Ralph, ick. Stop that." We sit for a minute and I say, "I know who the phantom is."

My brother's eyes bulge. He blinks an astonishingly large number of times. The milk shake maker grinds behind the soda fountain. Ralph swipes the back of his hand over his mouth.

"He's not in China. They made that up," I say. "He's not even Chinese!"

Ralph leans in, checks the vicinity for eavesdroppers, and whispers between his fingers, "Can I meet him?"

"You almost have. You've seen him anyway."

I tell Ralph everything I know about Michael Benton, the art and archaeology stuff and a little bit about his romance with Gone Mom, which gets Ralph intensely fidgety, and how their love pulled her all the way across the Pacific Ocean, and how I interrupted their plans to be together. I tell him about the cloud slipper match and that he is married now and that amazingly, I have a phantom half sister.

Ralph squirms, sloshes his straw in his glass. He's quiet for a long moment. He turns the color of wet newspaper. "Does Dad know?"

"What? Dad? God. No!"

Ralph frowns. Narrows his eyes, stares at the table. There's a long, awkward silence that I wasn't expecting at all. "I guess I've had a few days to think about this and you haven't," I say, which is exactly what the phantom said to me.

Ralph finger-paints drips of vanilla ice cream on the tabletop. "So . . . Michael Benton has got the other little Martian boot thing, the mate?"

I tap my palms together. "Yep. He has one and I have the other one. The pair. It's like Gone Mom wanted me to find *him*, not her, and I did."

He looks up at me. "So they have a family, with him and your sister, and his wife, who's all nice and all . . ." His face crumples. He swipes his eyes. His voice cracks. "Are you gonna go live with *them* now?"

WHAT?

He lowers his head. His shoulders start shaking. This is not a skinned-knee cry but an out-of-the-blue, tight, ripped-feelings cry. He's petrified that Dr. Michael Benton is going to explode our Firestone family still-life arrangement. This is a "prism moment"—my amazing little brother flashing all his hidden colors.

I slide him a napkin. "I won't ever go live with them, Ralphie," I say. He shakes his head. He's not buying it one bit.

On the bus Ralph mumbles, "Are you gonna tell Dad?"

"What do *you* think?"

"*Don't!* Dad'll beat him up."

"Are you kidding?" Not once have I thought of my father as having real human reactions of his own that are not either protecting his wife or protecting himself *from* his wife.

"And double do not tell Mom!" Ralph pleads.

"Okay. Okay. *I won't.* Right now only you and the phantom and his wife and Evangeline know. That's *it.*"

Ralph flashes me a look. "That's a ton of people!" he whispers. "Michael Benton is different than Gone Mom. He's walking around with a real name and everything— Mi-chael Ben-ton. He's *not* a phantom. Not anymore."

Ralph leans down, fumbles to arrange his kite under the bus seat, cranks his head to look up at me, and says, "It was neat finding your box, and the mirror placement technique, and the clues at the museum and stuff, and catching Mom and Dad red-handed, but now . . ."

I stare out the window. We pass the Country Club Plaza and Our Lady of Sorrows and neighborhoods with people walking their dogs, raking dead winter out from under their bushes, and little kids roller-skating and circling on their trikes.

Out of the clear blue, this question pops into my head and right out of my mouth. I turn to my brother. "Hey, why don't you have a kite theme for your birthday party this summer?"

"Nah."

"Why not?"

Ralph turns to the window. "I'm not *having* any more birthday parties."

"Why not?"

"Just not."

"Why?"

He starts to say and then he doesn't.

I sit back, a dull gong clanking inside. "What's wrong?"

Ralphie turns to me, pulls back the corners of his eyes. "Your ears are too tight." Then he rubs his index finger over his front teeth until they're dry, sticks his neck out, bucks his teeth. "You famiry chinkie."

"So . . . uh, is somebody making fun of you because of me?"

No answer.

"Like guys in Scouts?"

Ralph nods. "Yeah. They're falling all over themselves."

I feel sick. "School too?"

"Yep." Ralph turns, sneers, and snaps his fingers in my face. "What else you wanna talk about?"

"God! I *hate* that. Why didn't you tell me?"

He shrugs.

"Don't let them bother you!"

Ralph turns to me, his eyes wide. "Oh, really? *That's* interesting advice, Mom!"

Hmm . . . "Then why don't you tell them off?"

He turns. "Or I could just walk out, get a detention from Boy Scouts." He shakes his head and says to the window, "It doesn't matter, they're not my friends anymore."

"Did you tell Dad?"

Ralph turns. His look reads: *maybe your ears* are *too tight*. "Oh, that'd be rich. Either he'd laugh it off like with you or . . ."

Ralph doesn't need to say the rest—or Dad *would* rise to the occasion and help Ralph somehow, and expose a race discrepancy right in our house.

Ralph crosses his arms. He looks a million years old. "But if Michael Benton ever shows up, Dad better order him off our property."

I shake my head. "Right. And if he doesn't, *you* will."

Chapter 33

It's late Sunday afternoon. My parents have just finished their routine round of gin rummy at the kitchen table, unaware that they are about to *meet* Michael Benton. Dad gathers the cards, taps them into a neat stack, looks up when I step in. "Hello, Lily."

Despite my lurching stomach and the internal warnings, I walk over, grip the table edge, and blurt out this sentence: "Do you two remember how you said that my Chinese birth father was gone forever behind the Bamboo Curtain, never to show up again?"

Dad's forehead turns slick. His breathing becomes a string of sighs. Mother chews her manicure. Ralph walks in, sniffs danger, glares at me with his palms up—*what gives?*—and exits.

"Based on the circumstances, that is what we assumed to be true, Lily."

"Well, he's *not*."

Dad cocks his head as if experiencing a sudden hearing loss. There's a slight *say what?* eyebrow raise.

"My birth father is not in China. His name is Michael Benton." Mother's eyes turn to stone. I unfold the newspaper story onto the table with his picture next to the bodhisattva in the Chinese Temple. "I met him at the art museum. I was not searching for him; it happened by accident. He is an archaeologist and an expert on Buddhism and Chinese art. I was researching the old objects in my box from the orphanage and one thing led to another. He is a white, American person."

Mother scrunches her face. "What exactly *is* Buddhism?" she says, in a pathetic detour attempt. But I'm not fooled.

Dad holds up a hand. His voice shakes. "You are telling us that this man is your birth father?" His eyes narrow on me. "Based on what evidence? What possible proof?" He slaps his palm off the picture so hard we all jump. *There, Ralph, Dad hit him!* Dad sounds like a real person, no ho-ho-hokey announcer talk.

"All this time I believed what you told me. You let me believe he was in China."

"We thought it was best! For everyone. What's the difference, really?"

My hands and face tingle. "What's the *difference*? You didn't know if it was true! That's the *difference*! And it wasn't. You can't just change somebody's provenance."

Dad stands, snaps his words. "Dammit, Lillian, this has gone far enough!"

"Oops!" I shoot back. I feel tears spilling down my face. "I thought this was just a *crazy old world*, Dad. Heh-heh! You know, a real head-shaker old world full of goofy surprises." I lean in. I am unstoppable, out of my head. Fierce. I switch directions, glare at Mother. "I don't get why you ever adopted me. Why *me*?"

Dad spreads his hands. "Lily!" He sounds sharp, offended.

But Mother sits with a puzzled expression, as if she's waiting for *me* to explain why they chose me. Our kitchen is a sinking ship. Ralph is crying just outside the door. I'm crying, trembling, sparking. But before *I* can march out, they do. First Ralph grabs his parka, slams out the back kitchen door, and hops on his bike. Dad takes a cue from Ralph. He pulls out Mother's chair, yanks their coats from the hook, and steers her out to the garage. The car revs, and in a flash they are gone too.

Only the enemy remains at the table with her smoking tongue. Joy hops on my lap but doesn't lie down. She's not cuddly now. She's hungry. Or scared. Or both. I try to pet her, but she ducks her head away.

Never have I seen Dad that mad. Never has Ralph stormed out of the house. Never has Mother headed *out* instead of up the stairs. Never have I exploded like that— right from the gut.

Our house flattened by the Lillian Firestone tank.

I head up to my room and find my Gone Mom notebook, my insides a jumble. I sit on the floor astounded that I actually did it. I finally revealed what has been phony and wrong with us.

The house is silent. I thumb through my drawings and feel my heart slow down. Elliot finds answers in his art. He discovers himself and other people—uncovers what's true. I can't stand that I walked out on him. I press my lips to the back of my hand. Tears hit the page.

I miss you, Elliot. . . .

"Where's Ralph?" my father demands as he barges into my room.

A siren goes off in me. "I don't know."

"He's not in here with you?" Mother screeches.

"No." I run past them downstairs and out to the garage looking for his bike. All I can see is the bewildered betrayed look he gave me at the kitchen door. *Please, Ralphie, don't run away, do not be hurt or kidnapped or . . .*

Dad gets back in his car. He bumps the curb hard as he wheels down the street.

My mother calls two of Ralph's friends. He is neither place.

It's nine thirty. Ten. No Ralph. No Dad.

Ticking clock. Shallow breathing. Panic building.

Where is he? Where would he go?

Mother stands on the front porch in her coat with Joy beside her. She yells, "Ralph . . . Ralph . . ." It is the oddest sound, her calling out to him like that. Dad returns. No Ralph. He looks old and very tense.

"I'm calling the police!" Mother says. In a minute she's describing my brother to the police department. Her voice is shaky but determined.

I recheck the basement, the side yard, call up the attic stairs. I look under his bed. "C'mon, Ralph, don't do this. You're scaring us to death." Maybe he left a note, a clue. I check his dresser, his desk, my vanity, and the bathroom sink. *The attic!*

I hear Dad back out of the driveway. Round two of the hunt. Mother sits by the phone. I climb the steep attic steps. It's cold. The streetlamp casts huge dusky shadows on the rafters. I grope for the light chain, knock it away from my hand before finally grabbing it.

I yank the light on, squeeze my eyes, blink against the glare. Joy meows, darts up the stairs, and heads for Ralph's lap. He sits by the broken window, surrounded by ancient bird doo and scattered sunflower seed shells.

"*GOD!* Ralph!" I pant. "Wow! Thank you. Thank you. What're you doing?"

He points. "Watching Dad's headlights circle the neighborhood." His voice is tight and overly polite.

I tiptoe over. "I called. Why didn't you answer?"

Ralph shrugs.

"Where are all your birds?"

He looks at me—*duh* . . . "Pigeons don't like cats."

"Why are you just sitting up here?"

"Well, I wonder *why* . . . ," he says, supersarcastic. He's Ralph, but he isn't.

I stammer without forming a word.

"You lied. You said you weren't gonna tell them about the phantom and blow everything up and then you turned right around and did it." He raises his palms. "You promised me and you broke it. You're just *like* them, lying when it's handy!"

"But I . . . I thought it was the right thing . . ."

"For *you*!"

"I was trying to be honest."

"With them, maybe, but you weren't with me." He points in my face, shakes his pudgy hand. "So go on and live with your new people."

"What?"

"In Chicago."

"*No!*"

Ralphie stares out the window with his back to me. His shoulders jerk. Next comes a string of swooshing, gucky sobs. He wipes his face on his sleeve. "*Go away . . . !*"

"I'm awful. I lied, but I didn't mean to. I didn't realize I

was even doing it. I am so . . . mad and sick of them and . . ."
I start crying. "I get it. I just did to you what they did to me,
and I didn't even know it. You're right. My ears *are* too tight.
I love you, Ralphie. I love you more than anybody else on
earth. I didn't think of how it would . . . I'm sorry. You are
my best person. You are most esteemed brother of lowly
rice-face girl."

He flashes me a look and, after a minute, smiles a little.
"Okay." He sits up cross-legged with his shoulders bunched
up to his ears—a bodhisattva with a runny nose. "How'd
you think to look up here?"

"Messenger pigeon," I say. Ralph's birds coo in the
eaves outside. I pause a minute and say very carefully,
"You know, I hate to say this, but I don't think they're
pigeons."

Ralph nods. "I know."

"You *do*?"

"Yeah. I figured it out a while ago. They're *doves*." He
shrugs. "It's okay, I like doves better anyway."

We hear our parents talking in the driveway. "I've got
too many parents now," I say. "It's real hard."

"Yeah," Ralph says. "How many too many?"

"Four."

"Right. Four's a *load*." He stands, shakes out his hands
and shoulders. "So is *two*." He tiptoes across the plywood
planks and clomps down the stairs.

I'm sorry. I messed up, Ralphie. I love you. I turn to the attic window and watch the treetops—crisp black feathers scraping the sky. I imagine flying out, slicing the night, a kite soaring without a string.

Chapter 34

The whole class is ready and waiting on May 4, fifth hour, for Lillian Firestone's current event. Actually, nobody could care less, except me. I'm nervous for twenty people. My blouse is soggy and my tongue is glued to my teeth. I just pray I can go first and get it over with. I look toward the door, calculate the steps to escape just as Mr. Howard shows up with his ladder. *What?*

He nods politely at Miss Arth and points at the ceiling light fixture—*This will only take a minute.* He positions his stepladder right by the door. The bell rings. I look at Miss Arth seated under the American flag framed by a giant pull-down map of the world. Mr. Howard lumbers up his ladder with a hunk of building keys on a ring and a canvas bag of lightbulbs hooked to his tool belt. I'll bet he actually unscrewed some earlier so he could stage this moment. I stare at the gouged tornado on my desk until I hear my name.

My shoes and I walk to the front. I face my class. Miss Arth squints briefly at the drawings in black cardboard frames that I hold, one in each hand.

"I've got two current events to share. They go together."

Miss Arth checks her watch and clucks, "Those look like *artworks*, Miss Firestone. Current events are to be gotten from the newspaper."

Mr. Howard clears his throat.

Her tone is so infuriating it pushes me to say, "Oh, yes, you're so right, political cartoons *are* definitely works of art. These are related to events that have just currently happened." I show the class Elliot's drawing. "This artwork was done by Elliot James, who is a good friend of mine. It won first place in the Fine Arts Showcase. It's called *Atalanta and Meleager*, which is a marble sculpture at the Nelson-Atkins Museum of Art." Snickers. Sighs. The couple is so real it almost pops off the paper. They could have come from Michelangelo's own sketchbook. Elliot has angled and shaded the figures so we see their arms and their sides and legs—nothing too controversial.

I step closer to the front row and point to Atalanta. "She's been *ruined*." I stop to let "ruined" soak in. "See the mustache drawn on the woman?" I point to her upper lip. "A Fu Manchu mustache like these guys have." Kids crane forward, squint at the picture. I walk over to Neil's cartoon on the bulletin board with the army tank of raging Chinese soldiers. "A *chink* mustache."

I look out over the room. Shiver. Catty Piddle won't look at me. Neither will Anita. I glance up at Mr. Howard—an angel in work boots hanging above us all.

"These are marks of prejudice. Things like this happen to me every day." I tilt my head—*ching-chong*. I touch my eyebrow for *slant eye*. I demonstrate sidesteps in the hall. "Oh, and the buckteeth . . ."

There's the faint squeak of Mr. Howard unscrewing a lightbulb in the ceiling. Otherwise there's not a sound.

"Fear creates prejudice. Fear *thwarts* thinking."

The guy sitting next to my empty desk looks confused. "'Thwart' means to stop something. Thwarted thinking is the opposite of *using* your brain. It's letting your brain get *washed*." I wait for someone to cough "thwart." "During war we don't usually know the *enemy* as distinct people who live in another country. We typecast whole races of people from a distance." I know the word "typecast" is lost on everybody, but at least *I* know what it means. "The wars happening in this building are very quiet—an ink mark, a cough, a look, but they're deadly too."

Mr. Howard and I both know I am quoting him almost exactly. I hear my chest fill with air and exhale.

I hold up Elliot's new cartoon. "I would pass this around,

but since I have touched it, you might become *infected* with Communism." Neil sits, arms folded, legs extended, ankles crossed. I lock eyes with him for half a second. He stretches and produces an elaborate yawn with a long *huh* . . . at the end. I know what he's doing—waiting for the chorus of affirmative yawns from his classmates. But there aren't any today. I feel unexpectedly sad for Neil, who is still acting so stupid. I guess he doesn't know what to do. Maybe I wouldn't either.

"That's me in the crosswalk. The weapons pointed at me aren't guns, they're words." I cover my mouth and cough the word "commie." I sneeze "chink." Anger buzzes through me thinking of Ralph feeling the slap of prejudice because of me. Infuriating. "Any one of us might be in this crosswalk mistaking the thoughtless insults of others for truth. We draw mustaches on each other all the time."

I pause, my heart pounding. Mr. Howard hangs above the doorway—huge and immovable. Miss Arth is silent. She must know he will swoop down and eat her whole. My next remark, before I die, is just for her. "Witnessing slurs and doing nothing is silent encouragement."

I pin my two current events to the bulletin board.

Miss Arth checks the clock, traces her chipped purple fingernail down her grade book, and announces the next presenter. Patty Kittle!

Patty's report is about the fund drive the Red Cross Club

is sponsoring. "Uh, Elliot James is, uh, or *was*, donating his award-winning artwork for our auction," she says, slicing me with a look. "But . . . uh . . . now I don't know what he'll . . ."

Atalanta and Meleager. HA! I sit, feeling the flame jerking and fluttering inside. I can't get my heart to slow down. *I did the right thing, with help.*

Just before the dismissal bell, maybe on purpose or maybe not, Mr. Howard drops a lightbulb on his way down the ladder. It pops off the floor and shatters. "Oops!" He gets busy, a buffalo with a whisk broom and dustpan blocking the doorway so everyone has to congregate in front of the bulletin board before heading out. They peer at my current events, wordless, and inch out of the room—an army of snails, tucked under their shells.

I leave school and walk all the way to *The Thinker*. Our class acted dull as a dry sponge. Mr. Howard was amazing though. Bodhisattvas can climb ladders when they need to.

"I did it," I say to *The Thinker*. "I made a speech in front of my whole class. I will probably get a detention for insulting my teacher, which is *fine* by me. Detentions are doorways." Squirrels skitter all over the sculpture. A lady with two dogs shuffles up. They sniff my shoes and go on. *Hello, good-bye.*

I sit back, a chilly mist on my face, fighting the nasty tide starting to roll inside me—the front edge of a familiar storm of old insults—wondering if I'll be an even bigger target now, remembering how Neil tried to start an all-class yawn and how nobody did it. Funny how someone not yawning in your face can feel like a victory.

On Monday everybody will probably act like it never happened, the same way my parents act like Michael Benton never happened. They simply dropped the subject of him—a whole human poofed away—the *Firestone* way. All I notice is that Dad acts less joke-book and a little more man-of-the-house weird and Mother looks right through me. She's made me invisible, which is much worse than her disappearing into the bedroom.

I head inside the museum, straight upstairs, and sink onto a bench in the temple. I cry a little from relief and from knowing that life, that *I*, will never be quite the same.

My heart finally slows down. I look around. If a room could be the perfect *blanket*, the Chinese Temple is that room—the lacy carved gates, the trace of sandalwood, the warm light, the honesty between Michael Benton and his wife that I witnessed in here.

If a statue could be a perfect *person*, the bodhisattva is that person. Its crystal gaze ignites the air. Michael Benton called it *rasa*—the feelings an object evokes in us. A wooden bodhisattva reminds us of our capacity for compassion and understanding.

The power is not in the statue, it's in us—*waiting to surface.*

No wonder Gone Mom brought me here. She must

have known the bodhisattva would eventually live here too. She and Michael Benton worked hard together. This is their room, their temple.

I look up at the statue. *We're all just people messing up and trying again. Right?*

The bodhisattva is slow to answer. *That's right, which brings us back to the Elliot James issue, Lily. You need to thank him for the cartoon—in person.*

Okay.

Think of something to give him.

And kiss him back.

Hmm . . . so strange and startling—these sparky ideas of mine.

Have a double date with Atalanta and Meleager.

"Ha!" I cover my mouth, my face hot. I swivel around, praying nobody heard my shriek.

I stop at the case in the Main Chinese Gallery with Dr. Benton's single cloud slipper perched on a little platform in front. The empty space beside it is sad. Lien never got to live with the love of her life. She gave me up too. Just like that. I turn away, their whole love story stuck in a stale glass box. I shut my eyes and clench my fists, trying not to let the raw edge of that fact shred my heart.

When I walk downstairs Evangeline and Ralph are chatting at the information desk. I jiggle my head, sure I'm seeing a mirage. But before I can say a word he flashes Mother's compact at me. Ralph points behind the desk—*lost and found.* "It's been in the safe under there all this time." He glances at Evangeline. "It's where they keep the valuables." Ralph stuffs it in his pocket.

"I was just trying to decide what type of art your brother might like, Lily."

"Chinese!" Ralph says.

"Naturally," Evangeline says. There's wonder in her face, looking at the two of us. Wistfulness. She must be imagining her lost brother.

"Ralph is my favorite work of art," I say. "But no label quite fits."

"Do you want to go to Cooper's?" I say on our way out.

"What do you want from me this time?" Ralph says.

"I want to tell you about current events today before I keel over and die from exhaustion."

"Oh, I thought you were gonna say you were getting married."

"God, get off of that, would you? He is not even speaking to me right now, not that I blame him. Plus I've never been on a real date with him, which would include meeting Mother, who would look down her nose and notice that his fingernails are inky and that his hair is everywhere and that he's not in an ROTC uniform." I hold up a finger. "But he does have one very positive feature—he's not Chinese."

"Good point."

I flash on another fantasy scene—my meeting *his* parents. I see their crestfallen expressions, veiled aversion to tea-colored persons. Or maybe I'm wrong. Maybe they're not prejudiced. Maybe they're like Elliot.

We sit at the soda fountain. I tell Ralphie about the chink mustache on Elliot's drawing and my current-event retaliation.

"Yeah, I heard about the mustache thing at Scouts. Jerry Newcomer told me. His older brother goes to your school," Ralph says. "He thought it was pretty funny. And his Dad's our leader!"

"So did you say anything back?"

"Yep."

"What?"

"I called him Oodles, like everybody else does. I said he was a fat slob with no friends and BO."

"No, you didn't."

"No. I didn't. But he is."

On a napkin I sketch a messy version of Elliot's cartoon of me in the crosswalk and explain everything that happened.

Ralph's eyes light up. "Do you think he'd do one for me for Scouts? You know, something to punch 'em all in the face."

"No. No. And no." But just as I say this, somebody does

pop into my mind—the perfect hero for Ralph's troop. "How many guys in your patrol?"

Ralph looks suspicious. "Nine. Ten with Mr. Newcomer. Why?"

I tap the side of my head. "Just thinking." I make Ralph promise not to give Mother her compact yet. We need a plan for that, but right now my mind is finished—too dead to even get brainwashed.

Chapter 35

A miracle sentence marches out of my father's mouth. "I should meet Dr. Benton!" It's just the two of us in the kitchen squeezing oranges, on what *was* a normal Sunday morning until the world tilted and everything slid off into never-never land.

Oh, wait, I get it. He's kidding. Blowing smoke rings. "He's not a *joke*, Dad."

He turns to me. "I'm not joking."

If he'd said he was leaving home to marry Lucille Ball I couldn't be more shocked. "But . . . ?"

"It seems right somehow. I should meet the man. I'm not saying *tomorrow*."

"Have you told Mother?" I whisper.

Dad taps his palms on the countertop. "Nope!"

I feel a tiny shift, *relief*. Just the idea that he has actually had an individual thought about this topic, that he would bring it up at all, is jarring because Michael Benton was headed pell-mell for burial in the Firestone cemetery of unmentionable subjects. He was crushed down into being my burden and shame, like I should have chaperoned him and Gone Mom in China and kept myself from being conceived.

"Although, of course, your mother would disown me if I did. . . ." Dad says.

Would that be so bad?

I shoot him a glance. "Me too." *She owns us both, or used to, anyway.*

And that's the end of it for now. Short and sweet and baffling. Back to waffles and juice making. But he's thinking.

The long glass crystals are thirty cents each at the toy-and-science store. I get ten. They're skinny, but they will work fine, splashing the spectrum wherever the sun shines through.

Mr. Howard loved my idea, but he'd agree to come only if I did too. So here I am. Mr. Howard says it is his first speaking engagement and he needs coaching. He shows up at Ralph's Scout meeting in his truck with his stepladder in the back. He carries it into the church basement. I carry the prisms and fortune cookies.

I'm nervous. I pull in a deep breath like I'm holding Ralph

inside, protecting him. My eyes burn. Talking to eleven-year-olds should be a cinch compared to the halls of Wilson High School, but I'm furious at all these stupid boys for hassling my brother. We meet Jerry Newcomer, who thought my mustache was so funny, and his dad, who is the adult leader. They do some ritual stuff first—pledges and oaths and the secret sign for their "Flaming Arrow" patrol. It comes with an eerie whistling sound effect.

Jerry's father is polite. If Mr. Howard being a Negro puts him off, he doesn't show it. They shake hands. He tilts his head and asks Mr. Howard if he has served in the military. Mr. Howard answers "Okinawa." Mr. Newcomer's eyes get big. He seems to blink back a string of questions, shakes Mr. Howard's hand a second time.

Ralph introduces me. I smile at everybody, but I really feel like strangling them. They are pip-squeaks compared to my brother.

The guys are super quiet, sitting in a semicircle facing Mr. Howard, who seems to be moving especially slowly— laying out the crystals, a radish, and a gleaming silver meat cleaver on a spindly table. He takes forever unfolding his ladder at the front of the room, checking its position relative to the church basement windows, adjusting, checking, and adjusting again. Then he climbs two steps from the top and gazes down at everybody. A few boys wave self-consciously and exchange looks.

Mr. Howard cups his hands around his mouth. "Can y'all hear me down there?" They nod. Mr. Howard digs through his pockets, shifts his feet. The ladder creaks. The boys have stopped breathing.

"What's this?" Mr. Howard demands, pulling a big crystal from his pants pocket. It hangs by a piece of fishing line.

"Glass," somebody says.

"A crystal," Ralphie adds.

"So true." Mr. Howard pulls his head back and examines it himself as if he has never seen one before. "What color?"

Answers from the group: "Clear." "Clear with fingerprints." "Plain."

"Clear. Everybody agree?" Mr. Howard says. Nobody would dare disagree with Mr. Howard at this particular moment.

"Yeah."

He turns, steadying himself by holding his palm against the ceiling. Mr. Newcomer exhales for everyone. Mr. Howard reaches a bit too far out to hold the crystal in front of a ceiling light. "Still clear?"

"Yep!" somebody squeaks.

Mr. Howard lumbers down, repositions the ladder a few feet away, by the wall in front of a high window. The Saturday-morning sun is just right. The crystal explodes its spectrum of color on the boys. He tilts it, washing rainbows across the boys' faces, the floor, the ceiling. He angles it at me, and then holds it away from the window.

"So all of us who said it was clear weren't exactly wrong, we just weren't looking at it in the right light, from all possible angles. We were picking black and white instead of color. Lots of you guys probably knew this was a prism with much more hidden inside than on the surface, but you went ahead and called it clear because somebody else did. Scouts are no fools, but if you label something or somebody wrong, you can sure feel like one.

"You don't wanna be dumb, and neither do I. Right, Mr. Newcomer?" Jerry's dad gives Mr. Howard the Scout salute. "Every time you notice somebody mislabeling somebody, maybe calling them something bad or stupid because of what they see on the surface—light up the prism in your brain and think smart.

"Miss Firestone and I have been party to name-calling, and I'll bet some of you have too. It takes a hero to stop it, but you Scouts are brave by nature." He raises the prism. "I salute all you wise young men." Mr. Howard's voice has gotten more oratorical. He seems to have gained five inches in height.

He leans over us, his eyes flashing. "If any of us hears some kinda nasty name, especially if it's coming out of our own mouth, we risk being a fool. No words do justice to the hurt it causes. And if you are the victim of it from somebody else, I say put a stop to it—a little fury is good fuel."

Ralph is glued to Mr. Howard. So is everyone else.

"Are any of you fellas married?" Mr. Howard asks. The Scouts squirm, smile. Mr. Newcomer's hand shoots up. "Me too," says Mr. Howard. "I am lots of things besides being a Negro. I am a janitor and a Chinese chef at the House of Chow—by the way, if you haven't tried pot stickers, I suggest you get on it right away. I'm a husband and a dad with two boys about your age. I play the flute." He starts down the ladder, his boots scraping each rung. "I can even transform a piddly little radish into a rosebud. There's only one thing I'm sure I can't do—the splits!"

Mr. Howard stands at the table, pinches the radish in his fingertips, wields the cleaver, and with precise blade positioning and a twirl of his wrist, transforms it into a rosebud. He passes it to the boys and turns to me. "Miss Firestone, would you please allow these gentlemen to select a fortune cookie?" I pass the basket around. "Everybody gets a different fingerprint," Mr. Howard says, "and everyone gets a different background, just like everybody draws a different fortune from the basket of life."

He gives a prism to each boy and shakes each hand. "Polish these up to remind you to be a hero, stalk that nasty name-calling, and stop it in its tracks."

"Late lunch on me at the Chows'," Mr. Howard says, snapping us the Boy Scout salute as we exit the meeting room. "They're expecting us."

We sit three across the seat of his truck cab, still filled with the heavenly light he rained down on that crew of boys.

The minute we walk in, Auntie Chow steers Ralph to the aquarium. "Fish cranky. Stomach growl." She pushes a box of fish flakes at him. "You feed."

Fiery red fish with gold crowns, and copper and orange fish, brush the glass with frilly fantails. Water fire. Ralphie bites his lip, watches them, transfixed. I know he'd love to shrink down and jump in. "Water mean flow of life. Red for joy and happiness. Prosperity." Mrs. Chow points to a catfish. "Bottom-feeder. Keep tank clean."

Mr. Chow greets us waving a wooden spatula. He uses it to push a glob of steel wool around a gigantic wok. "Keep clean. No soap. Soap make sticky," Auntie Chow says. I picture Vivian Firestone's under-the-sink arsenal of scouring soaps and how she'd rather starve than eat from a wok. Mr. Howard helps Mr. Chow tilt the heavy pan, swish the hot cleaning water.

Auntie tosses me an apron printed with starfish and beach umbrellas. "Now, you! Come on." Gathered on the counter are a stack of pale, paper-thin squares of dough, a bowl of minced meat and vegetables, and a dish of water. "Make little hat," she says, demonstrating the construction of a wonton. She peels a wonton skin off the stack, sticks a pinch of vegetables in the middle, gathers the sides, wets them, and twists. Cute as can be.

She motions. My turn.

Lillian Catherine *Loo* Firestone's first-ever wontons are smushed, ripped pockets of dribbling vegetable bits, covered with fingerprints.

Auntie Chow beams at me, wiggles her fingers. "You practice, grow Chinese fingertip." We carry our wontons to a pot of hot chicken broth on a gas burner. Mr. Howard and Ralph come over to watch. Steam weaves around us as we toss the wontons in. They splash the boiling broth.

I wave my hands. "Hey, guys, be careful. . . . *Sim sam! Sim sam!*"

Chapter 36

I'm in my mother's closet looking for a shoe box. If she knew why, she would croak.

The movie I'm acting out in my head stars Julia Benton, my half sister. The plot involves her discovering *her* phantom half sister—*me*! Julia is going about her business being nine years old in Chicago and suddenly—*boom!* While they are making orange juice one morning, her father tells her that she has a half sister in Kansas City. She will drop her orange. She will not comprehend this news at all except maybe in a temporarily excited, *new pet* kind of way, and then she will learn that she will never meet me or know me and that I am part Chinese, which will be impossible to explain.

I sit back on my heels, lost among Mother's cardigans and zippered clothes bags. What makes me think my mother would have an *empty* shoe box in here? Hers are all labeled and packed with the original tissue paper still unwrinkled.

But worse than them telling Julia would be her parents *not* telling her about me and her finding out on her own and feeling betrayed. So my idea, this package, could help her someday to understand that I am real and connected to her. It will nudge her parents to tell her the truth.

I finally find a stationery box with one lone sheet of paper and an envelope in the linen closet. Perfect. My little Chinese doll from the House of Chow will fit in fine. My *send the doll to Julia* idea was pretty easy, but writing the note isn't. My pen and my brain are leaking.

To Dr. and Mrs. Michael Benton,

I want you to give this present to Julia when you tell her about me so she will know the truth and not live with a lie. Tell her that I hope she has a good life.

Thank you.

Zip, zap—note in envelope, envelope in box, box wrapped in mailing paper, taped, and tied with string. Ready. I ride to the museum, intending to give it and mailing money to Evangeline. I pray I don't lose my nerve. I pray she is working today.

She is. I sit on a bench in the entry waiting for her to get off the phone. All I can imagine is that she's talking with

Michael Benton. Or that he's going to step out of the men's room even though I know he's in Chicago.

Evangeline agrees to run my package to the museum mailroom, where they will forward it to Dr. Benton. No return address. She doesn't ask questions. She is all business, simply helping a museum patron.

Evangeline returns, grabs her sweater, and sits beside me. "Thank you," I say. "I . . ."

She interrupts in a loud whisper, "I believe you are acquainted with a young man, Elliot James?"

WHAT? "Y . . . yes."

"He was here earlier. Quite the talent. Is he your boyfriend?"

God. Help! "How do you know him?"

"Students who take classes with him at the art institute rent in my building. They talk."

"Could we sit outside?" I say, desperate to change the subject.

We find a park bench, sunny and private enough. "I need to know something," I say at the end of a string of Elliot-avoiding talk, including whether she has made any progress finding her brother, which she has not. She turns, her face open, inviting. "It's questions about adoption."

She looks off. "I'm sorry, but I am not at liberty to discuss that."

"Can we discuss adoption in general?"

She tugs her camel skirt over her knees. I'll bet she

wishes she had her habit to hide in. "Yes. As a process, a legal procedure."

"Okay, could you say some more about how orphans and parents get matched up?"

She looks right at me. "Different ways." She pats her hand on her chest. "I selected which of the available orphans would give prospective parents *tours* of the place— an initial introduction, a chance to get acquainted, so to speak. I watched for the spark, the connection. If I saw it— wonderful! If not, I tried again. The children at the Mercy Home were fascinated by you. You were"—she smiles—"a perfectly irresistible . . ."

"China doll?" I say.

"Yes. So small and beautiful. Mr. and Mrs. Firestone stood in the visitation room when you walked down the steps with Nancy. You wore a dress with peonies that day. I embroidered it for you. The minute you saw Mrs. Firestone you yelled 'Mamá!' You ran up behind her and hugged her legs as if you already knew and loved her. She just melted. She bent down and picked you up, and that was that!" Evangeline pats her hands together, still relishing the moment. "I'd never seen anything like it, the instant connection."

I turn to Evangeline. These words stumble out of my mouth: "Did Nancy feel bad that I got picked and she didn't?"

"She wasn't *available* for adoption, but she didn't know it.

Her mother said she'd be back, that Nancy's placement was temporary." Evangeline sets her mouth, shakes her head. "But she didn't come back."

"Did that happen a lot?"

"Yes. Parents with the best intentions. Pipe dreams. We didn't tell those children about their nonadoption status, because they would become fixed on their parents' return. A childhood locked in limbo."

"But my birth mother, Gone Mom, made it clear she would never return."

"Very clear," Evangeline says. "Some children were more difficult to place than others."

"Like me, right? A Chinese waif?"

Evangeline smiles slightly. She neither confirms nor denies this.

"It's not like my mother to pick someone, or anything, that's *different*."

"I wanted you two to work out together, Lily. You needed each other."

"Is that why you said the orphanage saved her? Because of getting me?"

She nods.

I think of the old photos of Mother with her long black hair over her shoulders and a big smile on her face. I wonder if Evangeline orchestrated all the adoptions with this level of heart and . . . *manipulation*.

"My father must have been so relieved to see her happy, he would have adopted a python or a laughing hyena," I say. "Cats and orphans shape themselves around the people who choose them. They want them to stay happy. I sure did." I look away. "But now she's miserable with her choice."

Evangeline's breath catches.

I look down. "She should never have picked me. Our match did not work out." Evangeline turns, a stricken look on her face. "I'm sorry." I want to die for disappointing her. But it is the whole truth.

"Are you miserable too, Lily?"

I explode into tears—long, knotted sobs and shudders. "Yes! It's terrible. Since the world fell apart and everyone hates Oriental people . . . she's so scared and stiff . . . and high school is so cruel and I'm not . . . I don't . . ."

"Have you told her?" Evangeline's voice is kind and firm.

"I've told them about Gone Mom and Michael Benton. That blew everything up."

"No, I mean, have you told her about your sadness and frustration with her?"

"She won't listen to it!"

"Hmm . . . Do you know *her* story? Have you asked about her life before you came, or when she was your age?"

"She doesn't talk about that. Ever."

We sit silent.

"Mrs. Firestone needed you to nurture. I was so often focused on the children in my care, I forgot the harsh realities adoptive parents had experienced—the years of disappointment, their ache for a child, the intense longing to spill their hearts. Adoption is not a perfect ending. It is a path. . . ." She taps her palms. "Lifelong."

The orphanage stories filed away in Evangeline must be endless. But orphans are not the only ones. Evangeline's own story is yet to be written. Maybe someday she'll tell me.

"So you do the same thing with orphans and museum visitors," I say. "Predict what will make a good match."

"Yes. I do."

"Do you direct visitors like my mother to silver tea sets and crystal, and men like my father . . . ?" I try to imagine her assisting a tough customer like Donald Firestone, yawning and checking his watch—so opposite from Elliot and Michael Benton, whose whole lives are art.

"Men?" says Evangeline. She grips her hands with a faint *Mona Lisa* smile. "The preferences of that breed, if they are over twelve years old, I would know nothing about!"

Evangeline's neck is as red as her hair. We both smile. I feel trust. For an instant I feel like we could be friends.

Chapter 37

Steam and starch. Mother's ironing.

I teeter on the top basement step. *Go down there right now. Stop thinking. Go do it.*

I grab the rail but don't move. Fear ends when you face what you fear? Maybe not. Fear might mean you should protect what's yours. I feel like Mr. Rochester in *Jane Eyre* ". . . paving hell with energy."

Mother and I have barely talked since the Michael Benton revelation, but I'm clinging to the tiniest thing— how she smoked a cigarette the night I told her about Gone Mom instead of leaving the living room. So weird, so un-Mother-like. Maybe there's a crack of hope she'll listen to me. Probably not.

I head down carrying my backbone and a prayer for the right words when I need them. I also have a peace offering—her compact. I've rubbed out all the finger-prints. The stiff Victorian ladies on top stare silently at each other. A bad omen.

The overhead lights glint off her metal hairclips—three rows of them across the crown of her head. She raises her gaze to me, no smile, then plows the hissing iron through a field of wrinkles in my yellow cotton blouse. The iron-ing board creaks under the shifting pressure of my mother and her iron. She is a steam-powered robot in satin house shoes. She changes position to stay out of her own shadow. Beside her is a suspended rod with empty hangers awaiting assignment.

I pat the felt jewelry bag with her compact in my skirt pocket. "Mother?" I say, halfway down.

She doesn't look up. The vertical wrinkles between her eyes are deep. No amount of ironing can smooth those out. She raises the cuff of my blouse to the light. "I couldn't get this out. What is it, India ink?" She sounds exasperated. *Look at all I do for you. . . .*

"Sorry. I . . ."

"No you're not."

Slap. "What? Why wouldn't I be sorry about the ink?"

No answer. Head down. Ironing board groaning.

Do not get deterred by a drop of India ink. This is the quicksand of my mother—taking in something I say, defining it, dissolving it.

"I know you're mad," I say.

No response.

"Because of my finding them, but I . . ."

Mother shakes her head. "I let my guard down and look what happened!" She raises the iron. "You have no idea what it was like all those years not getting to have a baby daughter of my own. I thought God had *had* it with me. And then finally"—she looks heavenward—"I *did*, and now you're ruining it. I don't know if I have a daughter or not! Everything you do is an *insult*. I can't go through this anymore, Lillian, you sneaking behind our backs, undoing all we've done!"

My mouth opens, shuts. Mother has stopped ironing. Her face is fiery. I stand silent, transfixed by the spectacle of my mother's real self exploding right here in the basement— awful and fascinating. If somebody storms out of here, it is *not* going to be me.

If somebody leaves this basement, it's not going to be Mother, either. She's caged. I am blocking her way out.

Silent seconds pass. I cannot take my eyes off her.

The silence gets louder.

Ralph's Scout shirt is yanked from the basket.

Ironing resumes.

Wrinkles resolve.

The air is starched.

A bolt of pure furiousness rocks through me. I'm standing here and it dawns on me that she's already *through*! And it's my fault. She's finished, so *I'm* finished.

I step toward the ironing board. "I'm not through, Mother. I have more to say. You know that I have been made fun of at school—*insulted*, harassed, called names, excluded, even back in grade school. Whenever I told you about someone taunting me, or making fun of your Jap monkey daughter with the ching-chong eyes, you acted like it would just go away."

Mother snaps a damp shirt in the air and positions it on the ironing board.

"It took me a long time to figure out that it was happening. I thought it was *me*. I let it go on so long without any help from you. You kept telling me to ignore it. To ignore myself. And now, when I told you and Dad about walking out of class and the discrimination and the detention, you only seemed worried about whether other people knew. That was all you cared about!

"Do you know Ralph's getting it too? Kids teasing him about his chinkie, rice-face sister?" Mother looks up. "When I need somebody to talk to or to help me, it's never you. I'm too Chinese for you. I belong to the enemy side. Did you know I overheard that comment you made to Dad one time about my not marrying another Oriental, magnifying the problems in my kids?

"I can't disown my face, but I've tried to. I've tried to be exactly what you wanted. I ignored everything, just the same way you ignore everything. You want me to disown my *reverse*, my whole life before you and Dad, to have me be born at age four because it didn't suit you. I wasn't looking for my belongings you hid in the attic, but I found them and I'm glad."

Mother glares at me. "What do you *want*? You think you've found something better now?"

"*What?*" I gulp for air. "You chose the wrong girl, didn't you? You wanted someone just like you. I don't *get* it. Why didn't you adopt a nice white baby in the first place?"

Mother takes a sharp breath. I wait.

"Why *did* you choose me?" I snap. "I have never understood that!"

Something drips from my mother's eyes. Tears? Poison? "You ran right to me at the orphanage, Lillian. You threw your arms around me, called me Mama. You latched on and would not let go. Why? Why did *you* choose *me*?"

And from my mouth explode these fatal words: "Because you were wearing a bright pink sweater and you had long black hair and I was little and I made a mistake. I thought you were Lien Loo, my birth mother, come back for me!"

I rock back, whipped by my words. Mother freezes, the steam rising around her. I burst into tears and stamp up the stairs, barely missing Joy on her way to rescue my mother. I end up in my bedroom and slam the door, leaving the pieces of my honest, exploded self in the basement for her to clean up.

Chapter 38

Mother's compact whacks against my trash can.

Pack? Sob? Scream? I dig my fingernails into my palms. I pace my room shaking and sweaty, listening to the house. Any minute Mother will slam the front door, get in her car, and *go* . . . run away from me.

It's done now—all secrets out. The raw truth of our mistaken starting point revealed.

Look for my bright pink sweater, Lily, that's how you can always find me.

Two moms *gone*.

I lie gathered up in a ball facing the wall. I sob and shudder, wiping my cheeks on the sheet. The room gets dusky. The doves coo in the eaves. My eyes sting. My throat burns. I drift, unhooked from everything. . . .

I awaken to a tap on the door. "Ralph?"

I roll over in the dark, stretch to click on my lamp, and look straight at my mother standing in the opening at three o'clock in the morning.

"It's one of the *Girdles*," she says, bumping in the door.

My eyes pop wide.

She sets a tray on my vanity, walks over, sits on my bed, and does something miraculous. She leans over and pushes away a strand of hair stuck to my face. We both burst into tears. The mattress creaks under the weight of us.

"I brought you some lima beans," she says, straightening up and pointing to the tray. "*Suffocated* to perfection."

"Thanks," I croak. I glance at her ivory robe. I don't reach out and touch it, but I could. I look at the straight side of her nose, her pale mouth, the creases under her eyes, the shadows under her skin. She looks real and ragged.

"It's ham and egg rolls, actually. And popcorn and bridge mix. I was starving. How about you?"

I nod.

In my mind the bodhisattva floats through the window, faces us across the room. "I have something I was going to give you in the basement before we loaded our weapons," I say. I get up and reach in the wastebasket. Mother's eyebrows shoot up. I hand her the felt bag.

"My compact," she whispers. There's a trace of something in her face—distrust, disdain?

"I know it's real sentimental to you."

"So you threw it away?"

"Yeah, temporarily. Sort of like how Dad hid my box from me." My mother nods, an *I can understand that* nod. "It was handed down from your grandmother, wasn't it, and then your mother gave it to you?"

Mother's face darkens. She twirls her wedding rings and draws out the word. "Wrong."

"But you've said a million times—"

"I know what I *said*." Tears slip from her eyes. "But they didn't!" Her voice is flat. "I made that up. I wanted it to be true. But it isn't. I bought it for *myself* at an antique store! I didn't inherit my crystal, either. I bought it too." Mother doubles over, with her fingers knotted together, and sobs. I get Kleenex. I know that this outpouring is not about me. "I hid the truth about it from everybody, except your father, and myself sometimes."

"You made up that story about your mother and grandmother?" She nods. "Like how you created that story you wanted to believe about my birth father still being in China?"

"That was to protect you."

"That was to protect *you* . . . and Dad."

She nods. "Protect all of us, I guess." She looks exhausted and wrinkled in a way that Vivian Firestone is *never* wrinkled. "But it didn't work, did it?"

"So you and Grandma didn't . . ."

Mother holds up a hand. Her voice shakes. "My mother

and I never chose each other, even though I was her naturally born daughter. We were not a good match."

"So I don't know your true story either," I say slowly. Mother stiffens, looks off. "I barely remember Grandma. Ralph didn't know her at all." Shadows from the streetlight play off Mother's face. She shakes her head, as if answering a question inside. I need to add Grandma and my great-grandmother to my family tree. Someday I am going to get her to talk more truth about them and herself. "I guess I don't know very much about you, do I?"

She nods. "Not everything."

"Should I get the Ouija board?" Mother smiles, touches my hand. "Mr. Howard, the janitor at school, who is my friend, says we can never replace a person who has gone. We can only face it, feel awful, and move ahead. That's it." My mother looks at me, so sorry and sad. "Then after lots of screaming and heartache the popcorn can start to pop and we feel better in the life that we *do* have."

I realize I have just strung more sentences together talking with Mother than ever before. *Thank you, Mr. Howard.* Joy comes in, hops on the bed. "I wasn't born the day you chose me, or I chose you, or we chose each other. I had almost four years already. You and Dad were the keepers of my little life story, my *provenance*, until I discovered your version wasn't true."

"I was doing something wrong for what I thought was

the right reason." She sighs, slides off the bed, walks to the vanity, and comes back with the tray. She puts a plate on my lap and one on hers. She puts an egg roll and a pile of popcorn on each. We bow our heads a moment, then bite into the sandwiches.

"Where are Dad and Ralph?"

"Father-son overnight."

"Oh, yeah, right. I guess I forgot about them."

Mother gets the bowl of bridge mix. "What's your favorite—raisin, nougat, caramel?"

We sit together pawing through the bowl, chewing, pawing. Ralph's doves sleep to the faint hollow chatter of bamboo wind chimes from the attic.

"I think that Gone Mom protected me by leaving me with the sisters. She wouldn't tell my birth father about me. She knew I couldn't go back to China with her. I'd die there—a half-breed girl. It took courage. She wasn't a Communist or a spy or a tramp or a *heathen*. I believe she was smart and decent."

Mother looks off. Says nothing.

I am not ready to talk about my cloud slipper. I may never be. I feel protective of my first parents' true story. But I do say, "It helps me to know the truth about her and *him*. I am not white, Mother. I'm not brown, either. I'm *golden*!"

Golden.

My mother looks at me a long moment, nods, polishes

her compact on her robe, and wipes her eyes. "Where was this? It's been missing for months."

I could make up anything but I don't. Her original story about the compact isn't true, but I have a true one.

"Ralph took it because he needed a little mirror at the art museum." I tell her about the parts of the bodhisattva on the table and his idea of sleuthing using strategic mirror placement and how we forgot it.

Mother almost laughs, which I haven't heard in an age, and I glimpse a little girl in the dim prism of her. Her provenance must be a patchwork of rough stories—some true, some not. I have no idea. But I bet Dad does. It's why he's so careful with her, why he dances around, talking out the sides of his mouth, cushioning her from everything. But, of course, it didn't work. As Mr. Howard said, if you look square at the gut-crushing loss, you can start to find your true self and get free.

Mother says, "Where did it turn up?"

"What?"

"My compact!"

I look her square in the face. "It turned up at the information desk in the lost . . . and found."

Chapter 39

It's Friday. Elliot's hanging around in the art room. He's probably getting a report from Mr. Howard about my current event. Mr. Howard must be telling Elliot that what he drew for me was perfect. I am running around the building to the side street where he always parks. Please. Please. Be parked here. Where's your car? Elliot's car! Yes!

Do not go chicken. Put a note under his windshield.

I rip out a blank notebook page and write so fast the plan practically shows up before I can think it.

Elliot,
Please meet me at the ramshackle old shed next to the Sisters of Mercy Children's Home on Waldo Avenue at 8:00 tomorrow night. I have something for you.
Lily

I fold it and shove it under his windshield wiper. *Do not blow away. Do not get stolen by somebody.* I hurry off thinking that people do not typically use the word "ramshackle" in invitations, but then, Elliot's car is ramshackle and so is his personality, so it fits!

Then I ride all the way to the orphanage, sneak through the side yard, and yes, the shed is still there and unlocked. I adjust the oilcloth window covers. Then I ride home, lock the bathroom door, take off all my clothes, and sink into the tub.

The phone rings. When I hear Ralph answer, I lower my whole self underwater until all that's left of me is steam and a skinny string of bubbles.

When I step out the front door at exactly 7:15 p.m. on Saturday to walk to our rendezvous, Elliot is sitting in his car in front of my house. Zip of nerves. Wonderment. I clutch my bag containing a shoe box and Ralph's camping stove. Elliot leans out the car window. "Were you going to walk the whole way over there?"

"Yes, I'm walking." I feel just the tiniest bit stupid.

"Do you want a ride?"

"Well . . ."

"Or I can just follow slowly behind you."

"Okay. Okay."

Me and my colossal case of the jitters get in the car. "It's dilapidated," I say. "The shed, it's by the—"

"I know where it is. I went by there already."

It looks like Elliot has shaved, and the regular rumble of artsy stuff on the passenger floor has been thrown in the backseat.

"It has a light," I say. "But I brought a heater."

He turns with a straight face. "Goodie."

I keep my mouth shut from this point forward. I make much more sense when I keep my mouth shut.

We park down the block, run to the shed, slip in like cats, and shove the doors shut. I turn on the light, which casts a dusty glow on the sawhorses and mowers and crates. I picture Sister Evangeline standing in here with me, handing over my bootie the afternoon she unhooked from her nun self and crawled into the secret passageway of her future.

Elliot makes a low seat with two crates and a plywood plank. I lock away thoughts of mice and spiders. He lights Ralph's camping heater, sets it on a shelf across the room. Tangles of dead vine spill down the inside walls, weave through an old wood-burning stove and across the floor. Curtains of cobwebs drip off the ceiling beams. We hear squirrels on the roof—at least I pray they're squirrels. It smells earthy and old. The shelves are filled with stacked shadows. Dusty shards of light are propped against the walls. Just as I start to apologize for the world's worst meeting spot, Elliot sweeps his hand and says, "This place is magic, an inside-out room."

We sit quiet a moment. "I used your cartoon for current events," I say.

"Good." Elliot rubs his hands together. I'm not sure I've ever seen them without a pencil or a brush. His fingers are long and thin and less ink-stained than usual.

"Mr. Howard was in there too, on a ladder. Did he tell you?"

"Yeah."

"The cartoon was perfect." My eyes fill up. I picture how he drew me striding in front of that tank. "If you want to help someone, try drawing her. Right?"

Elliot nods, looks down.

I can't explain how his one powerful ink stroke, the one that created my backbone, made so much difference, but I think he already knows.

I also cannot think of words to say sorry for not kissing him and for making him feel like an idiot. And what could he answer if I did—*Hey, that's just fine, happens every day, I'm used to it?* Or maybe, *Don't worry, it'll* never *happen again?*

Words aren't doing their job tonight.

I take the shoe box out of my bag and hand it to him. "It's for you. I didn't write anything on the box or decorate it, because I can't draw, or I guess I don't *know* if I can draw or not . . . but anyway, it's a plain old shoe box . . . and uh . . ."

Words still aren't working.

Elliot shakes it and lifts the lid. His fingers crawl over

a roll of powder-blue silk, looking for the end. I hear his breathing. I see it too.

Elliot unrolls until the wrist rest falls into his palm.

He looks over at me, says nothing, and then examines it in the light. Our abilities to talk seem to have crawled back down our throats. He holds it under his forearm, moves his hand like he's painting. He traces the carving of the Chinese characters on the flat side. "It's old, isn't it?"

"Really old," I squeak. "There's one like it—"

"In the museum," Elliot whispers. "I know. Where'd you . . . ?"

"M—my Chinese mother, my *birth* mother, gave it to me."

Elliot lowers his head, rubs his face, sighs.

"It's yours now," I say.

Elliot cups the wood in both hands, tilts his head back, and shuts his eyes. "God, Lily. I can't believe it." He turns to me. His expression is intense, serious. "Thank you."

Backbones and wrist rests—we've exchanged the perfect gifts and we both know it.

"You know those pictures you spilled in my car? They were that bodhisattva statue, weren't they?" he says.

"Yeah."

"So . . . ?"

"My birth mother helped find the pieces of it in China. Her father was an archaeologist."

"Wow. Did you know her?"

"No. *Yes.*" I pause a moment, waiting for a way to say it. "I knew her for three years. She gave me a box of things when she left me at the orphanage"—I point next door—"my *home* for one year. She's back in China now, I think. Her father was sick and she had to go back. I don't know if she's still alive." *Done. Said. Survived.* "I figured out that the things in the box, including the pictures, were part of our art museum somehow, and so I kinda happened upon learning about her."

I stop and look around this dusty spot that is helping me talk because it's small and feels safe, and because Elliot James is tall and feels safe. We just sit side by side staring into the overgrown spring jungle.

Elliot brushes his finger down one of my cheeks and up the other. I do not jump to my feet. I do not look away. I clasp my hands, force the words, "Okay, Elliot, stand up."

"I don't want to leave yet."

"We're not leaving. Just stand up. Okay?"

I step up onto the bench and face him, eye level under the light. I reach my arms around his neck, breathe in the air he has just exhaled, and kiss him. Actually it is three or three hundred individual kisses run together, who knows? But it is definitely a kiss back and it's going on and gaining strength. I don't remember being up this close to another person in a million years. He doesn't taste mad at me anymore. He's breathing brushstrokes. He's in every dimension swirling around me. I feel his hands move up and down my spine. I press back into them. He gathers my hair in his fist. Our lips move, match, open, brush, push. I taste the salt of tears on them.

A breeze flaps the oilcloth over a broken window. The Virginia creeper vines shiver in unison. We finally stop to breathe. I look down. Our shared shadow has turned Technicolor.

We've exchanged the perfect kiss and we both know it.

Chapter 40

Dear Dr. Benton,

I have returned my mother's cloud slipper to the Nelson-Atkins Museum of Art. Evangeline Wilkerson is keeping it in the safe at the information desk until your next visit. At that time, please put it in the case in the Main Chinese Gallery alongside yours.

Perhaps someday Lien will return to Kansas City and see the mates together. She will know we have found each other.

I pause, breathe, position my wrist and pen, and add my calligraphy signature—one upward stroke of ink full of flame and backbone.

ACKNOWLEDGMENTS

Xie xie!

Thank you,

Catherine Stuber, for educating me on the obstacles and triumphs of being *golden*.

Sister Rosalima Wilkinson, for sharing your astonishing provenance.

Bambi Nancy Shen, for translating Cantonese and Mandarin and for your thoughtful and thorough answers to my endless questions regarding all things Chinese.

Nelson-Atkins Museum of Art, for being my muse, my infinite source of mystery, and my inspiration.

Ann Ingalls, for introducing me to the pagan babies and the abandoned orphanage with its ramshackle, romantic, vine-filled shed. Thanks also to Liz Meyerdirk and Pat Cole.

Anne, for your nonstop, sisterly encouragement and faith that everything would turn out just fine. Thanks also to my amazing critique partners Stephanie Bunce and Judy Hyde, the members of Heartland Writers for Kids and Teens, and to my dear friends and early readers Judy Joss, Nan and Mark Meyerdirk, Jeanie Schmidt, Mina Steen, and Kathy Wells.

Karen Wojtyla, my exceptional editor, and assistant editor Annie Nybo, for so carefully polishing Lily's story. Enormous thanks to my agent, Ginger Knowlton, for your full-out enthusiasm and help.

Andy, Anna, and Austin, for being honest with your mother about your impressions all along the way. I trust you guys completely.

Jack, for our Sunday morning walks when you absorbed, untangled, challenged, and lifted the heart and soul of this story. I love you.

AUTHOR'S NOTE

Although *Girl in Reverse* is a work of fiction, the Nelson-Atkins Museum of Art in Kansas City is real. *The Thinker* by August Rodin sits on the lawn. The colossal, three-ton, Carrara marble sculpture of *Atalanta and Meleager with the Calydonian Boar* by Italian artist Francesco Mosca fills one corner of the Main Sculpture Hall. A world-famous jade, the *Chinese Ritual Disc with Dragon Motifs (Bi)* (one dragon indeed has a broken tail), carved between 475–9 BCE, may also be found there. The bodhisattva sculpture in the story was inspired by the remarkable eleventh- to twelfth-century seated *Guanyin of the Southern Sea* bodhisattva, which has been heralded as the finest sculpture of its kind outside of China. It is said to have been found dismembered, its pieces dusted with snow, in the yard of an antiquities dealer. I added the golden starburst halo.

The characters and events in this story are all imaginary, but Asian art experts did travel northern China in the 1930s. The accounts of their acquisitions and commitment to the restoration of their treasures are legendary. Knowing an artwork's backstory, its provenance, increases its value in much the same way that discovering her true creation story, her *reverse*, inspired and completed Lily.

Construction of the elegant Country Club Plaza, our country's first shopping center, began in Kansas City in the 1920s. It was the vision of real estate developer Jesse Clyde Nichols, not Donald Firestone.

When you visit the Nelson-Atkins Museum of Art, do not miss the astounding pair of two-and-one-eighth-inch-long Sui Dynasty (581–618 CE) cloud slippers with fancy upturned toes in the lighted glass case of Ming Qi Miniature Ceramics on the second floor.

What a joy it is to weave my love of art into stories.